BLOOD CURSED

THE WITCH'S REBELS BOOK FOUR

Blood Cursed

Copyright © 2018 by Sarah Piper

SarahPiperBooks.com

ISBN-13: 978-1-948455-09-1

TAROT ACADEMY

ONE

RONAN

The instant we stepped into the hell portal, I knew I'd lost her.

I was still holding her tight against my chest, but it wasn't her body that'd left us. I'd fucking *felt* it—the departure of her soul. The entirety of the woman I loved violently wrenched away as we'd tried to rescue her from the disaster blackening the skies in the Shadowrealm.

One horror after another, and yet for Gray Desario, they just kept on coming.

After what felt like a hundred years, the portal puked us out into the underground chamber beneath the Vegas desert —same spot where Darius and I had first entered. I hit the ground hard on my back, cushioning the blow for Gray.

I grunted at the impact, pain exploding along every bone-tired inch of my spine. She didn't make a sound, though.

Blinking the stars from my eyes, I laid her on the ground

and checked her over, feeling her head, her limbs, anywhere that might've been hurt. She seemed okay— warm and still breathing, heart still beating, blood still pumping through her veins, blue beneath the near-translucent skin at her wrists. But her eyes were—

Wait. *Blood...*

The thought tugged hard, yanking my attention away from Gray for a split second. Just long enough for me to recognize the wet, strangled gasps emanating from the other side of the chamber, shrouded in darkness. I sucked in a deep breath. The acrid tang of copper scented the air.

Fucking hell. Gray and I had not been the first out of the portal.

He'd beat us here.

"Beaumont?" I called, rising to my feet and creeping closer to the darkness. The shapes before me emerged slowly, revealing the gruesome scene one sliver at a time. A pair of shiny black shoes came first, attached to legs that jerked and spasmed. Clenched fists, split knuckles and pale skin turning white. A chest blackened and wet with blood. A face twisted in shocked horror—a face that had once belonged to the demon thug that'd escorted us here earlier.

And then, almost unrecognizable in his violent, blood-splattered stupor, our vampire came into view, looming over the body and siphoning its blood like a starved newborn.

I stood immobilized, watching with a mix of fear and fascination as this primal beast devoured his prey. All traces of the cool, composed man I'd known and cared for had vanished, leaving in his place nothing but sharp fangs and a deep, desperate need.

It was too late to backtrack, too late to grab Gray and make a run for it. He'd already noticed my presence—I could see it in the twitch of his head, the brief but detectable pause in his wet, incessant slurping.

My eyes darted around for another exit, a weapon, a miracle, anything, but there wasn't a damn thing I could've used to our advantage. Even the darkness worked against me, given vampires' superior sight.

As if he could read my mind, the bloodsucker formerly known as Darius flicked his cold gaze up at me, not bothering to detach his mouth from the victim's throat. In his eyes I caught a glimpse of something so horrid, so animal, it would probably give me nightmares for the rest of my long damn life—assuming I made it out of here alive.

His message was clear:

Move an inch, and I'll devour you next.

I had no choice but to let him finish, and hope to fucking hell the demon guard was enough to sate him. Because if Darius came at me in his current primal, blood-drunk state, I wasn't sure I had the strength—or the heart—to fight him off. Not with Gray lying behind me, soulless and unconscious. And if I died, she'd be next—slaughtered by the very hand of the vamp she loved. The vamp I was pretty sure loved her, too.

When he finally finished his meal, he tossed aside the body like an empty sack and rose to his full height, wiping his mouth on the back of his hand, his eyes never leaving mine.

"That gentleman tasted like shite," he announced.

"That's because he's a demon," I said firmly. The skin on my arm burned at the spot where I'd allowed Darius to feed after he'd turned up wasted and half-dead at Elena's house. "Vampires despise the taste of demon blood."

Darius took a step closer, stumbling a bit, then catching himself.

"And who might you be?" he asked, his words slurring together. His eyes were glassy and dark, his lips and chin shiny with smeared blood.

Drunk, lost, and feral. Seeing him like that... It nearly broke me. The beast wobbling before me was so far removed from the Darius I'd known that my brain kept rejecting the images, desperate to convince me that it wasn't real. That we were all trapped together in some heinous nightmare, or imprisoned by another cruel trick of the Shadowrealm.

But deep down I knew the cold, hard truth. We weren't lucky enough to wake up from this. It was real. It was now. And unless I figured out a way out of here, it was going to get us all killed.

I swallowed the tight knot in my throat, forcing out my response.

"Me? Just another shite-tasting demon," I said, but it seemed I'd already lost his attention. Darius's eyes wandered past me, an unnatural grin stretching across his face.

I didn't have to turn around to know exactly where his gaze had landed.

Fear soured my gut, spiking my blood with adrenaline.

"She's spent," I hedged, stepping in front of his path as he stalked closer to Gray's form. "Not worth your effort —trust me."

Ignoring this, he sidestepped me, a blur of color that vanished before my eyes, then reappeared right next to her. He knelt down and touched her face, fingering a lock of her hair, then pressing it to his lips to inhale her scent. A low rumble of desire reverberated in his chest.

But unlike the kind of desire I'd witnessed the night we'd shared her in bed, bringing her to the edge of ecstasy in a tangle of hot limbs and endless kisses, this was different. Dangerous. This desire meant to devour her, drain her of all that remained.

Every hair on my body stood at attention, my muscles tensing for a fight. But I couldn't make a move in here. Not without risking his ire. Risking her life.

Best I could hope for was a distraction.

"We need to get out of here," I said, forcing my voice to stay calm and steady. "You killed one of hell's soldiers. More will come. Let's go."

"Without this lovely creature?" He stroked her face.

It was all I could do to keep my heart rate in check. "Dead weight. She'll only slow us down."

"I could lighten the load a bit." He leaned in close and brushed his nose along her neck, his eyes so dark they were nearly black now. I felt my own shift into blackness as my demon instincts took over. "Maybe I'll just take a little off the top."

A glint of fang, and I was on him, barreling into him with enough force to knock him halfway across the room. I'd caught him by surprise, and now I used up the very last millisecond of my advantage by slamming a fist into his face.

The force of the blow dislocated his jaw, splitting the skin over my knuckles wide open. I waited for him to retaliate, but Darius merely smiled, licking my blood from his lips as his jaw snapped back into place.

"You're right," he said smoothly, malice soaking his voice as we rose from the ground. He'd lost some of his slur, and now he towered over me, menacing and cold. "You taste like shite."

"Told you."

The two of us circled each other like wild cats fighting over a wildebeest. He was clearly toying with me, and I was still holding back. I didn't want to hurt him any more than I had to, though I suspected he had no such hangups about *my* safety.

"So there's no reason for me to let you live," he said. "Unless you can think of one?"

"We're *brothers*, asshole. Let's start with that."

Darius laughed, hollow and chilling. "A vampire and a demon? Mom and Dad must be so proud."

"Genetics has nothing to do with it."

He zipped behind me, a blur in the darkness. When he spoke again, his breath was icy at the back of my neck.

"Try again," he whispered.

I dropped into a crouch and kicked backward, hitting air.

"Is that the best you can do?" he asked, already in front of me again. Taunting. Tormenting.

"Stand still and find out." I charged, but he went blurry on me again. Every time I blinked, he vanished, then reappeared behind me. Next to me. Across the room. Again. And again. And again.

Demonic strength could do a lot of damage, but vampires were still stronger. Faster. I was outmatched, and he was enjoying the game, batting me around like a cat with a caught mouse.

Then came the cruel grin.

A chill raced down my spine.

"Whatever you're thinking," I said, holding out a hand as if that alone could stop him, "don't—"

The plea died on my lips.

He came at me full on, and his attack was torrential, like a thousand powerful fists battering my jaw, my gut, my ribs, my kidneys, everything at once. My ears rang, my mouth full of blood, the blows coming so fast my bones hadn't even had time to crack yet.

They would, though. That much was certain.

A human would've died five times over, but I was still on my feet, my body desperately trying to heal itself. I was still swinging, still clawing and scratching, still hoping for that miracle, even as the adrenaline started to fade.

"Done yet, hellspawn?" he taunted, landing another solid punch to the gut.

I gritted my teeth against a wave of excruciating pain, my entire body throbbing, bruising, bleeding, everything at once. My vision swam.

Blackness crept in around the edges, whispering promises of sweet relief as Darius continued to unleash his fury. But I couldn't give in, couldn't slide into the bliss of unconsciousness. Not like this.

As fucked up as this was, I hurt for him almost as much as I hurt for myself. There was a chance, however minute, that he would remember me. Maybe not today or tomorrow, maybe not in a year, but one day might come when his memories rushed back like a river breaking down the dam. He'd remember our friendship. And then he'd remember this moment.

And it would eat through his bones like acid. All the gut-punches in the world wouldn't come close to the pain he'd feel on that day.

I wanted to spare him. To save him, even if I couldn't save myself. Even if I couldn't save Gray.

"Darius Beaumont," I panted, holding up my hands for a momentary cease-fire. "That's your name. Listen to me. You're the most powerful vampire on the west coast. You were born in London, many years ago. You own a club in the Bay called Black Ruby. Gray is… You're bonded to her, Darius."

He stopped the violence long enough to hear my words, but none of them seemed to be sinking in.

"You've suffered memory loss," I continued, spitting out blood. It was a struggle to stay on my feet, but I had to keep talking. Had to keep trying to get through his thick skull. "The three of us just returned from the Shadowrealm. We were trying to get Gray back to her own magical realm, but we were attacked by memory eaters and had to jump into the hell portal. Now her soul's trapped in hell, and we're here trying to kill each other."

"Hmm. Charming story," he said, his tone now light and teasing. "But how will it end, I wonder? The suspense is nearly killing me. Perhaps it will kill you, too."

"The ending hasn't been written yet." I took a deep breath to regroup, hoping we still had a shot at a good one. Hell, I'd settle for one where we all walked out of here alive. Broken bones and bloody knuckles would heal. Gray's soul was trapped in hell, but it still existed, which meant we might be able to get it back. And Darius's memories? I wasn't ready to give up on them yet, either. Somewhere, maybe they existed. In this realm or another.

Shitty as things had gotten, we hadn't yet crossed the point of no return—not with any of it. There was still a glimmer of light. Of hope.

"Darius, listen to me. We can still—"

"Sorry, demon. I'm afraid your part in this tale has come to its inevitable end." He grinned again, his eyes sparkling with fresh desire as they roamed over Gray's body. "It's time for my midnight snack."

"Not a chance, brother." I wound up for another hit—

anything to stall him from his end game of feeding on her—but stopped short at the strange look on his face.

Brother, the word that'd barely registered with him earlier, seemed to snag on a memory. His gaze went far away for a beat, then came back, and he cocked his head at me and narrowed his eyes. The whole thing happened in the span of two heartbeats, but I swear I saw the flicker of recognition pushing out from the depths of rage.

"Beaumont?" I called, unable to keep the hope from my voice. "Darius? Do you—"

His hand shot out and grabbed my throat, instantly choking off the words right along with my air supply. He hauled me up, my feet dangling a foot off the ground as his mouth twisted into another sick grin.

Then it went slack.

I thought he had another memory, a flash of something. But Darius gasped in pain, his eyes wide with shock. He dropped to his knees with a grunt.

Finally freed from his impossibly strong grip, I squared off with a new assailant.

I took in the sight of her, my mouth dropping open. With her short stature, wrinkled skin, and head of close-cropped white hair, she looked like she should be sitting in a rocking chair and knitting blankets, not taking out vampires outside the hell portal.

Yet there she was, still gripping the hawthorn stake she'd jammed between his shoulder blades. She shoved it in a little harder now, her mouth pressed into a grim line as Darius's head slumped forward.

Certain the vampire had been immobilized, she stepped back from him and brushed her hands together, finally meeting my eyes.

Recognition twisted my gut. My heart fucking stopped.

It was *her*.

TWO

RONAN

"Deirdre Olivante," I said, hating the shape of it in my mouth. Though we'd never met before, her name had been seared into my memory for decades, the echo of it like a ticking time bomb that haunted my every step.

She looked like I'd always imagined her. Short, small-boned, and old, but tough beneath her layers of crafted sweetness, with the same intense blue eyes and sharp cheekbones as her granddaughter.

I wanted to despise her, but right now I could only be grateful.

She'd saved us. Ironic, all things considered.

"Foolish boy," Deirdre snapped, the first words she'd ever spoken to me. "Rayanne's soul is trapped in hell, and you're playing around with a vampire. I thought you were her guardian."

I said nothing. She was right. Gray—Rayanne, to her—was my charge, and I'd failed her.

13

Again.

But the fire smoldered out of her words quickly as she took in the sight of Gray. Kneeling beside her on the floor, Deirdre brushed her fingers across her granddaughter's forehead for the first time in more than twenty years.

"She's beautiful," Deirdre said, momentarily lost in her own world. Her voice was thick with emotion. "So grown-up. I never thought…"

She trailed off as a tear slid down her cheek. In that moment, she looked vulnerable and wounded, a woman who'd seen more than her fair share of suffering and loss.

Behind us, Darius twitched on the floor, groaning at the pain of the poison coursing through his blood. Despite the fact that he'd damn near killed me, I hated seeing him in that state. I hated seeing Gray unconscious on the floor, the grandmother she didn't remember weeping over her body.

A fresh lump lodged itself in the back of my throat.

For so many years, I'd believed the worst thing I'd ever have to face was Gray's death—the event that would trigger the official start of her contracted servitude, requiring me to deliver her straight to Sebastian.

But now here she was, very much alive, her soul trapped in his hell. Was that worse than becoming a demonic servant? An eternal slave?

Was there any chance at getting her out of either disaster? Of any of the obstacles and terrible situations she'd likely face, even if we could free her from this latest round of torments? She was a powerful Shadowborn witch. To think she'd survive this life unscathed was a ridiculous pipe dream.

I turned away, unable to look at her another minute. I didn't have the strength for this. It turned me inside out, like someone had carved me open and set all my nerves on fire. It hurt to breathe. To blink. To think.

Gray's death? It would've gutted me.

But this... This was definitely worse. She wasn't dead, just trapped, condemned to an eternity of suffering, mere seconds after we'd liberated her from the last otherworldly prison.

Deirdre sighed, and I turned back to face her, our eyes locking once again. Hers were cloudy with sadness and regret, and for a brief instant, that shared pain connected us by an invisible thread.

In another life, we might've been family.

I wondered if she was thinking the same thing. Then she got to her feet and said, "Don't just stand there moping, demon. Sebastian is certainly expecting you by now."

"Fuck Sebastian." I closed my eyes, breaking the momentary connection. "There's nothing he can do for me now. And if you think for one hot second I'm taking her anywhere near him, you're—"

"She's lost in his domain now, Ronan Vacarro. He's the *only* one who can help us get her back."

"*Us?*" I opened my eyes and looked at her again, eyeing her skeptically. "You think there's an *us* in all of this?"

She folded her arms across her chest and jutted out her

chin, a look that was so very Gray, it shot a bolt of pain through my heart.

I stepped closer, staring her down. "Let me tell you what it means to be part of an us. Gray and I were an us. We had each other's backs. We cared for each other. We shared things, went through shit together, came out on the other side swinging. We didn't condemn each other to—"

"Enough!" Her eyes blazed, and she didn't back down, glaring at me as if she were the one towering over me rather than vice versa. "We've all done unspeakable things to keep her safe. Don't pretend you're above all of this. I know the truth."

"You know nothing about me, witch."

"Oh no?" Her steely gaze softened, and she reached up to touch my face, her palm soft against my cheek. "I know what you gave up for her. I know what she means to you. And," she said, her voice dropping to a whisper, "I know what haunts your dreams."

At first her touch felt kindly, like I'd always imagined a real grandmother's would. But then it turned icy cold, spreading across my jaw and into my head, boring into my skull. The feeling was like a brain freeze, like eating ice cream too fast, and everything else in me went still as she rifled through my mind—not my thoughts, I realized, but my dreams. My nightmares. I saw each one flicker and glow as she paged through them like stories in an old, dusty book.

When she finally pulled back and the warmth rushed

back into my head, she was looking at me with a mixture of righteousness and pity. Compassion.

"Do that again," I warned, "and you'll… I'll…"

I pinched the bridge of my nose and shook my head, letting the words die off. I didn't have it in me to threaten her. She'd been right. We'd all done things to protect Gray. Would do them again in a heartbeat. I had no right to judge her.

In a fluid, effortless motion at complete odds with her small physical stature, she hauled Darius to his feet and yanked his arm over her shoulder, taking the bulk of his weight against her body. Darius groaned in half-hearted protest, but he leaned into her, trying to find his footing.

"I'll deal with him," she said, then nodded toward Gray. "You get Rayanne to Sebastian. I'll meet you there as soon as I can."

I looked at Darius, the blood congealing on his lips and chin. His hands trembled, his head lolling sideways as if he didn't even have the strength to hold it up. His eyes held none of their earlier viciousness.

Fucking hell, Beaumont.

Deirdre must've seen the concern in my face. Adjusting him against her body, she said, "He would have killed you both had I not intervened."

"He would've tried, maybe."

"Ronan, we don't have time. I've got him. You need to help Rayanne."

"He's not himself," I went on. "But he's… he's impor-tant to her. To both of us." I stepped closer, putting a hand on his shoulder as if he was mine to claim. "I can't let you end him, Deirdre. No matter what he's done."

She sighed loudly, her patience clearly thinning. "I'm not planning to decapitate him, demon. He needs sedation and treatment. Unless you want me to release him into the wilds of Las Vegas, I need to relocate him somewhere safe, preferably before sunrise."

Safe? I almost laughed at that. Where the hell in this city was a safe place for a powerful vampire with no memory, out of his mind with bloodlust, currently neutered by hawthorn, completely at the mercy of a pint-sized, dream-stealing, elderly witch?

"I'll find you at Sebastian's casino once the vampire is secured," she said, the sternness in her voice leaving no room for argument.

Darius groaned again, but if he had an opinion on the matter, I had no idea what the hell it was. I had to go by instinct, trusting that I knew the real Darius well enough at this point to know what he'd want.

Like me, he'd want to protect Gray at all costs. He'd want me to focus on her. To find some way to get her out of this fucking bind.

I scooped Gray into my arms, holding her tight against my chest.

For a moment, Deirdre and I stood facing each other, looking over the charges each of us held close.

These are the most important people in my life.

"I'll take care of him, Ronan," she said, a little bit of that grandmotherly tone creeping back in. "You have my word."

Her gaze dropped back to Gray, her lips pressed into a tight line. The creases between her eyes deepened with worry, and she glanced back up at me, as though she wanted me to give her the same reassurances.

But I didn't owe her a damn thing. She knew who I was. Knew that I was perpetually obligated to keep Gray safe, even if I *wasn't* in love with her so deeply my heart would never hit a steady beat without her touch again.

With my best friend—hell, my entire life—cradled in my arms, I emerged into the lonely desert night, leaving Darius in the care of the one witch I'd hoped I'd never, *ever* meet in person.

The witch who—twenty-some years ago in her own dark moment of desperation at the crossroads—had signed her name in blood on a contract with the Prince of Hell, bargaining away her granddaughter's eternal soul.

THREE

LIAM

For all the power I possessed, for all the fear my presence invoked in humans and supernaturals alike, for all the incomprehensible vastness of my very being, I could not save her.

The pain wracking my human vessel was agonizing, guilt's red-hot lava boiling in my stomach, shame blazing a new fire in my chest, regret eating a gaping hole in my heart that could only be repaired by Gray's safe return. Shifting into my shadow form would've spared me, but the pain was no less than I deserved.

I couldn't risk depleting my rapidly waning energy with another shift. Not until I made my journey into the heart of hell.

For once, I wasn't speaking in metaphor.

"Ah, my old friend, the Lord of Shadows. Welcome to Sin City." Sebastian entered the conference room with a flourish, then sat at the head of the long, sleek table, his image perfectly framed by two large paintings depicting nude women pleasuring scores of demons.

How the natural order saw fit to keep this despicable being in power was beyond even my understanding.

"My assistant tells me you requested a meeting," he continued with a smirk. "Does this mean your rendezvous in the Shadowrealm didn't go as planned?"

"Let us not pretend you don't know *exactly* how things unfolded in the Shadowrealm." My temper flared, but quickly faded under the watchful eyes of the women in the paintings. They seemed to be disappointed in me, as though I'd managed to fail them as horribly as I'd failed Gray. I could hardly blame them.

Hanging my head, I said, "I'm afraid I've... miscalculated."

"An understatement, I presume." Sebastian chuckled, removing a small silver box from his inside jacket pocket. "Cigar? Something tells me you've got a doozy of a story to tell."

The greasy demon prince held out the box, his thrill at my misfortune—*Gray's* misfortune—plainly evident. When I waved him off, he removed and lit a cigar for himself, his cheeks billowing as he puffed the thing to life.

Smoke curled around his pockmarked face. I wished I had the power to bring disease to his lungs. To cause him a very long, very painful demise.

But Sebastian was immune to the powers of Death.

"So tell me. Did the witch refuse your proposition?" he asked. "Tell you to stick it where the sun don't shine?"

"The proposition, as you call it, is no joking matter. It's a matter of her true destiny. As such, it was not something to be entered into lightly. There are many facets, many details which must be explored and debated ad nauseam. We did not have the time to fully discuss her options."

"You never even told her there *were* options." Sebastian sucked on his cigar, the end of it crackling. His eyes shone even more menacingly in the orange glow. "There's a difference."

A thousand retorts swirled in my mind, but every one of them turned to dust on my lips. Sebastian was right. I'd kept everything from her—everything that mattered. Her true choices, and what each one would've meant. Her legacy. Consequences. Information that would've altered the course of her destiny and saved a lot of lives in the process.

I'd staked everything on my ability to train her in time, to persuade her onto the right path. I was so certain, so blindly convinced she'd accept, none of the myriad other pathways spiraling out before her seemed plausible.

After all, who could refuse the call of Death? According to the scrolls in the hallowed Hall of Records, no one in a hundred thousand lifetimes had ever dared.

Then again, I was fairly certain Death had never fallen in love with his protégé, either. That was a complication I could not have foreseen.

I knew I should regret it, but I couldn't. No matter the outcome.

Even now, the remnants of our kisses on the beach in the

Shadowrealm warmed me inside. I closed my eyes, allowing the moment to replay itself. I smelled the salt of the ocean, felt the grit of sand and shells beneath my back as Gray fell into my arms, her mouth warm and soft, her hair tickling my cheeks, her laughter like music I'd only just begun to remember.

If I lingered there, if I allowed myself to partake in the comforting opiate of human memory, the pain burning through my body might finally ease, ever so slightly…

"In any case," Sebastian said, wrenching me from that blissful haze, "she's in my possession now, and though I can't use her as I'd originally intended, what with her soul being trapped in hell and her body being—well, wherever that thing ended up, I'm not keen on relinquishing her. As you have failed to uphold your end of our bargain, it seems our partnership has come to its unavoidable end." He rose from the table in a cloud of smoke, the fat cigar lodged into the corner of his mouth. "Now, if that's all, I'm a very busy man, and—"

"You *must* allow me to reclaim her soul," I said, suddenly frantic. "To reunite it with her body before she dies. There's still time, Sebastian. She deserves better than lingering in hell, and you know it."

He glared at me a long moment, then said with another smirk, "The way I see it, Lord of Shadows, you should be thanking me."

"Whatever for?"

He resumed his position at the head of the table, taking another puff on the cigar. "I've spared you the ugly task of killing her yourself. This way she'll never even know about our arrangement."

"I *never* agreed to killing her. That was your term for it."

"What would you call ending her life as she knows it, then? Tearing her from the ones she loves, forcing her into a service from which she'd most certainly recoil? What would you call eliminated one's every last choice?"

"I did not sign her original contract."

"No, of course not. You merely agreed to alter the start date."

"I never should've accepted your terms." The lava inside me sputtered to life once again, burning a hot path to my throat, though I was admittedly more upset with myself than with the demon presently taunting me. "The natural order is not something to be twisted and bent to one's will, Sebastian. We must respect it at all costs, or what are we left with? What do we become but a rabble of unconscious ghouls, roaming the earth like the primordial beasts of old, tearing one another limb from limb for the pure sport of it."

"Save your philosophy, demon. You and I had a perfectly legitimate deal. You failed to deliver, ergo—"

"I am *no* demon, Prince."

"Ahh, but aren't you?" He stabbed the cigar into his ashtray, grounding it until his fingers were coated in ash. The room was hazy with smoke, and now it began to descend on us like a fog. "You've bargained with her life almost as many times as I have. And here you are at the final hour, once again begging me to make another deal."

"I've done no such thing."

"Then why are you here? To enjoy the many pleasures of my establishment?" He gestured toward a blackened window on the opposite wall. At his attention, the glass lost its smokey tint, clearing to provide a view into the adjacent room. A soft red glow emanated from the ground, just enough illumination to reveal the garish scene unfolding inside. It seemed to be a near-exact replica of the artwork on his walls, and though the almost-nude woman chained to the wall did not move as three male tormentors carried on, her haunted eyes told the story of her endless torture.

She couldn't have been more than eighteen years old. Twenty at best.

"Perhaps your human vessel is craving a bargain of the, shall we say, carnal nature?" Sebastian's eyes glinted as he drank in the sight of the woman's brutalized body, licking his lips as one of her captors tore off the last remaining scrap of fabric covering her breasts. "Violet is a client favorite. I'm told she's never refused a request, no matter how degrading or bizarre. Then again, she doesn't have much of a choice. Such is the way with the Devil's bargains."

"You are a monster," I whispered, unable to look away from Violet's pained eyes. There was nothing I could do to help her. She was a demonic servant, the details of her own bargain unknown to me. Even death couldn't save her now.

"No, I am the Prince of Hell," Sebastian bellowed suddenly. "You would be wise to remember that before wasting my time with your pathetic pleas. I am not the hero in this story, Shadow Lord. Nor have I ever pretended otherwise. So, if you'd kindly stop wasting my time, I do have other business to attend to."

His eyes glowed the same eerie shade of red as the torture room next door, cutting through the remaining blanket of smoke and reminding me *exactly* who I was dealing with.

"So be it," I finally said, resigned. He was right—I *had* come here looking for one last bargain, and now I would have it. "There's no deal I wouldn't make to save Gray's soul from Hell's grip."

"I'm very glad to hear it." At this, he snapped his fingers, and a manilla envelope appeared, thick with what could only be another contract. "The terms are rather simple, actually."

"State them plainly, Prince. I've neither the time nor the interest to parse through your fine print."

"Very well." He set the envelope on the table before him, then stroked his goatee, gazing through the window as if he were deep in thought. As if he were actually considering the options rather than simply pausing for dramatic effect and enjoying the sick view next door.

Sebastian was no fool. He'd known full well why I'd come today, and full well the terms he'd offer. Still, I let him play his games, hoping that the day would come where his confidence would so fully blind him that someone more powerful than I would slip behind his defenses and plant the trap that would usher in his final undoing.

"I will allow you to retrieve your beloved witch's soul and work your shadow magic to bring her back to life."

"At what cost?"

"No more or less than our previously arranged price. The cost of your failure. An excellent bargain for you, I do declare."

It was precisely what I expected, yet everything I most feared.

I'm so sorry, Gray.

I knew there was no room for negotiating here. Sebastian might let me bring Gray back to life, but he would not allow her to walk away from him unscathed. Not when he already had her soul in possession. He held all of the cards here, and I was out of ideas.

I had to accept. Leaving her soul to float untethered through hell was simply not an option.

"On one condition," I said. Sebastian raised an eyebrow, and I pushed on, gesturing toward the window. "Release Violet into my possession. I... I *must* have her."

He eyed me suspiciously for no more than a breath, then laughed, smug satisfaction distorting his already vile features. "Ah, so our fan favorite has tickled your fancy. She's quite remarkable, I'm told."

"You were right," I said, trying to appear both aroused and ashamed. "My human vessel does have certain... proclivities. The longer I retain this form, the more insistent those proclivities become. I will comply with your terms, and ask only that you grant me this gift of flesh as a show of good faith."

Still laughing, Sebastian slid the contract and a pen across the table. "You've got yourself a deal."

I signed quickly, and the entire envelope vanished.

"I will have Violet prepared and waiting for you in Suite 666. It's my personal favorite." He produced a keycard, and I took it without ceremony, sliding it into my pocket.

"Always a pleasure." He stuck out his hand to shake, but a sudden commotion outside the conference room door interrupted our farewell. The door crashed open, and Ronan shoved his way inside, cradling Gray in his arms.

The sight of her lifeless body... I nearly gasped.

"I'm sorry, sir." Another young woman stumbled in behind Ronan, breathless and trembling. "I tried to stop him, but he was very insistent that he see you."

"Indeed. And what have I told you about Ronan Vacarro?" he asked.

"That's R-Ronan?" She quivered, bowing her head low. "I didn't realize it was him, sir. He never said."

"Ignorance is not your savior, child."

"I know, sir. I'm very sorry."

"As am I. Now I'll have to find a new assistant." He whispered a brief incantation, and then she vanished, leaving nothing but a black wisp in her wake.

"And to what do I owe this honor?" Sebastian drawled. "What an unexpected surprise."

He couldn't hide the raw pleasure on his face as he approached Gray. Here in the flesh, after all this time, was the witch he'd been patiently stalking her entire life. Longer, even. From the moment he'd heard about the Silversbane prophecy, he'd known she was special.

Ronan and I remained silent as Sebastian looked her

over, barely keeping his greed in check. With her head resting peacefully on Ronan's shoulder, Gray was warm and alive, the color high on her cheeks, her curls glossy despite her ordeal in the Shadowrealm.

But her soul was gone, just as I'd known it would be. And unless I could find it and successfully reunite the two, her body would decompose, and everything about her that had ever existed would simply cease.

A world without Gray Desario... It was incomprehensible.

Though I didn't deserve to touch her again, I reached out anyway, brushing my knuckles along her jaw. Her skin was silky-soft, but it felt wrong—a great void where before there had been vitality and warmth and pure magic.

"Do something," Ronan barked at me, ignoring Sebastian. "Fix this." His commanding voice broke into something helpless and desperate at the end, heartache soaking his every word.

"I shall do my best," I assured him, but hopelessness was contagious, and the longer I stared into his desperate eyes, the faster I felt myself slipping into the same dark oblivion.

Neither of us had the luxury of giving up or checking out.

"I see you two are already acquainted," Sebastian said. "Excellent, that saves me the trouble of introductions. Ronan, your friend and I were just having the most fascinating conversation. I understand the witch's soul is lost in hell. Can you imagine? What are the chances that my sharpest demon guardian would make the mistake of bringing a demon sworn through the hell portal?"

"We were out of options," Ronan said, his jaw tight. And swollen, I now noticed. Blood dried in the corners of his mouth, and along a deep gash above his eye.

"Well, I'm nothing if not generous," Sebastian said. "It turns out there *is* one more option. One way—and only one —to retrieve Gray's soul and reunite it with her body."

Ronan closed his eyes and took a deep breath, composing himself. "What's it gonna cost me this time?"

"Not a red cent, boy." Sebastian grinned, jerking his head toward me as he slapped a meaty hand over my shoulder. "This one's on him."

Ronan's head turned slowly, his eyes blazing with twin flames of fury and fear.

"What," he whispered, "have you done?"

I opened my mouth intending to explain, but there was no time.

And at the moment, I was severely low on courage and valor.

I nodded once, my form of an apology, then vanished without a response.

Gray's demon guardian would have his answer soon enough.

FOUR

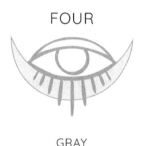

GRAY

I knelt in the bottom of a small wooden boat blackened with rot, floating on an obsidian lake. A striking orange-red sky bled across the horizon, beautiful like the dawn but for the faces looming in its dark gray clouds. They were the ghosts of hell, each mouth stretched and howling in torment, every one of them reflected endlessly in the black-mirror lake.

Their screams roared like the wind, but caused no ripples. When I reached over the side of the boat and trailed my fingers through the water, I felt nothing but air.

It was all an illusion meant to slowly drive me insane.

My predicament was neither a mystery nor a surprise. As a demon sworn witch, my chances of escaping the hell portal had been less than zero. I'd known the risks, but I'd taken them anyway; all I'd wanted was one more moment in Ronan's arms. To make him understand that I trusted him implicitly, no matter what the consequences. To leave him the parting gift of my unfaltering faith.

He'd earned it.

My eyes watered. The acrid stench of sulfur and burned flesh soaked the air, but I wasn't scared. Wasn't cold or hungry or tired or in pain. Stuck on my rickety boat in the middle of this endless yet nonexistent lake, I knew I wasn't in any real danger.

I was just... empty. Empty and alone.

Though I'd never met him, I was getting a crash course in Sebastian's precise form of cruelty. I'd no doubt that he'd crafted this version of hell specifically for me—his red-carpet welcome.

Unlike in the Shadowrealm, here I found no fire-breathing, flesh-tearing demons, or needling glass rainstorms, or Jonathan and his monstrous torments. Simply and ingeniously, the Prince of Hell had doled out the worst punishment he could've imagined for me: separating me from the ones I loved, leaving me to float helplessly on a boat that would never reach the shore while my rebels were left to fight their wars and face their demons without me. My memories would never fade, and I'd never be allowed to sleep. There would be no respite for me, no escape from the knowledge of all I'd lost. Just this boat, this lake, and all the ghosts that lived in my head. Every hour, every century. An eternity of regret.

That was his style.

But as much as I was learning about my new captor, it seemed he hadn't bothered to study up on me. If he had, he would've known that being a hostage wasn't really my strong suit. After all, Jonathan's cave prison hadn't been enough to hold me. And hadn't I managed to escape the Shadowrealm? Out of the frying pan and into the fire, maybe, but an escape nevertheless. One that should've been impossible given the fact that I'd banished an unwilling soul.

Yet Sebastian thought an unplanned side trip to Hell would stop me?

Hard pass, asshole.

I smiled, and something flickered beneath all that emptiness and despair inside. An ember of something that felt a lot like hope.

I got to my feet and climbed onto the narrow foredeck, the boat rocking but not tipping over as it probably should've. I knew my voice would never carry above the vicious howl of those ghastly clouds, but I felt the need to say my piece anyway.

"I am not your hostage," I called out. "You can burn my body, but my soul is and will always be mine. You hear me? I am *mine*. I am mine."

It started softly, but the words themselves were like a spell, magic gathering in the air before me, crackling with power, swirling into a hot wind around me that lifted my hair and gave me strength.

"I am mine. I am mine. I am mine." I repeated the words a hundred times, a thousand, a million, each time getting louder and louder until my soft calls turned into a powerful roar that echoed across the lake, drowning out the sounds of the damned, scraping my throat raw and reverberating through my bones. In one final, triumphant call, I lifted my hands to the sky, tossed my head back, and screamed, shattering the black mirror lake into dust.

"I. Am. *Mine!*"

"I want more than anything for that to be true," came a dark echo. "But there isn't enough magic in all the realms to make it so."

The magic wind surrounding me suddenly stopped, and when I brushed the hair from my face and opened my eyes, I found myself staring into the electric blue gaze of a massive white raven.

He flapped his great wings, then transformed into a pillar of smoke that roiled and churned before me, finally falling away to reveal a familiar sight.

A man with sun-streaked hair and a worn flannel shirt, gazing back at me with ancient blue eyes that swirled with all the mysteries of the universe.

My heart leaped. It felt like I'd conjured him. Like he'd heard the call of my magic across the realms, and then he'd appeared, ready to sweep me into his arms and escort me out of this terrible nightmare.

"My knight in shining flannel," I teased, unable to hold back my smile, even as fresh tears filled my eyes. "You have *no* idea how happy I am to see you."

I stretched up on my toes and kissed the corner of his mouth, wrapping my arms around his neck, but Liam didn't respond.

"Liam?" I pressed. "You... you *are* here to rescue me,

right?" Why else would he have tracked me down in Hell if not to help me fight my way out? To warn me against all my crazy schemes, and then back me up as I put every single one of them into motion?

"I'm so sorry, Gray. I'm not here to... I'm... Not this time," he sputtered, sounding as scared and uncertain as a child lost in the woods. He pulled out of my embrace and looked at me, eyes flashing with a deep and endless pain. He grabbed my upper arms so tightly I was certain he'd leave bruises.

"Liam?" I whispered.

"I am here to offer you a choice." Holding me just beyond the reach of his warmth, of his now-familiar strength, he said somberly, "The very last you will likely be allowed to make."

FIVE

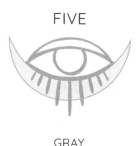

GRAY

I'd turned Hell's black lake into dust, and now our rotting little boat drifted on a sea of nothingness, our knees touching as we sat across from each other on cold, damp benches.

Minutes passed in deadly silence, time stretching before us like hours. Days. Even the ghostly clouds had drifted away, as if the trapped spirits had grown tired of waiting for Death to explain.

"Jonathan is trapped in your realm," he finally said. "I chased him through the black forest, but he eluded my capture. Something is very, very wrong with him. He's no longer part of the natural order, and therefore not subject to its rules. He didn't seem to recognize where he was, or how he'd gotten there—only that he wanted out."

"He's a hybrid now," I said. "Vampire, shifter, who knows what else. He jumped through the rune gate, and then..." I closed my eyes, my body trembling at the memory of the winged beasts that attacked us. That stole Darius's memories. "Liam, Darius lost his—"

"There's no need for you to relive that pain. I know what happened."

"Oh. Right." I opened my eyes, and he lowered his, his cheeks colored with something that looked a lot like shame, though I couldn't imagine what he had to be ashamed about. It wasn't Liam's fault he knew all possible outcomes before they happened. That was just one of Death's many burdens.

At least, that was how I saw it. God, I couldn't imagine carrying that kind of weight.

I reached for his hand, but his own was cold beneath my touch.

"I could do nothing to help you," he said, still not meeting my eyes. "Nothing to warn you or turn back the ceaseless march of time. The attack, Ronan's decision to bring you through the hell portal, Darius's memory loss... all of those things belonged to an infinitesimal set of possibilities in an infinite sea of others. I saw those terrible events unfold, but I also saw you arriving in your magical realm to meet me as we'd planned, and returning home safely. I saw other outcomes where Ronan died, where Darius was lost in the hell portal rather than you, where you were the one whose memories were swallowed. I watched you turn on your beloved demon, stabbing him in the chest with your blade because you perceived him as a threat instead of your guardian. I saw the three of you enter your portal at the Pool of Unknowing, arriving in the magical realm unharmed together. I saw you healing Jonathan rather than attacking him, reversing the damage his twisted experiments caused his own body and urging him to relinquish his evil quest. I saw you sending Ronan and Darius home through the hell portal, only to remain behind to fight the memory eaters yourself. In one version of events, you even became Queen of the Shadowrealm, sacrificing yourself once again for all those you cared for. And I saw Jonathan escaping into the material plane, unleashing his terror on the remaining witches of Blackmoon Bay... and beyond. It wasn't until I felt the pulse of your soul in this terrible place that I knew the final, irrevocable outcome from all of those possibilities."

"So all of those things... those were all actual possibilities?" I asked, still uncertain about how it all actually worked. Still in awe.

Liam nodded, then tipped his head back, gazing up at the now cloudless sky. It'd faded from orange to the palest gray, not unlike the skies of Blackmoon Bay just before a misty rain. I could almost taste the salty air of home on my tongue.

"Each one of those scenarios was equally likely until the decision just prior to it. In all things, Gray, with each decision one makes, hundreds of other pathways branch outward. No matter how large or small the choice seems in the moment—which side of your mouth you start brushing your teeth on, whom you confide in about your deepest secrets, where you decide to live, which route you take to work, the words you speak to express yourself, the way you style your hair on a given day—you are changing your possibilities, and therefore your fate, with every one. As Death, I see all of those possibilities at once, at all times. Unless..."

"Unless?" I prodded, losing patience with his obvious stalling. He'd come here to offer me some kind of choice, and so far, all we'd done was rehash the terrors that had landed me in this rotten boat. I didn't blame him for trying to ease into it, but really, what was the point?

"Rip off the Band-Aid, Liam." I spread my hands, indicating the hellscape around us. "How much worse could things possibly get?"

Liam finally met my gaze again and took my hands, his touch gentle, his eyes filling with an emotion I recognized instantly. I was intimately familiar with it, in fact; I'd stared it down in the mirror almost every day for the last decade.

Guilt.

"I see all of those possibilities," he repeated, so softly I had to lean in to hear the rest, "unless there are truly no other options."

No.

Other.

Options.

Each of those words echoed across the black sea, hammering into me like another nail in the coffin.

"Before you came into my presence," he said, his voice ragged with an ache so deep it made my own bones hurt, "I did not know it was possible to feel such a deep well of regret."

42

"You... you regret meeting me?" I tried but failed to keep the hurt from my voice. I couldn't imagine my life without Liam. Or Death. Or any of the ravens or owls or smoke-and-feathers illusions he'd embodied. He'd taught me so much, but I was starting to care for him so much more than as a mentor, or even as a friend. He'd come to mean something to me I hadn't even been able to put into words yet. In the absence of those words, the sparks we'd created on the beach had felt like the closest approximation.

I'd mistakenly thought he'd felt that way about me, too.

I released his hands, but he leaned forward and grabbed mine again.

"Look at me," he whispered. "Please. I need you to look at me. To hear this as well as see it."

When I finally did as he asked, I found him in tears.

"I could *never* regret meeting you, Gray. You have been a light I neither expected nor deserved."

"Then what is it? What are you trying to tell me?"

Crushing my hands in his grip, he shook his head and said, "I have wronged you, Gray Desario. More terribly and irrevocably than you can possibly imagine. And even if your soul is cursed to be hell's immortal prisoner and I remain here at your side, and together we gaze upon the very sunset of the human race, it still would not have been enough time for me to make amends for what I've done."

SIX

EMILIO

"The city of Blackmoon Bay has fallen under fae control," Jael said.

That was it. No small talk, no preamble. The Seelie Prince simply stepped into my sister's foyer, bringing in a gust of chilly air, and detonated the bomb.

"Explain," I said, holstering my weapon. Elena followed suit, but like me, she didn't take her eyes off him.

"The fae have taken the city," he said grimly, "though I'm loathe to call those monsters fae. Darkwinter are no kin of mine, I assure you."

At the mention of the brutal fae bloodline, a panicky buzz filled my chest, but there was no time to indulge it.

"I've been in touch with my guys at BBPD all night," I said. "No one mentioned anything about a hostage situation, especially not at the hands of Darkwinter."

"They are unaware of the circumstances." Jael lowered his eyes, almost as if he were ashamed. "Say what you will about my people, detectives, but the fae are quite subtle. No one in the Bay feels like a hostage. They are willing participants in this, thanks to the magic. *That* is the kind of power we're dealing with here."

"That's not power," I said. "That's manipulation. It's coercion. And it's against the laws of humankind as well as our own. I assume you've informed the Council?"

He met my eyes again, the shame replaced by a look of utter defeat.

The reality of the situation sunk like a stone in my gut.

The Council didn't need Jael to inform them.

"They already knew," I said.

Elena and I exchanged horrified glances. Our so-called conspiracy theories were suddenly getting a lot less theoretical.

"Talia was in the Cape tonight," I told him. "It's my belief that Darkwinter is partnering with hunters to eradicate witches in the Bay and possibly elsewhere, and I wanted the Council's help."

"Did she offer it?" he asked.

"Oh sure, Jael. Right along with a plate of cookies and a glass of warm milk." I pinched the bridge of my nose, breathing deep. Jael was probably the only fae ally we had left—I needed to cool it.

In a much calmer tone, I said, "Turns out she already knew about the Darkwinter-hunter connection. Looks like she just wanted to find out how much *I* knew. How much danger I would pose to her grand plans."

"Yes," Jael said. "She knew about Darkwinter and the

hunters. It's my understanding Talia is the one who brought the parties together initially."

It made sense. Talia had always stricken me as a climber. She'd probably been in league with Darkwinter for years, keeping them on speed-dial, just waiting for a chance to make her big move with the Council. Her earlier tirade about the witches echoed in my mind, each word taking on new meaning.

The witches are a problem that should've been dealt with long ago...

The Council has not been as involved as we should've been. That is changing...

We must find a way to make the distribution of power more equitable...

"Now she's convinced the rest of the Council that *you're* the threat," Jael continued. "She insisted Blackmoon Bay needs ongoing protection from you and your associates. They agreed. Late last night, she called in her hand-picked Darkwinter Knights to secure the city."

Late last night? So, after my frantic phone call, but before tonight's meeting.

She'd played me, of course. And I'd fallen right into her trap.

"The same Darkwinter Knights," I said, "who've teamed up with hunters to build an army of supernatural freaks and biological weapons with the power to kill and enslave entire races of beings."

I gave him the quick-and-dirty rundown on the situation in Raven's Cape and the prison we were still trying to locate, doing my best to protect Gray's privacy. Jael might've shown up here with helpful intel, but that didn't make us partners. I didn't yet know if I could trust him, and it wasn't my place to share details about Gray's magic or her current predicament.

"That does sound like Darkwinter," Jael confirmed. "They've had their eye on hybrid technologies and genetic manipulation for some time, though I had no idea they'd already had some successes."

"And now they're the de facto power faction in the Bay." I clenched my fists at my sides, my hands shaking with rage. It was a major effort not to totally wolf out. Not to track Talia back to Council HQ and take out the whole traitorous lot of them.

How could they sanction this? How could they sit back and let the supernatural community tear itself apart? By the time anyone inside the Bay realized what was happening, it would be too late.

Talia, Darkwinter, the hunters... I didn't know who'd be left in power when the dust finally settled, only that it wouldn't be the people. The citizens who'd lived and worked and played and built our homes there for decades.

Human and supernatural alike, most of the Bay's residents probably had no idea the city had been occupied. Jael said there'd been no physical attack, no bombs, no guns, nothing to actually fight.

No, that wasn't Darkwinter's style. Their real attack would simply unfold without a sound, slowly and subtly as a weed. Inch by inch, hour by hour, the residents of my city would be gently—pleasantly, even—coerced into relinquishing the very last of their freedoms.

Later, when they finally snapped out of the haze and realized how miserable and desperate their lives had become, they'd get angry. The supernaturals among them would take their anger to the Council, demanding answers.

And in response, the Council would give them exactly what they needed to turn the embers of that anger into a raging inferno: a common enemy.

Our community would destroy itself from the inside out, just as Elena and I had predicted.

"Is there *anyone* on the Council who's still an ally?" Elena asked.

"I don't know," Jael said. "But for the moment, I don't believe any of them can be trusted."

"*Jesús, María, y José*. This is insane." I still couldn't believe what I was hearing. The Council was our governing body. Ignoring a few supernatural skirmishes was one thing. A rogue Council member like Talia making a power grab—that made sense, too. Happened in the human government all the time.

But sanctioning an act of war against supernaturals?

I reached for my phone, instinctively ready to call Ronan and Darius. To rally the troops. But then I remembered they were fighting another battle in the Shadowrealm, trying to find a way home for Gray.

My heart twisted to think of her again. To think of all of them out there, lost, trapped, injured, or worse… Hell. Were we ever gonna catch a break?

"How do you even know all of this?" I finally asked Jael. I needed to stay on point. Worrying about things over which I had no control wouldn't help Gray and the guys any more than it would help the Bay. "You're not part of the Council, are you?"

"No, I'm not." He held my gaze for a long time, taking his measure of me, then looked to Elena, assessing her as well. I got the feeling he was trying to decide how much he could trust us—if at all.

I couldn't blame him. I was doing the same to him.

"You said yourself you don't want an all-out war," I said. "That you're one of the few remaining fae who feels that way."

"I am."

"If that's true, then we're on the same side, Jael."

"All of us," Elena said firmly, coming to stand at my side. Her shoulder pressed against my arm, the contact so solid and reassuring I had to blink back tears. It'd been a long time since we'd presented a united front. It almost felt like we were a pack again.

She seemed to pick up on my feelings, and surprised me again by sliding her hand into mine and giving me a reassuring squeeze. I squeezed her right back.

The crises facing our communities had converged here, and maybe that was the only thing holding us together. Maybe when this was all said and done, my sister and I would go our separate ways again.

But right now, we had each other's backs. And from the

grave look in Jael's eyes, it was clear we'd need all the strength and solidarity we could muster.

"Okay. It sounds like we've got a lot more ground to cover tonight," Elena said, motioning for Jael to hand over his cape. She hung it carefully in the hall closet, then shooed us into the dining room. "I'll put on fresh coffee and fix us something to eat. I don't know about you guys, but I can strategize much better on a full stomach."

As Jael and I settled into our chairs, I heard the unmistakable knock of the chef's knife against the cutting board in the kitchen, followed by the *tick-tick-tick* of the oven preheating. Despite everything, I smiled. Elena was so much like Mamá. Birthday, funeral, holiday, unexpected company, hostile fae invasion—there was no occasion that couldn't be marked with food, and no food worth preparing unless it was an outright feast.

"I hope you're hungry," I warned Jael. Then, getting right back to business, "What else can you tell me about the situation in the Bay?"

SEVEN

GRAY

The air rushed out of my lungs at Liam's dire words, but I forced myself to remain calm. "Tell me. Whatever it is, we'll work it out."

"It's a very long, highly complex—"

"Highlights version, Liam. Let's start there."

Liam waited a beat, then finally released my hands. He exhaled deeply and closed his eyes.

"I've told you before I'm not exactly as I seem," he said. "And that is only a modicum of my treachery. But it is where we must begin." He opened his eyes again, twin blue orbs that burned with new intensity and locked onto my gaze as if that alone could keep us from falling apart. "I was human once, Gray. A shadowborn, like you. In some respects, I'm *still* human."

Briefly, I wondered if that was the worst of it, but the fierce look in his eyes said otherwise.

I sat down on the bench and nodded for him to continue, unable to look away, to blink, to breathe.

Liam sat across from me and wove his tale. At first, each sentence came at an agonizingly slow pace, then built up, layer upon layer, finally rushing out in a deluge, so many confessions and images and beginnings and endings I could barely grasp a single thread.

"...and that is simply because Death is neither a being nor an entity," he was saying, "but an immensely honorable appointment—one which I was supposed to offer to you. Upon your acceptance, I would then transfer my responsibilities to you and resume the mortal life I relinquished millennia ago—in a different vessel than my original, of course. Instead, I withheld that choice from you, and as a result, watched you endure untold horrors, much of which could have been avoided if only I'd been straightforward about your destiny from the onset..."

Liam babbled on about the dawn of man and witchcraft and Shadow magic and Death's great big capital-R Responsibilities on the ever-turning wheel of life, but I was lost, my head spinning as I tried in vain to keep up, my ears ringing from the impossibly loud beat of my heart. Tears gathered in my eyes, but I had no idea why I felt so sad. So lost.

Finally, after the pale sky had turned black and the obsidian sea reformed in a glassy sheet beneath us, reflecting the wrongness of a million red stars, Liam paused to take a breath.

"Say something, Gray. Please." He reached for my face, his fingers stopping just short of my cheek.

"What... what are you?" I whispered. It was the only question that came to mind. A starting point at the center of a vast labyrinth I wasn't sure I could escape.

"I am Shadowborn, like you. A human. At least, I was. As I've said, that identity becomes murky once a human dons the mantle of Death."

"But... when?" I asked, wondering if he was as old as Darius and Ronan. Did he have a life before? A family? Did he remember them? Miss them? Had they been made to believe he'd died in an accident, like Darius's family had? "How long ago were you human?"

"In terms of years, I don't know. I no longer process time the same way humans do. But I can tell you that it was so long ago, I scarcely recalled the simple joys of even *being* human. When I felt the call of your power across the realms, I knew only that the time had come for me to reclaim my humanity, live out the end of my days, and eventually find my soul's peace."

"The call of my power? How—" But my words evaporated as the realization hit. It must've been the night I'd inadvertently resurrected Bean in the alley. He'd been there —the dark raven who'd watched me touch her soul. The same one who'd appeared in Sophie's room the night she'd been murdered. He'd transformed before my eyes into the hooded figure I later learned was Death, and we'd been entangled in each other's lives ever since.

"Ah. I see you are beginning to understand." He almost sounded relieved.

He was wrong, though. I didn't understand at all. If

anything, I was more confused than ever. Human? I couldn't have heard him right. "But you're... you're Death. The Great Transformer, older than time, vaster than the seas, more illuminating than a thousand and one suns."

"Yes. Death is all of those things and more. So much more. So *very* much more, in fact, that the energy of such a being cannot possibly be contained by a single entity. Boiled down to its very essence, Death is but another role. That is what I'm trying to explain."

"A role? Like a job? Liam, you're not making any sense."

"Sparing you the specifics, it happens thusly: In an ancient rite as old as existence, the mantle of Death is passed down from one Shadowborn to another of their choosing, revealed only when the time is right. It was bestowed upon me many, many centuries ago by the Shadowborn who'd held the position before me. So yes, it *is* a job. The loneliest, most difficult job one could ever be tasked with, as well as the very highest honor. To wear the cloak of shadows and balance the great scales of life is a responsibility few are ever given the opportunity to consider. None who've been called to serve have ever refused."

"*Could* they refuse?"

"Of course. To wear the mantle of Death is a choice. One that is entered into freely and fully informed, or not at all."

My head was spinning again. Of all the things Liam had ever shared with me, of all the lessons he'd imparted, this was the most baffling. "So this... this choice? It's the choice you mentioned earlier? You're saying I have to decide whether to become you? To become Death?"

A bitter laugh escaped his lips. "If only it were as simple as—"

"No," I said. I didn't even have to think about it. My life as an orphaned, Shadowborn, demon-sworn, deranged-hunter-targeted witch was a red-hot mess on the best of days, and at the moment, my prospects for getting off this hell boat were looking pretty grim, too. But my friends on the material plane were counting on me to find a way out. It was way too early to lose hope. "I don't want that life. Death. Whatever you call it. No. Final answer."

"You don't understand, Gray." Liam shook his head, his every movement weighted with sadness. "That choice is no longer before you. You see, I chose you to be my successor. I began your training. And then I neglected to give *you* the choice of accepting or declining. Now, you're here. You do not get to make that choice."

I nodded somberly. Here in hell, I didn't get to make *any* choices. That was kind of the point of this place.

"It doesn't matter," I said. "I would've said no anyway. I still would've ended up right here, and you'd have to go with your second choice either way."

"It doesn't work that way. The moment I chose you, I un-chose all others." Liam pulled his foot up onto the bench, absently picking at the laces of his boot, and I almost laughed. Dressed in a flannel shirt and dark jeans, rocking that messy blond hair, Liam looked like a regular guy. One I'd had the distinct and fairly recent pleasure of making out with—kisses I still felt tingling on my lips. Yet here we were, floating aimlessly on the black lakes of hell, talking about things that would make most people's heads explode.

And judging from the severity in his eyes, we were just getting started.

"If any chosen Shadowborn fails the training or refuses the call," he went on, "the current servant of Death is permanently bound and forced to serve for eternity. It is the risk we take when we make our selection, but I never considered it a risk. As I said, no one has ever refused before."

"Yet here I go, breaking all the rules again." I offered him a small smile and reached out to squeeze his knee. I was pissed at him for keeping me in the dark on this—it was a major revelation, to say the least, and I'd need time to fully process it later, and ask more questions and probably ignore him for a few days—but in the grand scheme of our current predicament, and everything that still waited for us on the material plane, Liam's sins of omission weren't exactly unforgivable. I had bigger battles to fight, and I was counting on Liam to stand by my side through all of them.

Besides, he'd picked me, and I'd refused. Now, he'd be stuck as the Grim Reaper for all eternity. That sounded like punishment enough.

But Liam didn't return my smile. His gaze darkened, his brow creasing with deep lines. "Yours was not a refusal as much as a... well, a different sort of complication"

"What sort of—oh." *Damn. Of course.* The labyrinth of

this insane tale just branched out in a thousand new directions. "Because of Sebastian. My contract."

"I named you as my successor, unaware of your existing bond. Regardless of the strength of your power or whatever greatness I believed you capable of, as a demon sworn witch, your soul was already claimed. I couldn't move forward without the permission of your master."

The sound of the m-word made my skin crawl with revulsion. Liam had the grace to look embarrassed, but it was too late.

"So you made a deal," I snapped, getting to my feet. This was his true confession—the real source of his guilt. I turned away from him and knelt on the foredeck, gazing out across the endless black mirror beneath us, shaking my head in disbelief.

Fucking Sebastian. What *was* it about him? Why did the men I cared most about always turn to him when the chips were down?

"You made a deal," I repeated. "With the Prince of Hell."

"At the time," he said softly, "I thought—"

"Yes, I know, Liam. You thought it was the only option at the time. You and everyone else who's ever signed on Sebastian's dotted line. That's why they call it a devil's bargain." I rubbed my temples, a new headache squeezing my skull like an overripe melon. I could forgive Liam for not telling me about the Death thing. But making a deal with the Prince of Hell? After everything I'd been through on that front with Ronan? "Just tell me what happened."

"Well, Sebastian heard my case, of course. He already knew how powerful you were—how powerful you were destined to become. And just as I'd bargained on you accepting the mantle, Sebastian had bargained on your refusal."

"Oh, I'm sure he did." I couldn't keep the sarcasm from my voice. "And the terms of this clandestine deal of the century?"

"For a small price, he agreed to grant me the opportunity to assess your magic, train you to the fullest extent that time allowed, and ultimately present this choice to you as I was meant to. If you accepted the honor, you would continue on in my stead, and I would be free to live out a mortal life, just as I'd planned."

Wow. So that's what all this had been about. Liam wanted his mortality, and he was willing to trade away mine for the privilege.

"And this so-called small price?" I asked.

"I was to bring him the soul of a woman who broke her contract years ago, and has eluded his capture ever since."

"Bring him the soul? How?"

"I would've had to take her life, Gray." He let out a deep sigh. "I'm not proud of that now. Please understand— when I made that deal, I did not think and feel as a human."

"No, that didn't happen until you became Liam Cole-brook, surfing philosopher, giver of advice and spreader of knowledge, Mr. Humanity himself. Right?"

"Not... quite. It is only in your eyes that I see my human

reflection. You look at me as if you truly believe I could be human. As if you truly believe I could be loved."

I didn't respond, and after a few moments of chilling silence, Liam said softly, "It's what I thought I wanted at the time, Gray. My soul was ready to move on."

"And now?" I asked, my own voice just as soft. Just as broken. I was still kneeling on the foredeck, and I couldn't bring myself to turn around and look at him. I was too afraid of what he might say. "Is that still what you want?"

"It doesn't matter. It's not possible now."

"But if it *were*, Liam. Would you want that? A mortal life?"

Liam didn't say anything for so long, I thought he'd vanished. That I'd only been imagining the feel of his heat cresting behind me, the imprint of his presence refusing to fade from my memory.

But when I finally found the courage to get back on my feet and turn around, he was standing right before me, solid and real, closing the small distance that remained. Fresh tears shone in his eyes.

"I did want that, yes," he admitted, resting his hands on my shoulders. "And I kept on wanting it, right up until—"

"Until what?" I felt my own tears gathering again, my throat tight with emotion, my heart heavy with the sting of betrayal. "Until you realized that mortals die painfully and that being the Great Transformation and the Vast Almighty Fuckwhit of Time Immemorial isn't such a bad gig after all?"

At this, he let out a small laugh, but it was hollow. I

tried to look away, but he took my chin between his thumb and finger, gently tilting my face up until I had no choice but to look into his eyes.

"What I realized, little witch, was that living a mortal life would hold no joy for me if you were not living that life by my side. Everything I thought I'd wanted vanished under the bright light of your smile, and every time I heard your laugh or tasted your magic in the air or felt even the barest touch of your hair against my cheek, I swore I'd rather die a thousand deaths by your side than be human for a single day in a world that you no longer inhabited—a world where I'd spend every night dreaming that the woman I was falling in love with was curled up beside me, only to awaken to the chill of her absence and the emptiest ache a human heart could bear."

"You... you're falling in love with me?" I gasped at his words, each confession a tiny flame that surged and burned its way through my heart.

Liam smiled again, his cheeks coloring. "Another unforeseen complication, I'm afraid."

God, that smile. I wanted him to kiss me. I wanted him to take me into his arms and promise me he'd find a way out of this for both of us. To convince me that his betrayals didn't matter. That love was enough, and if we only had the chance to find our way back to each other—to grow and nurture that love—we could get past this.

But we were in hell, and hell was the place where all wishes died.

We couldn't get past this any more than I could still

become Death. Not because of the secrets or even the deal with Sebastian. But because there was too much still uncovered. Unconfessed. I saw the guilt of it lingering in his eyes, felt his shame in his touch.

As if he could read my thoughts, Liam said, "I'm sorry, Gray. For all that I've done. For all that I've yet to confess. For all the ways my words and deeds will cause you more pain."

There was so much emotion, so much love in his eyes, anyone else would've melted before that gaze. But the longer Liam stared at me, the more enraged I became. It was more than the things he'd confessed, or even the secrets he still held. It was, I realized suddenly, that I'd started falling for him, too. And all along, he'd been something else—some*one* else—entirely.

Everything about us suddenly felt like a lie. Every memory was tainted. In that way, he'd stolen them from me —some of the most beautiful, meaningful moments of my life.

How could I have trusted him so easily?

Fury was lapping at my feet like a wave, and when I couldn't take another second of his intense gaze, I finally exploded, letting that fury wash right over me, sucking the last of my patience out to sea.

"In all your training and mentoring," I said, jabbing my finger into his chest, "you led me to believe it was for my own good, so I could learn to strengthen and direct my magic, to call upon my powers, to grow as a person. But it was really training camp for Death—a job that you no longer wanted. Something you called the loneliest, most difficult job ever. *That's* what you were to pass along to me."

"I would have told you in time, but—"

"No. You kept me in the dark because you made a deal with my soul and couldn't bring yourself to admit it. Meanwhile, you watched my best friend die, my other friends get kidnapped and tortured, the men I love risk their lives to save me from a Shadowrealm I banished myself to, all the while knowing you could've spared us this if only you'd been honest with me. No, I wouldn't have chosen to become Death, so all of those things would've happened anyway, just like they did. But I had a right to know there was another way, and you kept that from me."

"Gray, I—"

"All your rambling about choices and destinies and paths. All along, you were making my choices for me. I trusted you, Liam. I cared for you—more than you even realize. And when you told me things—about the realms, about my magic, about what I could do—I believed you."

I blew out a breath of air, my body shaking, my heart pounding. Somewhere along the line, I'd hopped on a roller coaster of understanding to frustration to forgiveness to anger to rage, and I still wasn't ready to step off this crazy ride. The longer we talked, the more it hurt. And the worst part was that none of this even mattered. Not if I couldn't find a way out of here. Eventually, Liam would have to leave, go back to his Death duties. And I'd be left here, alone with these feelings. With this blackness.

"I never misled you about your capabilities," he said. "You and I were only just beginning to tap into your potential. You *can* do all of those things. And more. So much more, Gray."

"Ah, but I can't. Remember?" Angry tears threatened to spill, but I eradicated them with a quick swipe. I would *not* let my emotions lead me back into his warm embrace. Not now. "I'm *here*. A permanent guest in Sebastian's playground. Banished. No better off than I was in the Shadowrealm. All that's missing is a visit from the Prince himself, come to introduce himself and gloat at his big win."

"Gray, this wasn't... Your ending up here had nothing to do with my deal." Liam's face paled, his shoulders slumping under the weight of whatever he was about to say next. "Remember, Sebastian was betting on your declining this opportunity. Per our arrangement, if I failed to properly train you or convince you to accept the honor, I... I was bound to burn your life scroll."

"My life scroll?"

"Do you recall the soul ferrier you met the night Sophie passed? The owl I entrusted with her soul?"

I nodded, the familiar sadness of Sophie's death clawing at my heart. It was a pain I'd learned to live with, but now it flared anew, as bright and strong as it had been in those first few days after her murder. For her, I did let those tears fall. They slid down my cheeks and into my mouth, the salty taste a reminder that I could still feel.

Liam cupped my face, gently catching my tears with his

thumbs. I let him, desperate for the comfort, however brief it had to be.

"They take many forms," he continued. "Owls, ravens, bats. Ferriers ensure safe passage of the recently deceased to the Shadowrealm. But that is not what marks a human's death in the cosmic sense. Deep within the cosmos, at a distance beyond infinity, lies the Great Hall of Records. A library, essentially, that contains the life stories of all creatures. Their life scrolls."

"Literally," I said.

"*Quite* literally, yes." He dropped his hands, and I canted forward, already missing his touch. Liam continued speaking, pretending he hadn't noticed. "Every being is issued a blank scroll upon birth, upon which their life stories are written. Of course, what are stories but a series of choices, and as such, they are never written in permanent ink, for they are ever-changing. The only chapter that is final, immutable, is death. So, when a being dies and passes into the Shadowrealm, it is Death's responsibility to see that their scroll is burned. The burning is symbolic of the great transformation of the soul, and it's how the natural order is kept in balance. There are never more scrolls—or living beings—than intended."

In typical fashion, Liam's explanation left me more confused than ever.

"So Sebastian wanted you to... to kill me?" I asked. "Like the woman who'd escaped his capture?"

"No. He wanted me to burn your life scroll. As I said, that is a symbolic gesture—it does not literally *bring* your death. It merely *records* your death, as far as the natural order is concerned."

"But I wouldn't actually *be* dead? Just *listed* as dead on an old dusty scroll that you would then set on fire?" I closed my eyes and shook my head. Hell's atmosphere must have been screwing with my logic circuits, because clearly I was missing something. "Liam. If all Sebastian wanted was for you to record my death on paper, why wouldn't we just do that?"

"It's so much more complicated and devastating than that, Gray." He paused, his eyes electrified with pain and guilt. In a voice so low I had to read the words on his lips, he said, "Remember what your death—even on paper— actually means for him."

The full horror of Liam's deceit hit me then, all at once, like a thousand glass rainstorms pelting me from all directions. I collapsed onto the deck, all my bones turning to dust. I couldn't breathe.

Liam really had bargained away my soul. If I'd accepted his offer, I would have become Death. If I'd failed or refused, I would've been marked as "dead", a tiny loophole just big enough for the Prince of Hell to step through.

A loophole just big enough to allow him to collect on my original contract, years—decades—before it was meant to begin.

In exchange for a shot at his own mortal life, Liam had sold me into demonic slavery.

EIGHT

GRAY

Blurred by my tears, three women appeared on the boat behind Liam, dressed in white and carrying their silver swords, just as they had in my dream in the Shadowrealm.

We told you not to follow him, they said.

"Where is my sword?" I asked, nearly delirious with grief. "There are supposed to be four."

I was vaguely aware of Liam kneeling down on the deck before me, his warm hands wrapping around my calves, his blue eyes scanning my face, searching for signs of life. But I looked past him, reaching instead for the women.

You must seek your own sword, they said, their voices unifying into a single, shadowy echo. *Before you no longer have the strength to rise.*

They vanished in an instant, leaving their swords behind, suddenly embedded in my chest. Blood leaked from the wounds, soaking my shirt and staining the wooden slats of the boat.

"Do something," I whispered to Liam.

Tears glittered in his eyes, and he leaned forward and pressed a kiss to my temple, the scent of his skin like summer and the beach and the ocean and everything I'd come to love about him. "I'm trying, little witch. Please let me help you."

I leaned into his touch, and just as quickly as it had appeared, the dream-haze lifted. I was whole again, my mind focused, the blood no more than a nightmare receding in the dawn.

Liam pulled back, watching me intently. Waiting for me to speak.

"I don't know what to say to you," I admitted. "Part of me wants to hate you. The other part can't imagine letting you go."

"I understand." He lowered his eyes, shame coloring his cheeks once again. "I… I've utterly failed you."

"Liam, don't—"

"In guiding you through your magic without revealing my own secrets," he pushed on, "I have failed you. In withholding this choice and its ramifications from you, I have failed you. But most of all…" Liam cupped my face, each of his words a struggle that seemed to wring another drop of life from his being. "In falling in love with you, I have failed you. I wanted to keep you whole and unbroken, to hold on to the sweetness I tasted in your kiss, to believe in the fairy tale I saw in your eyes when you looked at me that day on the beach."

"Then why didn't you?" I reached up to touch his lips,

soft and lush. Tiny sparks danced across his mouth, making my fingertips tingle. "Why?"

"Oh, Gray. Your heart was never mine to claim. That is why these sparks—the lightning—why it followed our every kiss. You and I... We were never supposed to exist in that way. There was no room for that possibility in the natural order. I broke it when I tried to make it so. I broke *you*."

My heartbeat sputtered, twin halves pounding very opposite rhythms. One half for the new love I'd only just begun to feel for him during our time in the Shadowrealm, fizzy and hopeful and as delicate as lace. The other half for the black rage still coursing through my blood, heating up all over again.

"Say something," he whispered. Desperate. Lonely.

"I never want to see you again." I closed my eyes. Apparently, I was a good liar, too. "Go."

Liam sighed, but he didn't make a move to leave. "I'm afraid I can't. Not until I've offered you this final choice. It is why I've come, Gray." He got to his feet, pulling me up with him. Grabbing my shoulders tight, he said, "You must hear me out. Please. It is your *only* chance at leaving this realm."

"Go," I said again. I needed him to leave. I needed him to stay. I needed him to undo all of this so we could avoid this soul-crushing pain and skip to the good part. The falling in love, learning about the universe together part. The kissing part.

"Go," I repeated.

Liam ignored me. "Now that your soul is trapped here, you are no longer free to accept the mantle of Death I was meant to bestow upon you. You are Sebastian's possession, and I am meant to continue eternally as the Great Equalizer, Lord of Shadows, Bringer of Transformation. Death."

Fresh anger welled inside, and I jerked out of his grip, shoving him hard in the chest. "You've condemned us both, all because of your stupid ego! You're supposed to be above all this human crap!"

"I am supposed to be a lot of things, Gray. As are you. Yet we keep defying those expectations at every turn." The smoldering look in his eyes brought me right back to the beach. Our kiss. The lightning. He said we broke the natural order, and maybe we did.

But in that moment, breaking the natural order had made me whole.

The part of my heart that still cared for him beat harder, and I almost reached for him again. Almost pressed my lips to the hollow of his throat where his shirt opened up, licking the salty taste from his skin. Almost felt a thousand tiny sparks exploding between us.

With every image, every fantasy, my heart started to shift, making room for the possibility of forgiveness even now. Was that what it meant to love someone? To accept their flaws and fuckups, no matter how disastrous, as long as they were willing to bare their soul in front of you? To strip everything down, admit their mistakes, apologize? Mean it? Was it enough? I had no doubts that Liam was sorry. That he'd do anything to take back his actions and heal this great rift he'd opened up between us.

But did that mean I was strong enough to cross that rift?

My heart thought so. My skin, my eyes, my body, all the places that wanted to drink him in thought so.

But in the end, my brain just couldn't be convinced.

I broke away from his fiery gaze and backed off, folding my arms across my chest to keep him from getting any closer. "What do you want, Liam?"

"There is a final choice for you here, as I mentioned on my arrival. This time, I'm giving you the options equally and honestly, as I should've done before."

"Honestly?" I laughed, but the harshness of it hurt my ears. "Well, *honest* would be a good start, coming from you."

"A good start? No, little witch." He dropped his voice to a whisper, his face falling into a look of utter devastation. "It's the end."

"Of course." I sighed. I was out of anger, out of rage. Out of patience for his melodramatic declarations. "Just... just tell me, Liam. Get to the point."

"Option one," he began, the heaviness of his words pressing on my heart before he'd even finished his sentence. "We concede to this loss. I will return to my eternal work, donning the cloak of shadows for all time, and you... remain."

"Remain what? Where?"

"Here, Gray. Exactly as you are now, only without my company." He looked out across the vast emptiness surrounding us, the black sea still wholly unbroken by land or other vessels or even a cloud on the horizon. "This moment, this place, this view, this life, these memories, endlessly haunting you."

"In other words, live out eternity trapped in the most fucked-up Groundhog Day in the universe?" I shook my head. "Hard pass."

"You might reconsider, once I've shared the rest."

A tremble rolled through my body, head to toe, but I held it together. "What's behind lucky door number two?"

"I burn your life scroll, as Sebastian intended from the moment we made our first deal."

"First. So this is part of a new deal, then?"

"It is. We have no other choice in the matter, Gray. This is his domain."

"What does he want?" I asked, though I suspected I already knew the answer.

"He'll allow me to escort your soul back to your body and reunite the two, restoring your life force. You'll be physically alive and integrated, just as you were before you entered the Shadowrealm."

"And my magic?"

"Shall be restored as well. Your power will continue to develop—to whatever extent you are allowed to continue your magical training and studies—and you will grow and age and transform as you normally would. Upon your natural death, you'll... you'll remain in his possession, per the terms of your original contract."

I closed my eyes, the last of my hope evaporating. Of

course Sebastian had thought of everything. *The devil is in the details.* For the first time in my life, I was starting to understand what that actually meant.

"So that's it, then," I said. "Stay here, or start a new life as the Prince of Hell's magical plaything."

Liam had the good sense not to try to soften the harsh reality of that situation. "If you need time to consider this, I can come back—"

"Oh, I've already made my choice, Liam. But you were wrong about one thing."

"I was wrong about a great many things."

"I'm talking about the part where you said this would be the last choice I'd ever be allowed to make." I opened my eyes and glared at him. "I *guarantee* you it won't be."

Liam said nothing, but his lips held the hint of the same smile I'd caught in the Shadowrealm after I told him I wasn't giving up hope—that I'd find a way out of there, no matter how impossible it seemed.

"So what have you decided, then?" he finally asked.

I tipped my head back and looked up at the sky, gazing across the spray of red stars. They were beautiful, yet eerie. Not home. Not true.

I took a deep breath, calling up the magic from deep inside. It answered immediately, swirling in my chest, buzzing through my nerves, across my skin, into my blood, right down to my very bones. I might not be able to use it here in Hell, but this magic was a part of me, something even Sebastian couldn't take away.

I was done running from him. Done prolonging the

inevitable. It was time to meet my so-called master and let him know exactly what I thought of *that* little arrangement.

Lowering my face once again, I met Liam's intense gaze with my own brand of ferocity. He flinched in surprise, and I let out a laugh.

Then, with a smile on my face and all that beautiful, dark, incredibly powerful magic racing around inside me, I made my choice.

"Burn it, Liam."

NINE

EMILIO

"All non-fae travel has been restricted," Jael said, helping himself to a second serving of Elena's *canelones de espinaca*. "Communications into and out of the Bay are glamoured. I'd advise you not to trust any reports you receive from your men or anyone else in town, and don't bother trying to warn them, either. They won't receive your messages as you intended."

I pushed my own plate away, my worries about the situation back home killing the last of my appetite. "They can do that? Glamour cell phone conversations?"

"Cell phones, texts, emails, handwritten letters, telegraphs, photos, websites, on and on. Anything can be glamoured to seem like something else, especially when the targets don't realize they're being targeted."

"So coordinating a rescue from inside the city is out," Elena said. "We'll have to get in, but you say they're restricting travel. Is there a way to get close, sneak in below their radar? Maybe send in undercovers?"

"You won't get within fifty miles of the Bay," he said. "You'll drive your normal roads, of course, but then you'll suddenly forget to make the turn. Or you'll make the turn, only to end up right back where you began. Or you'll swear you left for the Bay hours ago, only to find yourself in the bathtub enjoying a good soak. Fae glamour has many facets."

Did we even stand a chance? Darkwinter seemed to have the advantage at every turn. And they had the Council's backing, besides.

What a mess.

"How did this even happen?" I asked, more to myself than anyone else, but Jael answered anyway.

"My sense is that Darkwinter and their allies have been planning this for some time, Talia's involvement notwithstanding. Recent conditions in the Bay have made the city ripe for such a takeover."

"How so?" Elena asked.

"The Bay was already in a state of chaos," Jael said. "After word spread of the rash of violence against witches, many of the others began to flee."

"It was safer for them to go," I said defensively, thinking of Gray and Haley. Of Reva. If they'd gotten out earlier, maybe they'd be safe now, too. Maybe Gray wouldn't be trapped in the Shadowrealm with a madman bent on killing her, and Reva and Haley wouldn't be locked in that awful prison. "What would you have them do instead? Wait around to be caught by a hunter? To be carved up and experimented on, slaughtered in their own beds?"

Jael finally set down his fork, deep pain flashing in his eyes.

Too late, I realized my mistake.

He'd lost someone he loved in exactly the way I'd so gracelessly described.

Nice move, asshole.

"Jael, I'm sorry. I didn't—"

"I wanted to take her away," Jael said softly. "But she wanted to stay. Sophie loved the Bay. It was her home. She loved Gray, too. I understand why you're so upset about this situation, detective." At this, he met my eyes again, his gaze fierce despite the calm, almost detached tone in his voice. "I'm asking you for the same understanding."

"I… Of course," I said. "I'm sorry, Jael. I should've been more… I'm sorry."

"Apology accepted."

In the awkward silence that followed, Elena cleared away some of the dishes and brought back a fresh pot of coffee, even stronger than the last one. She poured us each another cup—her fourth, my sixth, Jael's second. It seemed we'd all accepted that sleep wasn't an option tonight.

"I don't blame the witches for leaving," Jael finally said, stirring about half a cup of sugar into his brew. "I'm merely pointing out the facts. The power balance their absence created didn't cause this, but it *is* a factor. One we must consider if we're going to find a way to restore that balance."

"A factor, yes," I said. "Along with Darkwinter's aspirations, Talia's betrayal, and the hunters' endless quest for the magic they believe is rightfully theirs. Not to mention the Council's total fucking betrayal of their own oaths." I gulped down half my coffee, ignoring the burn in my throat. "Looks like we're about three kinds of fucked here, *amigos*."

Jael didn't disagree. "Another challenge we're facing is the existing unrest within each supernatural sub-community. The vampires in particular have become unstable. Several factions are vying for Darius Beaumont's territory. A group from the south has already taken control of his assets in town, including his apartment and the Black Ruby property."

"What?" This was news to me. Vampire hierarchy had a lot of very definitive rules. One group couldn't just move in on someone else's territory—not without a whole lot of bloodshed. "Darius hasn't formerly relinquished any of his holdings, and he isn't dead. Who are these upstart vamps?"

"They're unknown to me, but my understanding is that Darius lost respect in recent months after the slaughter of several of his own kind at Norah Hanson's home. His involvement with the Grinaldi family has not helped matters. None of the squabbling vampire underlings seem to know where his loyalties lie, other than with a witch who up until a couple of months ago was utterly unremarkable. And now the vampire seems to have vanished altogether."

"That's ridiculous, Jael. The vamps we eliminated at the

Hanson house were sent there to kidnap Gray and kill the rest of us. Hardly innocent victims."

"*Allegedly*," Jael said. "Remember, detective. The official story is typically the one written by those in power, regardless of how they came into such power. At the moment, they've set up camp in our city, while you and your allies appear to have fled. Whom does that leave to tell the tale?"

I conceded the point, despite the fact that it made my blood boil to imagine some rag-tag bunch of bloodsuckers invading Darius's territory. He'd rip their throats out if he knew. Hell, I'd save him the trip and do it myself if I could get back there.

"So who's pulling the strings?" Elena asked. "Darkwinter and the hunters are doing the dirty work, but someone must be financing the operation. Coordinating the takeover. Do you think it's Talia?"

"I wondered about that, too, but..." Jael sipped his coffee, considering, then finally shook his head. "No. Talia has always thought very highly of herself, and her position on the Council does afford her some measure of power. But I'm fairly certain she's not the ultimate player here. Someone—or someones—is leading the charge at a much higher level."

"Probably sitting in a cushy office somewhere, keeping his hands clean."

"Or hers," Jael said.

"Or hers. Exactly." I pushed back from my chair and got up to help Elena clear the last of the dishes.

Jael had given us a lot to consider, and it all felt legit.

But something was still bugging me about it all.

Jael wasn't on the Council. As far as I knew, his family made an honest living in the Bay through Illuminae—at least, as honest as a fae could be. Back in the fae realm, he was Seelie court royalty, but here in our world, he was a club deejay. Venerated by the groupies who flocked to Illuminae to hear him spin, but not someone I'd typically think of as a covert operator.

How, then, had he come across so much intel about Darkwinter's actions?

I opened my mouth a dozen times to press him on it, but after putting my foot in my mouth about Sophie's death, I didn't want to risk offending him again. We needed him on our side.

Thankfully, Elena spared me the trouble.

Setting out a plate of homemade *alfajores* so thick with dulce de leche they were probably going to be the death of us all, she said, "Unfortunately, we can't make a move on this intel until we verify it. The last thing we need is to expose ourselves because of a misguided operation based on incomplete or unverified information."

"That's going to be difficult," he said, reaching for a cookie. "As I've said, communications into and out of the Bay are not reliable."

Diplomatic as ever, she waited for him to take a bite, then went in for the kill shot. "So, who's your source on this?"

Slowly, he finished chewing his cookie, clearly considering his next move. He held Elena in his gaze, but there was no malice there. If anything, he looked impressed.

Reaching for another cookie, he said, "My sister Kallayna has been working to infiltrate Darkwinter for quite some time. She'd heard whispers at Illuminae that the old lines were gathering strength, preparing to make a move in the Bay. Frightened by the possibilities, she encouraged these rumors, hoping to find out more information. Eventually, she became aware that a Knight of Darkwinter had been spending time at the bar. She took her time, slowly getting him to trust her. To enjoy her company. They became quite close."

"How close?" Elena asked.

"They'd started dating, and then Kallayna sensed things were getting more serious. He asked her to move in with him—he'd recently bought a home in the Bay. She was scared, of course, but she saw the opportunity for what it was and accepted his offer, pretending to be dissatisfied with our family."

"And this Knight... He believed her?" I asked, finally sitting down again.

"As far as we know, yes. Though communicating with her has been difficult. We staged a very public, very brutal fight over her decision to move in with him, all to lend credence to her claims. She broke ties with me and turned her back on our legacy. Since then, she's been sending me encrypted messages through a secure, non-glamoured channel magically routed through our home realm, but the only way for her to access it is to leave the Bay, and she can't do that often without arousing suspicion."

"If you knew what Darkwinter was planning," I said, "why didn't you come to us sooner?"

"Just like you, I needed to be certain before acting on the intel. We didn't know exactly what they were planning—if anything. They could have just as easily been setting Kallayna up for a fall. I couldn't risk that."

"When was the last time you heard from her?" Elena asked.

"Two days ago—before the Knights secured the city." He pressed a napkin to his lips and closed his eyes, his shoulders stiffening. It was the closest he'd come to losing his composure in my presence. "The thought of losing someone else I love…"

He trailed off, but I knew the "someone else" he'd been thinking of in that moment. I realized just how much restraint he'd shown tonight in not asking me for details, for updates on the case, not even when the subject of Sophie had come up earlier.

He had a right to know where things stood.

"Jael, we know who took Sophie's life," I said gently.

"Oh?" he asked calmly. He didn't look up, didn't show any outward reaction at all, but I sensed the need in his voice, that one-word reply heavy with equal parts pain and hope.

"Sophie and the other witches in Blackmoon Bay were murdered by Jonathan Reese," I said. "He's the man currently imprisoning Gray and the others. We don't know whether he acted alone in the killings, but my gut says no. We already know he had accomplices in other attacks, including the one at Norah's house, so it's not a stretch to assume this is connected to the larger crime waves in the Bay as well as the Darkwinter takeover. I just wish I understood how all the pieces fit together."

"Jonathan Reese?" Jael met my eyes across the table. I could practically see the wheels of his mind turning. "Possibly a relative of Phillip Reese?"

"Yes," I said, recalling the name from what little I could find in Jonathan's public records. "Phillip is his father—the hunter who killed Gray's mother when she was a teenager. Do you know the man?"

"Kallayna has reported that her Darkwinter Knight has accompanied a human named Phillip Reese to at least three or four meetings with other Darkwinter soldiers. I don't believe she knew he was a hunter. She hasn't been privy to the meetings themselves—only to his comings and goings."

"We already know from another source that Jonathan's motive isn't murder," I said. "He's developing the hybrid technologies, but his experiments often result in the death of his subjects. I just couldn't figure out how he was getting his research to Darkwinter, or if they were running their own operation. But that's it—it's his father. Phillip Reese is the connection."

"I thought Jonathan was estranged from his father," Elena said. "That everything he does is in direct opposition to his father's legacy."

"That's what we heard from one highly unreliable

85

witness," I said. "Fiona Brentwood is a vampire with an ax to grind."

"Many people believe my sister and I are estranged," Jael said with a casual shrug. "Perhaps the rift between father and son was also an act."

We were all startled by my sister's phone. She hopped up from the table and fished it from her pocket, disappearing into the living room. "Alvarez. What have you got for me?"

I turned my attention back to Jael, who'd just snuck in a third *alfajor*. When all this was over, we'd have to send him a whole box of them.

"You could be onto something with that estrangement act idea," I said. "We hadn't considered it from that angle."

I popped an *alfajor* into my mouth, trying to process everything. It was entirely possible that there were multiple factions of hunter groups working together with Darkwinter, or that Jonathan and his father had set aside their differences to work against their common enemy. For all I knew, the prison was just one of *many* hybrid research sites.

The Bay needed our help, but right now, we needed to find out what was going on in that prison. That was the key to toppling the coup in the Bay—and anywhere else they'd set their sights on. I was sure of it.

"We need to get into that prison," I said. "We've got good intel that says it's here on the coast. Problem is, we can't actually locate it. It's fae spelled."

"I might be able to intercede," Jael said. "It's doubtful I can destroy the spell completely—Darkwinter have powers the rest of us can only dream about—but if I can weaken it long enough for you to get inside, that might be a start."

"It's worth a shot," I said. "But Jael, if Darkwinter figures out you were the one who brought down the spell…"

I let the silence speak for itself. Jael knew what Darkwinter would do to him if he got caught. He didn't need me to spell it out.

"They are, either directly or indirectly, responsible for the death of someone I love," he said, his catlike golden eyes suddenly blazing. "Possibly the torment of others. There is nothing I won't do, nothing I won't risk, to hasten their end. Are we absolutely clear on that, detective?"

I nodded once, accepting his offer. There was no point trying to talk him out of it. I knew what it meant to lay your life down for someone you loved—for vengeance, for a shot at saving them, for all of it. There would always be consequences, but not taking the risk at all? That was a shame I could never live with.

I sensed Jael felt the same way.

Elena returned from the living room, pulling on her jacket and gloves. "That was Lansky. We just got a hit on Norah Hanson's credit card."

"What does that mean?" Jael asked, reaching for another cookie.

"It means you'd better get a doggy bag, Prince." I grabbed the plate out from under his hand and rose from the table. "We've got a rogue witch to track down."

TEN

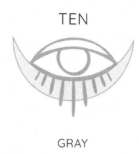

GRAY

It felt like someone had pulled the plug on my soul, and now I was being sucked down into oblivion, crushed by the weight of too much gravity as I spun and swirled and vanished down some ancient cosmic drain.

But just when I feared my bones would be pulverized, the spinning stopped, and I was breathing again, gulping down the precious air I'd been deprived of. I was alive.

And I was back on the material plane.

When I finally opened my eyes, I found myself resting on cloud-fluffy bedding, gazing up at a pristine white ceiling fitted with a stainless-steel fan that gently stirred the air. I'd been bathed and dressed in soft stretch pants and a loose gray hoodie that smelled like... like Ronan.

Like home.

God, how I wanted to close my eyes and sink back into that dream—the one where none of this was real. Where my rebels and I had never left the safe house, and instead spent our days cooking meals together and drinking good wine and playing Scrabble and making love. So much hot, passionate, incredible, amazing love in a bed big enough for the whole pack.

My core ached to think of it.

But despite the softness of his sweatshirt and the luxurious sheets beneath me, this was no dream. I'd just been betrayed by someone I trusted and evicted from hell, only to end up in a fancy hotel room I could never afford even if I *hadn't* lost my job at Waldrich's Imports.

Everything about Blackmoon Bay, about my old life, felt like it belonged to someone else.

And now, so did I.

I let out a tired sigh. The Prince of Hell would be expecting me soon, if he wasn't already. This hotel was probably his property.

Just like me.

Welcome to the first day of the end of your life, Gray Desario.

I waited another beat for the tingling in my arms and legs to subside, then sat up slowly, leaning back against a sleek ebony headboard. The room spun again, and when it finally righted, something else came into sharp focus.

The sight of him stole my breath all over again.

"Ronan," I gasped.

He stood at the foot of the bed in dark jeans and a black v-neck tee that clung to his muscles, a dark shadow of a beard lining his jaw, his hair practically begging for me to run my fingers through it. I wanted to touch him. To feel his hands and mouth on me.

But something was... different. His face had been bruised, with new, pink scars cutting across his jaw. His rigid, unmoving form was flanked by two terrifying canine beasts I recognized from our previous run-ins. There was no mistaking the matted, coal-black fur, the razor-sharp teeth, the glowing red eyes.

Hellhounds.

Despite the frightening and unexpected appearance of the hounds, a surge of gratitude swept over me. Ronan was here. Alive. He'd made it through the hell portal, and I'd made it back to him, and even if we only had one minute to say our goodbyes, I'd take it.

I couldn't help but smile.

"Ronan," I said, finding my full voice. "It's *damn* good to see you."

But Ronan wasn't smiling at me in return, or moving to capture me in a passionate kiss, or reaching for his phone to call Emilio and let him know I was okay. He was just standing there, still as a statue, his eyes blazing with fury while the hounds growled menacingly at his sides.

Ronan waited a beat. Two. Three. Made sure I'd finally seen the anger flashing in his eyes. Then, those beautiful hazel eyes that used to look at me as though I were the only person in the universe that mattered, turned demon black.

"Ronan?" Was this another trick? Maybe I hadn't made it out at all. Maybe I'd only found my way into another chamber in hell, full of fresh torments and hallucinations.

"Gray Desario," Ronan announced, his jaw clenched so

tightly I thought he'd shatter his teeth, "your contract has been called."

His tone was stiff and formal, every one of those words pushed through lips that didn't want to yield.

But they did yield.

"I'm here in my official capacity as Guardian at the Crossroads to inform you of your eternal imprisonment and to escort you to your..." He paused, swallowing hard, stumbling. "To your master. Do not attempt to renegotiate. The terms of your contract are binding in accordance with the laws of the Crossroads and upheld by all the courts of the realms."

Ronan rattled off a bunch of rules and regulations, each one clearly regurgitated from memory. The ice in his voice reached into my heart, freezing me all the way down to the bone.

I wondered how many times he'd had to do this before. How many times he'd have to do it again once I was "escorted" into Sebastian's possession and no longer Ronan's responsibility. He was, after all, a crossroads demon, oathbound to serve at his master's pleasure.

From the sound of it, it was only a matter of seconds before that master was the very last thing Ronan and I would ever share.

"Stop!" I shouted, climbing out of the bed and rushing over to Ronan.

"Oh, but I can't," he said sardonically. "This is my job. You always wanted to know where I disappeared to all those times. What I did. Now you get an up-close-and-personal view."

"Don't do this," I whispered. "Just... wait. Five minutes."

He clamped his mouth shut, and I reached for his face, running my fingers along his jaw. A shiver rolled through him, but before he fully leaned into my touch, he reached up and grabbed my wrist, yanking my hand away.

"Don't," he said. Cold. Dead.

Fear and confusion flooded my heart. *This* was how he wanted to say goodbye?

"What's *wrong* with you?" I asked.

Ronan took a breath, but before he could answer my question, the skin on my wrist—all the places where his fingers touched—began to smolder.

He released me as if I had the plague, his lip curling in disgust.

"Stay away from me, Gray." He held his hands up in front of him, slowly backing away. The hounds followed his every move, never leaving his side.

When I reached for his face again, they snapped at me in warning.

So that's how it's going to be.

"Let me guess," I said, pulling away and rubbing the heat from my wrist. "This new little trick of yours is courtesy of Sebastian, Prince of Hell, He Who Thinks He Owns Me?"

"It's not a trick, Gray. It's a price." Ronan sighed, finally dropping the stiff formalities. "He *does* own you. I've been fighting with him for a decade, looking for some technicality that could get you out of this mess, all for nothing. The only thing that kept you safe was the fact that you fucking stayed alive. But now?"

"Newsflash, Ronan. I'm still alive." I waved my hand in his face, displaying the red, angry welts quickly rising on my wrist. "Case in point."

"Colebrook was supposed to bring you back unharmed. Did he say anything about this?"

I took a steadying breath, trying to gather my thoughts. I didn't want to rehash the whole Death mantle thing right now, or give Ronan a reason to hate Liam. Despite my own anger toward him, I couldn't rule out the possibility of a future reconciliation. I already missed him so much—the flannel, the sun-kissed hair, the annoyingly philosophical conversations, the stupidly kissable lips. The whole situation was impossible, but that didn't mean it wasn't worth fighting for.

And Liam owed me a fight. That was for sure.

As much as I wanted to deny it, Liam—Death—was a part of me, stitched into the fabric of my soul. I couldn't imagine my world without him.

"Liam and I came to an agreement with Sebastian," I said, glossing over the details. "The only way to get my soul out of hell and back into my body was to fake out the universe. We had to trick the natural order into believing I'm dead. Unfortunately, that means—"

"It means you're dead," he said with a defeated sigh. "At least as far as the contract goes. That son of a *bitch*!"

Ronan looked like he wanted to pulverize something. Or someone. I was grateful Liam wasn't here.

"It was the only way," I repeated. "I never would've agreed to it otherwise."

Ronan didn't argue the point. He bowed his head, shaking it slowly. "I never should've brought you through the hell portal. We wouldn't be in this mess if I'd found another way."

"We wouldn't be *anywhere*. We'd be dead, or zombies with no memories. We wouldn't even remember each other, Ronan." I took a chance and stepped close to him again, ignoring the protests of the hounds. Ronan's eyes locked on mine, his lips pressed tight together, the muscles of his jaw flexing.

I brushed my fingertips along his jawline. They came away singed, leaving a trail of charred hair in his beard.

I wasn't allowed to touch the man I loved. Sebastian's cruelty was truly limitless.

Swallowing the knot in my throat, I said, "What happened after we got through the portal? Where is Darius? Is he... Does he remember anything?"

Ronan met me with dead eyes. No longer black, but no longer warm and familiar, either. It was as if he was shutting down.

"He's in rough shape. He attacked a demon—the blood-lust is hitting him hard. And... No, Gray. He doesn't remember anything."

Tears blurred my vision. "Where is he?"

"Somewhere safe."

"I need to see him. You owe me that much."

"Gray, Sebastian—"

"Sebastian can wait."

"Try telling *him* that."

"He owns me for eternity. Another hour won't make a difference."

Ronan didn't respond.

"What about Emilio?" I asked. "Is he still with his sister? Have they found Asher?"

"Sebastian hasn't let me get in touch with Emilio yet." He shoved a hand through his hair, the sudden movement making the hounds jump. "All of this happened so fast… I barely had time to think from the moment those memory eaters attacked."

"I need to see Darius. Please, Ronan. He needs to know he's not alone in this."

"It doesn't matter, Gray. Don't you see?" He turned away from me, his body stiffening again. "I was *summoned* here. This is it. Game over. Don't even bother packing your shit, because everything you own belongs to him now. *You* belong to him now."

"I know."

When he turned to face me again, his eyes were rimmed in red, flooded with pain and regret.

My insides twisted into a pretzel. It was one thing to make the decision with Liam, floating on a hell boat with no other escape route in sight.

But this was really happening now. I was about to become Sebastian's eternal slave.

"It's time," he whispered. He held my gaze for another heartbeat, letting me see the real Ronan one last time.

"I love you," I whispered back.

A tear spilled down his cheek. Just one. In his eyes, I saw the immensity of his love for me, his devotion.

Then he turned away, the hounds close at his heels, all of them expecting me to do the one thing I thought I never would.

Follow them back into hell.

ELEVEN

GRAY

We walked briskly down a long, carpeted corridor decorated with garish orange-and-gold walls and a ridiculous number of chandeliers. Ronan stayed a few steps ahead of me no matter how hard I tried to match his pace, his angry footfalls audible even with the carpeting. The hellhounds trailed on my heels—Sebastian's insurance policy that I wouldn't bolt the first chance I got.

It was almost laughable. Where would I go? How could a demon sworn witch on a death march back to hell via some chintzy, overdone Vegas hotel possibly escape?

You must seek your own sword...

The voices from my vision on the hell boat floated through my mind, but at the moment, I had no idea what to do with that bit of advice. My own sword? From the sound of things, I'd be lucky if Sebastian even let me use a nail file again.

Better for him to keep me away from sharp objects. First

chance I got, I'd be jamming something into his jugular, whether he was an immortal demon or not.

The corridor continued on forever, twisting and turning, taking us past doors that remained shut and walls that revealed nothing about my destination. After what felt like hours, we finally reached a large oak door that looked different from the rest, carved with strange symbols that glowed faintly at our approach.

Demon codes. Hell glyphs. Runes. I couldn't decipher any of them.

Ronan pressed his palm to the door, and the symbols pulsed brighter, rearranging into a different pattern. He turned to look at me over his shoulder and met my gaze, our noses nearly bumping, the warmth of his breath brushing my lips.

"Whatever you do," he whispered, "whatever you say, do *not* anger him. Sebastian is prone to melodrama and overreacting, and no matter what you might think, he *always* has the upper hand. Remember that."

"You don't know that. Maybe there's a bargaining chip we haven't—"

"There isn't, Gray. As long as you stand to lose something, he'll find it and exploit the hell out of it. There's nothing you can do here but listen and obey."

Obey. The word sent a shiver down my spine even as it filled me with indignation. I'd known what I was signing up for—at least, as far as committing myself to Sebastian before my time—but at the time I was more concerned with getting out of hell. Sometimes, you just had to deal with one shitstorm at a time.

But now the next storm was upon me, and I had to figure out my game plan—preferably before I was put in irons or sent into the fiery dungeons.

Because no matter what the contract said, no matter what the laws and order of the crossroads and hell and the Shadowrealm and everywhere else maintained, I was *no* one's prisoner.

The runes faded back to a faint glow, and the door swung open, the force of whatever was on the other side beckoning me to enter. The room was small, and as dark and cold as a refrigerator. I'd barely gotten a glimpse of it when the big door slammed shut behind me, the sound of it making my heart rattle.

There were no windows, and every corner was hidden in shadow. I could just make out a long table at the center of the room, with two figures seated in high-backed chairs at one end. The only light came from a thick black candle flickering at the center of the table.

"Gray Desario," a slimy voice called forth from the shadows. I couldn't see the man's face, but I knew immediately who the voice belonged to. Ronan had always said Sebastian sounded like Colonel Sanders peddling used cars. "We've been waiting a long time for your arrival."

He leaned forward, his face illuminated by the candle. Instinctively I took a step back, reaching behind me for the familiar solidity of Ronan, but I was suddenly immobilized. I no longer had control of my body—it lurched forward, then marched itself forward to the table.

"Is that really necessary?" Ronan asked.

"Remember your place, boy," Sebastian barked.

Inside, my magic stirred, bringing my blood from a simmer to a boil. But outside, I was a prisoner in my own body, unable to move. Unable to blink. Unable to breathe. It was a wonder my heart was still beating. I was pretty sure Sebastian could've stopped that, too.

I'd never felt so utterly powerless. Not even when Travis had me pinned in the alley, or Jonathan had taken me prisoner. Not when Norah put a hold spell on me. Not even when I'd been trapped in the cellar watching my mother burn.

He'd wanted me to feel that way. To know the score here.

Just when I thought I'd explode from the fear, Sebastian's invisible bonds released me. I gasped, sucking in air, stumbling to the nearest chair and collapsing in it.

Ronan stood at my back, the hounds taking their places at my sides. Though he hadn't said another word since Sebastian's reprimand, I could feel the anger rolling off him, the ferocity of his love for me warming the air around me. I clung to it—the one good thing still standing in this place, no matter what curse Sebastian had put on us.

"Now that we all understand each other..." Sebastian drawled. "Gray. How are you feeling after your long journey?"

You are going to die a slow, painful, horrific death. I will carve you into pieces. Set the pieces on fire. And eat the ashes of your bones.

Out loud, I said nothing.

"It's natural to be a little nervous your first time, Miss Desario. But you have nothing to fear from me. As long as you behave yourself, I think you and I will get along like butter on grits."

The figure on his left shifted, and I caught a brief glimpse of a face. A woman's face, I was pretty sure. She had short white hair and light eyes. Blue, I thought. Like mine.

Did Sebastian have a wife? A *willing* wife?

"Do you know why I've worked so hard to bring you into the fold?" he asked, stealing my attention from the woman.

Again, I said nothing.

"Speak plainly, girl," he said. "No use standing on ceremony."

"It's okay, child," the woman said. She sounded old. Sweet, almost. I immediately relaxed, though I couldn't tell if it was because I actually felt better, or if she'd spelled me. "Answer his questions. You're safe in my presence."

Sure I am. But even as I had the thought, some part of me believed her.

"It is not enough to seek your own sword," she continued. "You must learn to use that sword as well."

I gasped. Had she read my thoughts? Was she actually

encouraging me to kill Sebastian? What the hell was going on?

"Are you alright, girl?" Sebastian asked.

I blinked at him slowly. Numb. My eyes drifted back to the woman.

"He can't hear me," she said. "Only you."

Her mouth hadn't moved. It hadn't moved, I realized then, from the moment we'd stepped into this room.

Everything she'd said to me, she'd said in my mind.

I'd heard of witches who could telegraph their own thoughts into the mind of another. But how could she have known about my vision? I hadn't told anyone about that. Not even Liam.

I closed my eyes and took a deep breath, quickly trying to regroup. Despite the unconventional delivery method, the swords of the Tarot must've had a message for me, but what? Both the Three and the Four of Swords had come up in Sophie's book of shadows, in the reading she'd done just before she died. I'd seen the swords again in my nightmare in the Shadowrealm, and then again on the boat, when they'd pierced my heart.

But in the Tarot, swords weren't just about conflict. They were also about thoughts. Speech. Learning to harness your personal power and standing up for yourself and for those who needed protection.

Maybe that was the message I needed to hear today. It was time to stop cowering in the face of this devil and pick up my damn sword.

"Why have I brought you here, Shadowmancer?" Sebastian asked, and this time, I was ready for him. A surge of hot anger melted away the lingering fear.

"Let me guess," I said. "You want me to raise you an army full of corpses. Or better yet—magic up some poor lost souls and convince them to come work for you. Or maybe you want to run experiments on me, cut me open, see if you can figure out what makes a soul manipulator tick."

Behind me, Ronan shifted, a low growl rumbling in his chest.

"Simmer down, demon," Sebastian ordered. Then, to me, "Intriguing ideas, witch. But I'm afraid you've misunderstood. Soul manipulation is an extremely rare power, I'll give you that. But I'm not interested in your ability to raise the dead. Not today, anyway."

"You want to enslave my soul," I said. "That's obvious."

"Miss Desario! Wherever would you get such a preposterous idea?" He said preposterous like *pree*-posterous, and laughed as though I were the funniest girl in the world.

"You *are* the Prince of Hell, correct?" I asked. "Or is your whole dark, brooding, evil schtick just a smokescreen compensating for something else?"

Careful, the woman warned. *Don't push him too far.*

I kept my eyes fixed on Sebastian, not wanting to give her away. But why was she helping me? Was she a prisoner as well? She sat at his side as though they were on equal footing, and the way he angled his body toward her suggested a much more intimate relationship than master-servant.

So, whose side was she actually on?

Ignoring my dig, Sebastian cleared his throat, leaning forward so his face was once again in the light. The flickering candle made the pocks in his face deeper, his eyes more menacing. For all his southern-fried smoothness, Sebastian was downright frightening when he wanted to be.

"I don't need your soul today, witch," he said, his menacing tone sending shivers down my spine. "I need your blood."

"My... blood?" The same fear from before pulsed in my chest, but I let it pass, taking comfort in the familiar hum of my magic. I couldn't manifest it here, but I could still feel it simmering in my blood, tingling. Liam had been right about that, at least. My magic was still with me, even here.

"Why?" I asked.

"For a summoning." He said it as though it all made perfect sense, but I was lost. A summoning? Of what?

I glanced back up at the woman, who nodded slowly. Soothingly. I didn't know how, but we'd... connected somehow. Not just the telepathy, but some kind of link. I felt it tethering us, an invisible thread that allowed me to feel her emotions.

She was sending them to me. Infusing me with them.

Calmness. Reassurance. Support. And most oddly of all —love.

I lifted an eyebrow in question, but she remained stoic, her gaze fixated on the candle in front of her.

I was so thrown off by the whole thing that it took me a minute to realize Sebastian was talking again.

"...powerful line of witches that dates back millennia," he was saying. "Your bloodline was thought to have vanished centuries ago, relegated to the status of an urban legend. But some of us knew better, of course. When the opportunity arose to put you under my protection, well. Only a fool would have turned that down. And thanks to a series of unfortunate events perpetuated by some of your associates, here you are."

He spread his hands and beamed at me, waiting for me to speak. What did he expect? A thank you? A pat on the back for all his cleverness?

"I have no idea what you're talking about," I said, which was the truth. My bloodline? My biological mother had died when I was too young to even remember her. I knew nothing about my father. As far as I was concerned, Calla was my true mother. And if she'd been part of any ancient, urban-legend-inspiring legacy, she would've told me.

"You are Silversbane," the woman said reverently, her crystal-clear voice cutting through my thoughts. It was the first sentence she'd spoken out loud so far, and the sound of it reverberated through my very bones, igniting the magic within me and filling me with an odd sense of... belonging.

"But I've never even heard of Silversbane," I said. Ronan shifted behind me, his energy suddenly antsy. Did he recognize the name? "I'm not—"

My thoughts cut off abruptly as a memory arced

through my mind, flashing behind my eyes like a bolt of lightning.

A woman enraged, her dark hair swirling around her head, whipped into a frenzy by the wind. A storm raging, inside and out. A creek, icy cold and rushing by my face so fast...

"I am Silversbane! This magic is my *legacy. Mine! Why should you have it when it was promised to me? My birthright! You have stolen it, Shadowborn filth!"*

Cold hands pressing on my shoulders, sharp nails digging into my flesh, and then... ice. Freezing. Gasping. A bolt of pain in my skull, pressure, my lungs on fire...

"Stay down! Stop squirming, little bitch!"

"Unfortunately, Silversbane was your mother's legacy, not your father's," the woman said, yanking me out of the memory. Or vision. What *was* that?

"Unfortunately?" I asked, blinking away the last of the images. I couldn't shake the cold, though. I rubbed my arms, pulling the sleeves of Ronan's sweatshirt down over my hands.

"Power is as much a gift as a curse," she said. "Though I suspect you already know as much."

At this, I arched an eyebrow. "Says the witch sharing the head of the table with the Prince of Hell? Not to be rude, but you seem a little old to be a princess."

"I'm not a princess, child. I'm Deirdre Olivante," she said matter-of-factly. "Your paternal grandmother."

"My... grandmother?" My mouth dropped open in disbelief. I had a grandmother? Alive? In league with the Prince of Hell?

We will speak of this in private later, she whispered in my mind. *I will tell you everything. Please just remain calm, no matter what he says.*

Before I could even process what she was saying, not to mention the fact that I suddenly had a grandmother I'd never heard of, Sebastian was rambling on about the blood-line again.

"Your ancestors are extremely powerful, even in death," he said. "I require access to that power. Unfortunately, as they have already passed on, I can not retrieve them through normal means. But you, Miss Desario, can."

Show interest, Deirdre said, her tone growing more insistent. *The sooner you let him get to the point, the sooner we can leave.*

I hoped she was right. I also hoped her apparent help wasn't a trap.

"How can I get the souls if they've already passed on?" I asked Sebastian.

"Through the blood summoning. You are their legacy. The souls will not be able to resist the call of their descendent—especially one as powerful as you."

"What do you want with their souls? Don't you have enough to choose from?"

"I do not owe you a reckoning of my affairs, Miss Desario. I'm simply informing you of your first assignment."

"I'm not—"

Let him speak, Deirdre snapped.

"You *will* summon their souls as required," he said,

"then use your powers of manipulation to reintegrate them into new vessels, which will then be made available for my purposes."

I didn't bother telling him that Liam and I hadn't quite gotten to the Soul Reinsertion 101 portion of our lesson plan. Even if I wanted to help him summon my ancestors, there was no way I could do what he was asking.

"Let me get this straight," I said. "You want me to yank my ancestors out of their eternal rest by tricking them into thinking I'm summoning them, then imprison them in mortal bodies, and turn them over to you for some creepy purpose you refuse to divulge?"

"Well, you make it sound rather crass, but yes. That is your first duty to me, in a nutshell."

"*Oooh*-kay," I said.

I'd meant it as a pause, a breath before I told him exactly where he could stick his bloodlines and evil plans. But Sebastian clearly took the word as my acquiescence. His eyes lit up, the overeager smile making his lips twitch. He was doing his damnedest to hide it, but he'd just shown me his full hand.

This wasn't just some random errand he was sending me on. Something any one of his lackeys could do. Sebastian needed *me*. And only me.

And despite his bluster, a blood summoning wasn't something he could force me to do, either. It was magic. It required intention. Cooperation. You couldn't fake out a spell. If my heart wasn't in it, the magic would know, and it would backfire.

I pressed my lips together, hiding my own smile.

So, I *did* have a bargaining chip here. Maybe not the upper hand, but something close to an equal one, which was a hell of a lot more than I had when I'd walked into this dungeon.

"I'm so glad we've come to this agreement," Sebastian said. "Now, if you'll just—"

"Wait." I held up my hand, cutting him off cold. Now that I had his attention, and knew what he wanted, I decided to test the boundaries a bit. "If I do as you ask, I need something from you, too."

"Gray." Ronan grabbed the sides of my chair, his knuckles turning white. "Stop."

Sebastian let out a smarmy, patronizing chuckle. "Oh, let the girl speak her pretty little mind, son! There's no harm in hearing her request." Then, to me, "What would you like, Miss Desario? A shopping spree? A makeover? Some chocolates?"

"Actually, I'd like you to stop interfering in my relationship with Ronan. It has nothing to do with you, and I'd appreciate it if you'd undo whatever mojo you put on him to make us catch fire at every touch."

"This again?" He rolled his eyes. The Prince of freaking Hell rolled his eyes. "Sorry. No can do."

"That was never part of my deal," I said. "My relationship with Ronan didn't exist when my contract was executed."

"You're right," he said plainly. "It wasn't part of your

deal. But it was part of his." He nodded toward Ronan, his smile stretching all the way to Texas.

"His?" Heart hammering a terrible new rhythm in my chest, I turned around and tipped my head up, trying to catch Ronan's eyes. It was a long time before he finally looked at me.

"I had to," he whispered. Regret filled his eyes. "It was the only way he'd agree to let us use the hell portal."

His earlier words came back to haunt me, their meaning clear only now.

It's not a trick, Gray. It's a price.

"What, exactly, did you pay?" I asked.

"You know," he said softly. His voice was breaking. So was my heart.

"Say it," I whispered.

"Oh, for the love of all that is unholy." Sebastian slammed his hand on the table, making the candle flame flicker. "You two are pathetic. It's your own damn fault for giving in to this temptation anyway. I'm doing you both a favor by putting an end to it."

I closed my eyes, willing myself to remain calm. Grief and misery were banging on the door of my heart, but I couldn't afford to let them in. Not with so much at stake.

I couldn't afford to lose it. I needed to hold on to that damn sword and figure a way out of this.

Opening my eyes, I looked across the table at my grandmother. "Could I speak to the Prince alone please?"

"No," Ronan said, at the time Deirdre said, "I don't think that's a good idea."

Ignoring the protests, Sebastian nodded, gesturing for Deirdre and Ronan to show themselves to the door.

Deirdre went first, and Sebastian's eyes never left her. For a brief instant, I saw the flicker of something almost human on his face. It was gone in a blink, but not before he'd given me another clue into his motives.

I had no idea what it meant. Only that what I'd seen was unmistakable.

Sebastian was in love with my grandmother.

"Gray," Ronan called, and when I looked at him, I saw the trepidation in his eyes. The worry. He didn't want to leave me alone with Sebastian, but I couldn't think straight with him in the room. Not after what I'd learned—what his deal meant for us. I needed to stay focused on Sebastian, on what I could use as leverage to buy myself some more time.

For so long, Ronan had been my rock. My protector. My best friend.

But at the moment, he was no more than a distraction. One I couldn't afford.

He lingered at the threshold with the two hellhounds, awaiting my response, refusing to join Deirdre in the hallway. But in the end, Sebastian showed him a single raised eyebrow, and Ronan caved.

I knew he would. That's how it was in this place. All of us were bound to Sebastian, forced to follow his orders or risk the life-altering consequences.

For now.

TWELVE

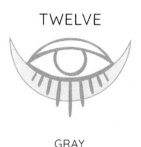

GRAY

Finally alone with the man who'd bought my soul, I squared my shoulders, sat up straight, and got right to the point.

"I'm sure you're aware that witches and the supernatural community at large are facing a massive new threat," I said. "Those who haven't been murdered outright have been taken prisoner, experimented on, tortured, and worse —used to create hybrid breeds and unstoppable supernatural weapons."

Sebastian stroked his goatee. "And you've come by this knowledge, how, exactly?"

I gave him the rundown on Jonathan and the prison—the horrors we saw there. "I don't know how or when, but the hunters are planning to unleash pure chaos. The entire supernatural community is in grave danger, as are humans."

Sebastian's oily laugh filled the room. "And this should concern me because…"

"You may not care about the fate of humanity, Sebastian. But if humans die off, you'll have fewer resources to exploit. Your demons will have fewer vessels to inhabit. Without the human capital that keeps this show running…" I spread my hands, indicating the tiny dungeon of the room, as well as the demon himself. "The whole seedy underbelly of your operation will come to a screeching halt."

He leaned back in his chair and folded his arms over his chest, not saying a word. His brows were stern and serious, but I saw the flicker of concern in his eyes. He'd heard me. Knew that the picture I was painting wasn't such a farfetched possibility.

"Get to the point, Silversbane."

"My name is Desario."

"I don't care what you call yourself. Just get to the point. Your obstinance is starting to grate."

I rose from the chair and crossed to the end of the table, standing before him. His lip twitched—the only indication that my presence affected him at all.

"My whole life, you've been making deals for my future —for my *soul*—with other people." Again, the magic inside me flared, giving me strength. Purpose. Power. "Now you're going to deal with me."

"You *are* a rebellious one, aren't you?" He laughed again, but it'd lost some of its earlier bravado. "You've spent too much time with demons."

"We could solve that right now." I jerked my head toward the door. "Let me walk, free and clear. Your absence from my life would mean one less demon to mess with my head."

"That's not how this works."

"Explain it again, then. I'm new here." I took a step closer, forcing him to look up to see me—to reveal the truth in his eyes. I unnerved him. He couldn't figure me out. He didn't like that one bit.

"If you refuse your assignments," he said, tapping the table for emphasis. "I return your soul to hell. There will be no brokering for its release after that. No deals, no trades, no begging, no rescue missions mounted by the bumbling, craven men who can't seem to think clearly where you are concerned. That, my dear, *will* be your eternity."

I watched him carefully. For a guy who owned a casino, his poker face left much to be desired.

He was totally bluffing.

"Do you think that scares me?" I asked, pressing my advantage. "That black, empty place Liam pulled me out of? That's not hell, Sebastian. Hell is turning your back on the people you care about and living the rest of your days knowing you could've helped them, but failed. Hell is watching someone you love burn before your eyes, power-less to save them. Hell is losing the people who matter to you most, no matter how hard you try to hold on. So let me tell you something, Prince." I leaned forward, making him flinch. "I'd rather spend a *lifetime* in your hell than one more minute in mine."

He lifted his hand, and a wave of power hit me, shoving me backward. I managed to stay on my feet, but barely.

I righted myself, and Sebastian smiled, thinking once again he'd gotten the upper hand.

"That's very poetic, girl, but this isn't open mic night at Luna's Café. Nor is this a negotiation. You're mine, and you're—"

"*Done*." I drew myself up to my full height and stared him down, my voice unwavering. "Send me back to your so-called hell. Now."

"Don't play games with me. You won't like the outcome."

I glared at him, wondering how far I could push him. This was a dangerous game, with stakes higher than any I'd ever fought for.

But that was exactly why I couldn't back down. It was too important.

"You need to maintain the status quo in our communities, Sebastian. This isn't about games or me rebelling or anything like that. It's simple math."

"Okay. Let's say, for curiosity's sake, I consider your request." Sebastian glared at me for much longer than necessary, letting the echo of his forced Southern drawl creep over my skin like spiders. When I could no longer hold back my shiver, his eyes glinted at my response, and he offered me a twisted smile. "What exactly are you offering me, witch?"

I took a deep breath and closed my eyes, seeking reassurance from the magic inside.

This was it. My one chance at getting this right. So many had come to negotiate at this table, and so many had walked away in chains. I couldn't let that happen.

"I will do as you ask," I said calmly, opening my eyes. "I'll fulfill the contract and complete the assignments to the letter. I'll summon and bind my ancestors—no loopholes, no tricks."

Sebastian grunted. "And in return?"

I'd kept a respectable distance from him since he'd hit me with that invisible smackdown, but now I approached the table again. "In return, you'll allow me to return to Raven's Cape with Ronan and Darius, liberate Jonathan's prisoners, and deal with the immediate threats facing the witches and the supernatural community at large."

"I see. And how long will that take?"

"However long that takes," I said. "Unfortunately, there's not a manual for these things."

Sebastian shook his head. "And you think I can divert my resources for this little rescue mission of yours? Help you save the day and skip off into the sunset, everybody's favorite little heroine? A poster child for all the witches across the land?"

"No, Sebastian. I don't need you to help me." I leaned forward on the table, looking straight into his evil eyes. My magic surged, the electric hum of it making the hairs on my arms raise and the candle between us flicker. "I just need you to stay the hell out of my way."

THIRTEEN

EMILIO

From the outside, The Phoenix's Flame metaphysical shop was an unassuming little cottage tucked into the woods about fifteen minutes outside of the Cape, complete with a garden full of gnome statues and a curl of smoke rising from the chimney. There wasn't even a sign outside—this was strictly a word-of-mouth business.

Inside, the place was a witch's paradise. The main level had been opened up, filled with a mismatched collection of metal, wood, and glass shelving, display cases, and table-tops, each piece from a different era yet somehow working together seamlessly. Every surface displayed tools of the craft—crystals, wands, incense, books, DVDs, statues, beads, bells, cauldrons, jewelry. An entire wall of built-in bookcases was devoted to fairy, gnome, and gargoyle stat-ues. A massive counter at the center of the store held a sprawling Tarot card collection that Gray would've loved.

"Merry meet, friends." A middle-aged woman with

startling green eyes and a messy bun of curly red hair emerged from the back of the house, carrying a tray of pastries and tea. I got the distinct sense she'd been expecting us. "I'm Verona Braden. Please, make yourselves at home."

She gestured toward a small room off to the side, set up like a regular living room with two small couches and an armchair surrounding a coffee table made out of a massive tree stump.

It was seven in the morning, and Elena and I had just knocked on the door after staking the place out overnight. Jael was keeping an eye on things outside. At the moment, Darkwinter's focus seemed to be on the Bay, but there were still dark fae here in Raven's Cape, and we couldn't take any chances.

Elena and I thanked her and took a seat on one of the couches. When Verona set down the tea tray and sat across from us, I noticed she wasn't meeting my eyes, but staring at a spot just above my shoulder, her own eyes slightly unfocused.

She was blind, I realized.

"Have you met Roscoe yet?" she asked.

At the sound of his name, a russet-colored golden retriever padded out from the back of the house and joined us, sitting on the floor at my feet. I leaned forward and held out my hand, which he happily sniffed. Seconds later, he leaped up on the couch, curling up between me and Elena and promptly falling asleep.

"He likes you," Verona said with a kind laugh. "Okay.

Now that I know you're good people, we can relax. Please, help yourselves to tea."

She remained amicably silent while Elena poured three cups from a teapot shaped like a cat.

Reaching for a pastry, Verona said, "So what brings you to my little corner of the woods? I don't get many drop-in visitors these days."

Elena introduced us and handed over our badges for the woman to inspect by touch.

"We're looking for information on a customer who came through here late last night," Elena said. "A witch by the name of Norah Hanson. Mid-fifties, highly knowledgeable. She's a coven leader from Blackmoon Bay."

The woman's eyebrow twitched—so slight a human wouldn't have noticed, but my shifter instincts picked up on it immediately. She'd recognized the name—if not from a personal acquaintanceship, then probably from the raised lettering on Norah's credit card.

"We don't believe she's a regular customer of yours," I said. "Just passing through town. She paid with a credit card and made a fairly large purchase—just over five hundred dollars."

The woman nodded, concern tightening her warm features. "Yes, that name and purchase amount sounds about right. But the woman I helped felt much younger to me—in her early twenties at best."

"What makes you say that?" I asked.

"Obviously I can't see people the way sighted folk can, but I do have a different sort of sight. I get a sense for people, Detective. Everything from the way you speak, the words you choose, your scent, the feel of your skin when I shake your hand, the sound of your shoes against the floor, the swish of your clothing when you walk—all of those things reveal a lot about a person. If that customer was in her fifties, then Roscoe here is a toy poodle."

Roscoe let out a whimper of discontent.

"Do you think the credit card was stolen?" Elena asked me.

"Possibly," I said. "Or Norah has an accomplice."

"Would you like to see her?" The woman gestured toward the checkout counter in the center room. Next to the cash register sat a pale, milky-green orb about the size of a grapefruit.

"Is that a... crystal ball?" Elena asked.

"Indeed. But not just any crystal ball. Green aventurine is an excellent stone for attracting luck, money, and success." Verona winked at us, her smile sly. "Also, that one's got a hidden camera."

She headed out to the register and grabbed her tablet from beneath the counter, her steps quick and sure.

"Security footage," she said, then used voice commands to queue up the video. "I don't like to judge my customers, of course, but I have to tell you... There was something quite odd about her."

"How so?"

"For starters, Roscoe refused to go anywhere near her, which is very unusual for him."

"Do you think he sensed something sinister?" I asked.

"Not sinister, exactly," she said. "He would've warned me if he thought I was in danger. No, this was more like... confusion? Like he didn't quite know what to make of her. And then there was... Well, see for yourself." She handed over the tablet.

Elena and I leaned in together over Roscoe, peering down at the screen. A young woman approached the register with a basket full of supplies. She was blonde, with chin-length wavy hair, brown eyes, and a heart-shaped mole above her left eyebrow. Her right brow was pierced with a tiny silver ring.

"Verona," I said, "would you mind giving us a moment?"

"Of course. Take all the time you need." She and Roscoe headed back into the main area of the shop, leaving me alone with Elena and the woman on the screen.

I felt like I'd just seen a ghost.

"Verona was right," I whispered, heart galloping. "This isn't Norah. It's Delilah Pannette."

Elena narrowed her eyes at the screen. "Who?"

"She's a witch from Norah's coven who went missing from the Bay not long after Sophie's murder. We feared she'd been killed, too, though we never found any evidence of foul play."

"Looks pretty alive to me," Elena said.

It was true, but there was something... off about her. When I'd spoken with her at Norah's house after Sophie's death, she was understandably upset, but I also sensed a fiery disposition inside her. She was talkative, alert, opinionated. The kind of witch who speaks her mind and doesn't back down from a fight.

The woman in this video was the exact opposite. She looked like a zombie, with glassy dead eyes, limp hair, and slow, jerky movements.

"Something is definitely wrong with her," Elena confirmed. The longer we watched the video, the more obvious it became. When Verona rung up the purchase, Delilah struggled to get her wallet from the purse, dropping the card several times. She never smiled, never asked questions, never said more than a few words, despite Verona's attempts at friendly small-talk.

"She looks like she's sleepwalking," Elena said.

"Or under a spell." My gut told me that was the answer.

Norah was staying out of sight. Whatever she was planning—whether an escape from the country, or something more sinister—she'd coerced Delilah into doing her bidding. Using the credit card had been her first mistake.

Elena and I rejoined Verona at the register, tablet in hand.

"Would you mind if I forwarded myself a copy of this footage?" I asked.

"Of course not," she said.

"Do you remember what she purchased?" Elena asked. The camera angle hadn't really allowed for a clear view of her items. "Or if she said anything about what she needed the items for? Maybe when she first arrived at the shop?"

Verona shook her head. "She knew right where everything was, got it all gathered up so quickly I'd barely had time to ask if she needed help. I offered her tea, but she declined."

"But what did she buy?" I asked, at the same time Elena said, "Did she say anything about Norah Hanson, or where they might be heading?"

Verona hesitated, clearly uncomfortable at the sudden barrage of questions. "I'm sorry, detectives. I don't typically disclose information about client purchases. Some of the items we carry are rather sensitive in nature, as I'm sure you can imagine."

"Of course," Elena said, backing off. "We're just trying to do our jobs."

"Anything you can share would be a big help," I said.

Verona put the tablet back under the counter, then knelt down beside Roscoe, scratching his ears. The dog sighed happily, his tail swishing across the hardwood floor.

"What is this about?" she asked. "Has this Norah woman committed a crime?"

Elena and I exchanged a quick glance. After a beat, I nodded. Verona was a witch. She could be in danger. She had a right to know what was happening. Besides, maybe if she heard some of the gruesome details, she'd be more willing to share intel.

"Norah Hanson is wanted for questioning in connection with the disappearance of a teenaged witch from Blackmoon Bay and is a suspect in the kidnapping and murder of several others," I said, "including the woman seen here using Norah's credit card. The two may be working together, or there may be some sort of coercion going on, but it's clear that something is not right about the situation."

"But… you said Norah was a coven leader," Verona said. "You believe she's killing her own witches? That seems highly—"

"Ma'am," Elena said, the last of her patience finally snapping, "I appreciate your desire to protect your clients' privacy, but this is a police matter. If you're not comfortable volunteering information, I can go through more formal channels, but quite frankly that would be a waste of your time and our department resources."

Verona stood up, her mouth pressed into a grim line, her green eyes revealing nothing. They matched the aventurine stone, I realized now.

"We're talking about a child," I said gently, good cop to the rescue. "A runaway who was taken in by a very powerful witch, and possibly imprisoned and harmed as part of a larger crime we're only just beginning to uncover."

At this, she finally softened. "Perhaps we should have another round of tea."

We reassembled in the living room, though Roscoe had abandoned Elena and me, taking a seat at Verona's feet instead.

"There have been whispers of trouble," Verona said, stroking the dog's head. "Several practitioners have brought their concerns to me in recent months, seeking protective spells and amulets, advice, private places to meet. They say witches are being targeted again. That within the next few months, we'll experience another Great

Hunt. At first, I didn't want to believe it. Rumors and old ghosts, I told them. Forty-five years I've been here, and though we've had our ups and downs, we've persevered. But this feels different now. Many have left Raven's Cape and the surrounding communities. Witches in other towns are getting worried, too." She shook her head, tears gathering in her eyes. "I keep assuring them that we'll get through this as we always have, but I'm not so sure."

"You *will* get through this," Elena said, surprising me by leaning forward and placing a comforting hand on top of Verona's. "We all need to work together, now more than ever."

Verona smiled. "Thank you. I know. I guess there's just a part of me that doesn't want to believe this sort of thing could happen again. Not in my lifetime."

She finished her tea, then said, "The woman pretending to be Norah did not tell me why she bought her supplies, but the combination of tools and ingredients she selected could only be used for one thing—a highly complex protection spell. One that, if done correctly, essentially erases a person's existence by changing her appearance and identity, altering her public records, and manipulating the memories of all who knew her."

"People actually do that?" Elena asked.

"Not often. If one thing goes wrong with that spell—the wrong word in the incantation, a single caraway seed more or less than called for, a mistranslated sigil, the wrong moon phase—the caster could die."

"Talk about erasing one's existence," I said.

"Precisely. There are other strong protection spells—those are the more common ones witches use, even in dark times. This one is not one to be trifled with."

"You didn't try to talk her out of it?" Elena asked.

"It is not my place to offer unsolicited advice to sisters of the craft, nor to pry too deeply into their affairs."

We finished our tea in silence, each of us contemplating what these revelations meant.

When we rose from the couch to say our goodbyes, Elena reached for Verona's hands. "Please be careful, Verona. It's not safe for solitary practitioners right now. Even covens are in danger. You must do everything you can to protect yourself."

"Don't you worry about that," she said, smiling at us both. "The witches of Raven's Cape will continue to do what we've always done. We will weather the storms upon us with a little bit of magic and a whole lot of common sense."

After promising to get in touch if Delilah or Norah returned, or if she thought of anything else that might help, Verona escorted us to the door.

"I'll be right out," I told Elena, lingering in the doorway. "There's, ah, there's something else I need to get from Verona."

FOURTEEN

GRAY

"Rayanne! Are you hurt?"

Deirdre Olivante was waiting for me outside the chamber, concern deepening the lines between her eyebrows. In the sudden bright light of the hallway chandeliers, she looked even older than I'd originally thought, but her eyes were sharp and clear, the exact shape and shade as mine. It seemed I'd also inherited her cheekbones.

There was no denying our resemblance.

Wow. I have a grandmother.

"I… I'm fine," I said as the door shut behind me, blissfully separating me from the sleazy demon inside. Unfortunately, the moment the door sealed, the hellhounds reappeared at my sides, glaring at me with their mean red eyes as if they were daring me to try something.

I was too tired to be shocked, but their presence was as unsettling as ever.

"They do that sometimes." Deirdre waved her hand

toward the hounds, careful not to get too close. "I'd say you get used to them, but I'm afraid you never quite do."

"Why don't you have a pair?"

"I'm not a flight risk." Deirdre sighed. "I've been with Sebastian a long time, Rayanne."

"Well, I don't plan on being here that long. Sebastian and I came to an understanding about a few things."

She arched an eyebrow, a smile playing on her lips. It warmed her face considerably. "It seems he's taken a liking to you. Sebastian doesn't usually give his demon sworn an opportunity to renegotiate."

"Lucky me." I was still wearing Ronan's sweatshirt, and now I pulled the hood up over my head, losing myself in a wave of his cloves-and-campfire scent. The back of my nose stung with unshed tears. "Where is Ronan? I really need to see him."

"He's taking care of some other business, but he'll meet up with you soon." Deirdre held out her arm. "Come. I'll show you around the casino while we wait."

I nodded, numb, grateful to let someone else make the decisions. The conversation with Sebastian had worn me out, and the unspent magic inside was making me feel fidgety, like I'd had too much caffeine. A walk would probably do me some good.

The hounds and I accompanied Deirdre back through the corridor maze to a sleek and silent elevator, which we took to the lobby level below, forty-two stories down. I had no idea what time it was; there were no windows anywhere in sight.

The casino, I learned, was called Inferno—a little on the nose for my taste, but the decor was a good fit, with deep reds and oranges on the carpeting and walls, accented with golden lights and a massive fountain in the center, lit up to look like real flickering flames.

If I didn't know so much about the owner, I might've been impressed.

The main gaming area looked exactly like the ones I'd seen on television—bright and glitzy, screaming with the sounds of music and cheers and beeping, blaring slot machines. The only difference was that this casino was packed with supernaturals, all of them blending right in alongside the clueless humans.

"I guess no one's immune to the siren call of the slots and the tables," I said, watching a fae woman blow seductively on the dice of her vampire companion.

"Sebastian's built quite an empire on our many vices," she said. "This is one of six properties he owns in Nevada." She told me a little bit more about the casinos, the demon security team, and the live shows, painting a glossy sheen over the less savory but even more lucrative parts of the business—prostitution. Drugs. Smuggling of all sorts. I pretended to be interested, and she pretended to be happy to give the tour, and a million unsaid things hung in the air between us.

I had so many questions for this woman, and under normal circumstances, I would've leaped at the chance to spend time with her. My grandmother. The mother of the father I couldn't even remember. A witch, like me, who'd somehow ended up in Sebastian's service.

But each time I opened my mouth, I lost track of my words. Every potential question felt loaded and dangerous, a Pandora's Box of possible pitfalls and fresh heartaches.

"Tell me about them," I said instead, indicating the hounds behind us, still glaring at me with those creepy red eyes. "I take it they're not invisible." People were definitely noticing them. The humans in the casino shot us curious glances, but the supernaturals gave us a wide birth.

"To humans, they look like service dogs," Deirdre explained, just as a man backpedaled out of our path. She let out a soft chuckle. "Big, scary service dogs, perhaps, but nothing so horrifying as their true form. Supernaturals can see them as they are."

"Are they always going to follow me around like this?"

Deirdre nodded. "They are charged with keeping you safe as well as preventing your escape."

"They've got their work cut out for them," I grumbled, but if Deirdre heard me, she ignored it. "Do they have names?"

"Sebastian has never bothered to name his beasts. As far as he's concerned, they're possessions like any other."

For some reason, that made me sad. Every being deserved a name. Even grotesque, cranky hellhounds. Especially hounds that were going to spend the rest of eternity getting up close and personal with me.

The last time I'd been this close to hellhounds, they'd damn near killed me protecting me in my magical realm. I hadn't forgotten the sharp pierce of their claws, the weight of those massive paws knocking me to the ground...

Toughen up, buttercup. You've stared down a lot worse than hellhounds in recent weeks.

Swallowing my fear and revulsion, I knelt down before them, meeting them at eye level. Their eyes glowed like hot coals, their breath carrying the stench of rotten meat and blood.

I really, really hoped I wouldn't be in charge of feeding them. Or cleaning up after them.

"Male or female?" I asked Deirdre, tentatively holding out my hand for them to sniff. They approached at the same time, their noses cold and wet as they pressed them to my palm.

When they didn't attack, I took a gamble and shifted my hands to their heads, rubbing just behind their ears. Their fur was coarse and matted, but not all that different from a dog's.

And, just like dogs, they melted into two happy, goofy puppies at my touch.

"Aww, you're not so tough after all, huh?" I laughed, moving in to scratch a little more. When I started showing one more attention, the other one nipped playfully at my hand.

Sophie had always wanted dogs. Two of them, actually. *Witches need familiars!* she'd said. *And we can't just get one. Two at a minimum. They need companionship, just like we do.*

I'd always shot down the idea—I didn't need a familiar,

because I wasn't a witch. Not out loud, anyway. Besides, dogs seemed like a lot of work.

But now, as they snuffled and licked at my hands, wagging their tails as if we'd always belonged to each other, I was overcome with a sense of rightness so intense, it brought tears to my eyes.

It was crazy—this whole *thing* was crazy—but I suddenly knew without a doubt that these animals—these hellhounds—were supposed to be with me. Not because Sebastian had ordered it. Not because of any stupid contract or demonic spell. We just... belonged to each other.

"They are both females, actually," Deirdre said, surprise and amusement in her tone.

"Really? That's the best news I've heard all night." I laughed. "I could use a testosterone break."

"Couldn't we all."

"Sparkle and Sunshine," I said suddenly, the names Sophie had always imagined for our non-existent dogs now coming to mind. Her words replayed in my memory.

But don't let their sunny disposition and happy-go-lucky names fool you. Our dogs are some seriously *badass bitches...*

With a smile on my face and a little more lightness in my heart, I got to my feet and joined Deirdre once again.

"Sparkle, Sunshine. Come on, girls." The dogs padded closer, pressing against my calves. I wouldn't go so far as to call them doting pets just yet, but it seemed we'd made a little progress.

"Well!" Deirdre said, astonished. "I've never seen anything like it."

"What do you mean?"

"The hounds belong to Sebastian," she said. "All of them. They're assigned to demon sworn souls as needed, but their loyalty has always been to him. This is the first I've ever known them to bond with someone else."

A human couple loaded down with shopping bags bumbled past us, inadvertently nudging Deirdre closer to the hounds. Her hand brushed over one of their heads, and the beast let out a contented yelp, licking her wrist.

Deirdre laughed. "Well okay, then. Hello there, Sunshine."

"She's Sparkle," I said. "Sparkle has the underbite, see? And Sunshine has this notch in her left ear." It looked like something had taken a bite out of it, poor thing.

Deirdre stared at me for a beat, her eyes sparkling, her smile broad. In that moment, she really did look like a grandmother. Like someone who wanted to bake you cookies or teach you how to play bridge.

I was pretty sure I would've liked that.

"Would you like to get some coffee?" she asked. "I know the perfect place."

At the mention of coffee, my stomach did a full-on summersault, letting me know just how hungry I was. Shockingly, I couldn't even remember the last time I'd eaten real food. The safe house? It seemed like a thousand years ago, and suddenly all I wanted to do was wolf down a giant cheeseburger, six orders of fries, and a chocolate shake. And maybe some apple pie, too. And possibly some cheese sticks. And also, bacon. So, so much bacon.

I smiled at my grandmother, linking my arm in hers. "Throw in some dinner, Grams, and you've got yourself a deal."

"Careful mentioning the d-word around here," she said with a wink. "Deals are what got us all into this mess in the first place."

FIFTEEN

GRAY

Deirdre took me to a quaint little fifties-style diner a few blocks away from the casino, tucked down a side street just far enough off the main strip to give us a break from the crowds.

I wasted no time in ordering a full-on feast, and after I shoveled in enough greasy goodness to give me heartburn for a month, I finally felt human again.

Finally felt ready to face some of the questions swirling around my head.

Deirdre must've sensed the direction of my thoughts, because she ordered herself a double bourbon, then looked at me sternly and said, "Ask away. Now might be our last chance to talk freely in this city—Sebastian's goons don't come down this way. The place is spelled against demons."

The ominous tone in her voice made me shiver. I hoped she was wrong—that we *would* get another chance to talk. Despite the immediate chaos I had to deal with, including but not limited to the epic disaster formerly known as my love life, part of me hoped that my grandmother and I would get the chance to spend more time together. Maybe not right now, and maybe not even on the material plane. But she was beholden to Sebastian, too. I wanted to believe our paths would cross again, even if it was in this city.

It would've been nice to have an ally here.

It would've been nice to learn more about my family— my father—her son.

It would've been nice if we'd been reunited under any other circumstances but the ones that had actually brought us together.

I sighed, trying to mask my disappointment. The clock was always ticking, and right now, I needed answers. Answers that would help me understand what Sebastian really wanted with me and my ancestors. And more importantly, how the hell I could get out of this deal.

I waited until the server returned with her drink, then dove right in. "Back in that room, when I heard you talking in my head..."

"Projection," she said. "That's part of my particular brand of magic. I can transfer words and thoughts, images, emotions. But only to other witches—it doesn't cross any other barriers."

"So that's why Sebastian couldn't hear it? Or sense it?"

"Right. He knows I have that power, but he can't access it. It drives him crazy that he can't control it or even know for sure when I'm using it." A sly smile stretched across her face. "One of the few pleasures I take with him."

Again, I wondered if they were somehow… involved. But I wasn't ready to go down that path just yet. I needed to understand more about her powers, and my connection to this whole Silversbane legacy, whatever that meant.

"So can you read minds, too?" I asked. I reached for a French fry, then slipped it under the table. Sunshine happily lapped it up, but Sparkle didn't seem to like fried food. She'd had no problem dogging down half my burger patty, though.

"It doesn't work both ways," Deirdre said. "Not unless the other witch has the same power and can transfer thoughts to me."

"But you knew about the sword-seeking thing," I said. "From my vision."

She nodded somberly, then took a healthy swig of her drink. When she set her glass back on the table, her smile had turned grim. "I, too, am Shadowborn. But my shadow powers manifested in different ways. I can read a person's nightmares."

I stared, open-mouthed. That sounded absolutely horrifying.

"It's not like watching a movie," she continued, "so the details are often hazy. It's more like… I can pick up on the images and imprints left behind. The stronger, more visceral effect a nightmare has on a person, the more clearly I can connect with it. Sometimes it's a visual thing—I can see an object or a person that appeared in the dream. Other times, I can hear words. Sometimes I can only sense the lingering fear—and that feels very, very real to me." She took another sip of her bourbon. "Unfortunately, unlike with my projection power, I can't turn this one off or choose when to use it. Touching someone makes it stronger, sharper, but even without a touch, it's always there, tugging me into other peoples' darkness."

I blew out a breath, then reached for another fry for Sunshine. Reading nightmares? I'd never heard of anything like that. Psychic powers, mind reading, empathy, yes. But to connect with something so specific, so painful... That sounded a lot more like a curse than a power to me.

God. There was still so much about witchcraft I'd yet to learn, to explore. For so long, I'd denied that part of myself. Now, all I wanted to do was dive into it and research everything I possibly could.

I just didn't have the luxury of studying anymore. It was trial by fire, or not at all.

"Do you know what the swords mean?" I asked. "I've had similar nightmares a few times now, and the Four of Swords turned up a few times in Tarot readings with my best friend, Sophie." I told her about Sophie's book of shadows, and the readings I'd done since. "Sophie insisted the cards were about me. She'd said the four swords represented four witches—that the one in the ground was supposed to rise up, find the others, and give them purpose. She thought it had something to do with uniting the covens, but I wasn't so sure." I lowered my head. "She died before I could ask her anything more. She... she was murdered."

I wasn't sure how much if anything Deirdre knew about

the story—about Sophie's death, the hunters, all of the things we'd faced in the Bay and in Raven's Cape—but I didn't want to rehash all of those details right now.

Then again, if she could read my nightmares, she'd probably seen every last bit of darkness in my soul.

I reached for my half-finished milkshake, taking a big, slurpy gulp. For an instant, I closed my eyes and allowed myself to pretend that I was a kid again, a normal one, out on the town for a day of fun with my grandmother.

But like all fantasies, this one came to an end much too quickly.

"Gray," she said gently. Tentatively. And when I looked into her eyes again, I saw the change come over her. Eyes that only moments ago shone with clarity and confidence now held a nervous, contagious urgency that made me squirm in my seat.

Beyond that, I saw only one thing.

Fear. Not the kind that came from bearing witness to someone else's nightmares, but the kind that came from knowing your entire world was about to go up in flames.

Deirdre reached across the table and grabbed my hand in a bone-crushing squeeze. "We need to talk about the Silversbane prophecy."

SIXTEEN

GRAY

"The Silversbane witches can trace their lineage all the way back to the first witches," Deirdre said. "It was the Silversbane bloodline that carried forth the honors bestowed upon all witches and mages by the Elemental Source."

"To become the guardians of Earth's magic," I said, recalling the history. The strongest human bloodlines were selected to receive and care for the magic, but the mages went mad for it, screwing everything up until the Source finally revoked their privileges, making witches the sole guardians. The mages didn't like that one bit. They blamed the witches for "stealing" the magic from them, and over time, their anger and desire for vengeance warped them into a vicious, bloodthirsty breed of humans we now called hunters.

"Precisely," Deirdre said.

"So how does the prophecy come into play?" I asked,

picking up my pace to match hers. We were back on the strip now, losing ourselves in the anonymity of the crowd. As always, Sparkle and Sunshine kept watch—one up front, one behind, clearing the path from anyone who got too close.

"The original prophecy was said to be delivered directly from the Source, in a series of visions that appeared to a Silversbane oracle in a cave in the lands that later became Ireland. It was passed down orally for millennia, but never came to fruition.

"Some centuries ago, the matriarch of the family— Dubheasa Silversbane—was concerned the oral traditions would be forgotten. She commissioned the greatest calligrapher known at the time to record the prophecy and other knowledge of the craft in a series of scrolls to be passed down from generation to generation through the maternal line."

"Let me guess," I said. "The scrolls were lost."

"Lost, destroyed, no one really knows. Witchcraft historians have found remnants of them—herblore, some spellcraft, details about certain rituals, references *to* the prophecy but nothing of the prophecy itself. Still, echoes of the original visions remained even after Dubheasa's time, and were once again passed down orally." Deirdre shook her head, disappointed. "So much of the original meaning has been lost in the translation since then, or embellished, or downplayed. Most consider it no more than a legend now, but there are many who still believe."

The reverence in her eyes told me that she was one of those believers.

"What does the prophecy say?" I asked.

"Loosely, it states that four sisters will come to power, led by the third in their line—a Shadowborn, third daughter of a third daughter of a third daughter. She will be the strongest Shadowborn witch to live, and through her leadership and the bond of their sisterhood, the four will come to power with the strength to unite the fractured underground covens."

"Unite them to what end?" I asked, ignoring the goose-bumps rising on my skin, the magic pulsing just beneath.

"Those who've studied the lore and the history believe that it's saying the unified covens will rise out of the ashes of oppression, reclaim their power, defeat the enemies who would stand against them, and bring the sisterhood back into the light. Remember, Rayanne, we were revered once. Beholden and respected as the true guardians and stewards of earth's magic. We kept all things in balance. Somehow, all of that got lost along the way."

"Thanks to the hunters." Bile rose in my throat. They'd been hunting us for millennia. Longer than that, even. Longer than they'd even called themselves hunters. And unless this prophecy was true—and the four witches could be found—they'd continue hunting us long after the current generation of witches was dead.

Deirdre stepped aside to let a group of jugglers pass. One of them dropped a tennis ball, and Sunshine bounded after it, but one growl from Sparkle had her running back.

I smiled, wondering if the hounds were sisters.

"Hunters, demons, supernatural factions who don't believe witches should've been entrusted with earth's magic," Deirdre continued. "Many have been seeking the witches of prophecy, in hopes of killing them and preventing the rise of power. But the hunters are less discriminating. They'll kill any witch, prophecy or not. They just want to eradicate us. Somehow, they think wiping us off the map would restore them to their former glory, complete with all the Elemental magic they once had."

"What about the Fae Council? Are they trying to get in on a piece of this prophecy action, too?" It wouldn't surprise me. Witches in power—in a big, united group—could really pose a threat to them. They'd be outnumbered for sure, and probably out-magicked.

"Officially, they've dismissed it as bunk—a rumor crafted by witches during the European witch trials as a way to legitimize themselves and avoid persecution. But there are many fae who believe magic is *their* sole domain, and they don't feel witches ever should have had access to it."

A small crowd had gathered on a corner, and we stopped alongside them to watch a group of street performers—a cellist and two guitarists. The blend of their music was as smooth and rich as dark chocolate, lulling us all into a state of peaceful contentment. They played with their eyes closed, their faces simultaneously serious and happy, and I couldn't help but envy them.

I knew nothing about their lives, their struggles, but in

that moment, they were free, carried away by the art of their music, their passion and talents bringing a group of random strangers together on a street corner. For five minutes, all of our problems were suspended. Nothing else existed but the music and the connection, a thread that held us all together in this strange city.

And then the moment passed. They finished their song to a round of applause, and Deirdre slipped a few dollars into an open guitar case at their feet.

"This," she said, smiling as she watched the musicians pack up their instruments, "is one of the few things I truly love about this city."

We walked on in silence, each lost in our own thoughts. My head was already spinning, but I sensed there was so much more to this story. So much more we hadn't even begun to touch on.

"So if I'm a Silversbane," I finally said, "Sebastian must think I'm connected to this prophecy somehow. That I can find these four witches for him. Right?"

It made sense in my mind. He either thought they'd already died and could somehow be resurrected into new vessels, forced under his control, or he thought they were still alive and could be located with the help of their ancestors. *Our* ancestors.

Either way, he wanted control of those witches. He wanted the power promised by the prophecy.

"*Connected* to it?" Deirdre gripped my arm, stopping me in my tracks and leaning in close. Her blue eyes were fierce, her voice low and serious. "Rayanne. You *are* the witch fore-told to unite the covens. The Silversbane heir."

The Silversbane heir.

The magic inside me roiled at her words, rising to the surface. Blue sparks lit up my hands, and I shoved them into my sweatshirt pockets to hide them.

"That makes no sense, Deirdre. First of all, I'm an only child. And second—"

My words evaporated as the truth marched across her face, plain and obvious and... *No.* It couldn't be. It was completely impossible. Absurd.

"You're wrong," I insisted, shaking my head vehemently even as I felt the truth of it in my gut. In my bones. In my magic. Everything inside me was buzzing and warm, pieces clicking together in my mind, gaps filling in to form a complete story I hadn't even known I'd been missing.

As hard as I tried to fight it, I couldn't ignore the rightness of her confession.

I was the Silversbane heir. That's why Sebastian had wanted me. Why the guys felt compelled to protect me. Why even Death himself couldn't predict my future. Why I kept defying expectations and breaking rules and doing things I never should've been able to do, even as a powerful Shadowborn.

The force of that realization nearly knocked me over.

"Breathe, Rayanne. Just breathe." Deirdre cupped my face, her smile kind once again. Her eyes twinkled, shining with something that looked a lot like pride. "It's true. You are one of the four Silversbane witches of prophecy. The

Shadowborn. That is what the Tarot was trying to tell you."

"But... I have sisters?" My eyes misted, my heart hammering inside.

"Three of them. You were separated from each other when your parents died, adopted into different homes in an effort to protect you from those who sought to kill you."

Separated.

Sisters.

Parents died.

Adopted.

Kill you.

The words were coming at me so fast, I couldn't even grab onto any of them, let alone make sense of everything Deirdre was telling me. I closed my eyes, sucking in a deep breath of warm Vegas air.

Focus, Gray. Focus.

"I was practically still a baby when I was adopted," I said, opening my eyes. "Why would someone kill babies? We couldn't have had much power back then, even together."

"As the witches foretold to unite the covens under a single banner, you had immense power. Just by *existing*, you were a threat to anyone who benefited from keeping witches subjugated. We reasoned—"

"We?"

"My coven. You four were in my care after your parents died. We knew you would be hunted, especially as you came into your powers. Together, you'd be so impossibly strong, so clearly the witches of prophecy, we wouldn't be able to hide you. But we thought if you were raised in separate homes, there was a chance you might survive. As long as you didn't reunite, the prophecy could not be set in motion."

"But we were sisters! And we never had a chance to know each other!"

Sympathy and sorrow filled her eyes. "I regret that. Truly. But understand, Rayanne. If you'd been allowed to stay together, you never would've survived."

"And now? What happens next? Where are they? How can I find them?"

"Now it's out of my hands, and in the hands of fate. It seems the time of the prophecy is upon us. There is no way to stop the wheel of time, and no way to prevent you from reconnecting with your sisters. They will be called to you through the blood spell to contact the souls of your ancestors. Whether you want this or not, Rayanne, the four *will* reunite. And you will lead them."

An image flickered through my mind—the three women I'd seen in my dream, all dressed in white, carrying their silver swords. The muscular blonde. The dark-haired girl with a braid wrapped around her head. The one with a shaved head, dressed in a hospital gown—the only one who'd sparked any sense of familiarity.

Their images sharpened in my mind.

"Yes," Deirdre said softly, undoubtedly reading the imprints from my nightmares. "Those were your sisters.

Their essences are reaching out to you. Consciously or not —they, too, sense that the time has come."

"Why does one of them feel so familiar to me?" I asked. "I don't think I recognize her, but there's something... I can't put my finger on it."

"Serena," Deirdre said. "She's the first born."

The first born. The oldest. My big sister. I have a big sister. Hope flamed in my chest.

"She's familiar to you because you... You've already met her."

"Serena?" I scanned my memory, but couldn't recall a single person I'd ever met with that name.

"You know her under her adopted name." My grandmother met my eyes, her own cold and steely, unwavering in their brutal honesty even as my heart threatened to burst.

For so long, the closest thing I'd ever had to a sister was Sophie. As far as I was concerned, she *was* my sister, blood or not. When I lost her, I lost a piece of my heart I'd never get back. I lost Sophie as a person, as a friend. I lost her light, her magic, her laughter, her love. But I'd also lost the chance to be a sister. To have that bond with another woman. I'd grieved it, just as I'd grieved Sophie herself.

Now, Deirdre was about to change all of that. The next words out of her mouth were going to shake my foundations to the core. Change my world forever. Bring the impossible, amorphous idea of "you have three sisters" into a solid, firm, and very real person. A person I'd already crossed paths with at some point in my life.

A name had infinite power, and Deirdre Olivante was about to unleash that power on me.

"Who is she?" I asked, my voice shaking. "What's my sister's name?"

Deirdre closed her eyes and took a deep breath. "Haley Barnes."

SEVENTEEN

ASHER

"That stench is starting to become a situation." Haley wrin-kled her nose at the dead heap of flesh and bones formerly known as Benson. "I can't believe they just left him here. Aren't they supposed to be brothers or something?"

"Brothers?" I thought of Ronan and Darius. Emilio. Hell, even Liam had a better chance of earning a place on my favorites list than these hunter pricks.

I kicked Benson's boot through the bars. "These assholes don't know the first thing about brotherhood."

"Apparently they don't know the first thing about biohazard contamination, either." Haley resumed her pacing, trying to breathe through her mouth. "We need a plan. My hope-o-meter is starting to run dangerously low."

"*You* need to sit down, or it's not just your hope-o-meter you'll have to worry about, not that I ever want to say that word again. They're not feeding you enough to fuel all this fidgeting." I grabbed her shoulders, gently steering her to the center of the chamber to sit with the other witches. The rest of the group had gone eerily quiet—including my favorite trouble-maker, McKenna. Energy and hope were both in short supply.

Shit, Jonathan had really done a number on them. It was a wonder they were still alive.

I hope you're ripping that mother fucker a dozen new assholes, Cupcake. Preferably with a sharp knife.

"We'll figure this out together," I assured all of them. "But right now, we need to conserve energy."

"You seem to be doing okay," Haley teased. "And you haven't eaten anything either."

Of the twenty-seven witches imprisoned in this room, she seemed to be in the best spirits. I needed her to stay that way, to help keep the others relaxed and upbeat. The second doubt started creeping in, we'd all be doomed.

"I'm different," I told her. "I don't need food the way you do."

"So I've heard." She flashed a devilish smirk. "You know I'm going to make Gray spill all the details once we get out of this place, right?"

"You can try, Hay. But trust me. Gray is *not* a kiss-and-tell kind of girl."

Her eyes lit up, and she jabbed me with an accusatory finger. "So you *did* kiss her! I knew it!"

"You'll have to ask her," I said, not bothering to hide my own goofy-ass grin. Damn, just thinking about Gray again made my whole body buzz. I tried to imagine her telling Haley about our time together, her creamy cheeks blushing as she rehashed all the juicy details, acting out her soft moans of pleasure as we…

Fucking hell. I was hard already. Talk about a situation.

Turning away from Haley, I adjusted my pants and said, "No more talking. I need time to think."

Haley laughed. "Whatever you say, incubus. But I'm telling you. As soon—"

Her words died at the sound of new footsteps in the corridor. A whole fucking lot of 'em.

"Everyone stay back," I whispered to the witches, slipping back into the shadows just before a group of fae soldiers marched into view.

Marched? Scratch that. It was more like a glide. I heard their footsteps like any other soldiers, but their feet never seemed to touch the ground.

They were elite, that much was obvious. Every movement coordinated, not a step or breath out of place. Their uniforms were pristine—black, form-fitting fatigues that allowed for a full range of motion and plenty of places to stash weapons. The black-and-gold insignia on their armbands marked them as Darkwinter.

Orendiel was at the head of the line.

Fuck.

They lined up in perfect formation, and once they were all assembled, they fell so completely still and silent, I wasn't sure they were even breathing.

Gone were the lackey, ragtag hunter pukes Jonathan had hired. These guys meant serious business.

My fucking hope-o-meter just dropped by about a thousand.

"Good afternoon, witches," a deep, commanding voice called.

From the back of the line came the shuffle and stomp of a pair of boots that most certainly didn't belong to the fae. They were clunky and intrusive, unleashing a grunt with every labored step.

A man appeared before the bars—human, about sixty-five, limping slightly, with broad shoulders that hunched beneath a loose-fitting flannel. His face was tired and weather-worn, the lower half covered with an unkempt white beard. His eyes, though. They were sharp. Deadly. Unfeeling.

Seeing him was like a straight punch in the gut. I solved the damn mystery before he introduced himself, and it took every last ounce of willpower I had not to rush the bars and tear out his fucking throat.

Dirty Beard. The fuckface, cowardly, piece-of-shit hunter who'd burned Gray's mother alive right in front of her.

"Most of you knew my son, Jonathan," the old man began, dragging his baton along the bars. The fae magic keeping us locked in here popped and buzzed at the contact. "I'm sure you're all great admirers of his work, as are we. Sadly, he's decided to move on to... other opportunities. I've brought in some new management."

Other opportunities? I wondered if this jackoff had any clue that his precious baby boy was probably being mutilated by the witch whose mother they killed ten years ago.

Probably not. Seemed unlikely he'd even care. From the looks of things, he and his little army had been waiting in the wings for the first opportunity to storm the castle. Now, with Jonathan missing and the rest of the hunters he'd commanded bumbling around in the chaos, it looked like daddy dearest was taking his shot.

"I'm here to assure you that Jonathan's work will continue," he said. "However, we'll be making a few changes to better suit our needs—starting with the location. Later this evening, you'll be transferred to another facility in the city—one with more equipment and better security. Any questions?"

"Where's our food and water?" one of the witches asked.

"Rations will resume upon arrival at our new location. Provided there are no *incidents* along the way. Next question?"

"Where are we going?" Someone else asked.

"That is classified. Anyone else?"

Man, I wanted to throttle this prick. He was really letting this fake-militia shit go to his head. Problem was, no matter how much of a toolbox he looked and sounded like —and it was a damn big one, don't get me wrong—deep down he was as badass as they came. One look into those dead eyes told me everything I needed to know. He was definitely the type of guy who spent his childhood mashing spiders, pulling wings off butterflies, and plotting revenge against every motherfucker who'd ever pissed in his Cheerios.

I'm guessing it was a long list.

Someone else was asking about the food again.

I nudged McKenna with my elbow. "Hey," I whispered. "Ask him about the escaped incubus." I needed to know how much they knew about me—where they thought I'd gone.

"What about the d-demon?" she asked, injecting a little fear into her voice. Nice touch.

"Demon?" Dirty Beard scoffed. "I presume you're talking about the incubus? He's been apprehended. Nothing to worry about."

I bit back a laugh.

You dumb fuck. I'm going to apprehend my boot so far up your ass, you'll be shitting footprints for a month.

As Dirty Beard rattled off the rules and regulations he expected all the witches to follow during the transport, Haley, McKenna, and I huddled close, trying to come up with some semblance of a plan.

"What kind of fae are they?" Haley whispered. "I don't think I've ever seen any like that."

"Darkwinter," I said. "Take every terrible nightmare you've ever heard about the winter courts, and multiply it by a thousand. Oh, and that hunter yammering up front? That's the sonofabitch who murdered Gray's mother."

"Oh, shit." A chill rolled through her body, but Haley stood firm. "I'm not going to let them torture us for one more fucking day."

"Same page, Hay. But, ah, you got a plan?"

"I have one," a small voice said from the shadows behind me.

"You're the super-demon, Ash," Haley said. "What's *your* plan?"

I gestured toward the bars, where Dirty Beard was gearing up for another round of demands while Orendiel and the Douchebag Brigade stood around like stiff, well-dressed corpses. "In case you haven't noticed, I'm in a bit of a bind right now."

"I know a way out," the voice whispered again.

"What about Detective Alvarez?" Haley asked. "Surely he's found the cave entrance by now. They're probably working on a breakout plan as we speak."

"We don't even know if he got Reva's message," I said.

"Guys!" Reva shout-whispered, finally getting our attention. I looked down at her and sighed, hating that she had to spend even one night in this dank place. She was so small, so thin.

No matter how long I lived, I'd never stop being surprised at just how monstrous men could be.

"What was that?" Dirty Beard asked, and I froze, clamping a hand over Reva's mouth.

"Someone in the back there. Another question?"

McKenna caught my eye, flashing me a cocky grin. Before I could stop her, she was on her feet, stalking toward the bars.

"Hey, asshole," she said. "I got a question. You know what happens to guys who fuck witches?"

Dirty Bead laughed. "No, I don't. Do you know what happens to witches whose food rations are cut in half?"

McKenna imitated his laugh. Had to hand it to her—she didn't back down from a fight. "No, I don't. Do you know what happens to a hunter when a pissed-off, half-starved witch puts a curse on him?"

He slammed his baton into the bars, sending up a spray of sparks from the fae magic locking us in here. "No," he said. "I don't."

"Neither do I." She laughed again, high pitched, totally mental. "It's a new recipe I'm working on. Come back tomorrow and we'll all find out together."

"That's enough," Dirty Beard said. Unlike his son, he wasn't so easy to rile up. McKenna kept at him, though, giving us just the opportunity we needed.

"Alright, Reva," I whispered. "What've you got for me."

"I know a way out of here," she said.

I thumbed toward the retinal scanner at the front of the bars. "You got a spare eyeball?"

"Not out of the cell. Out of the whole prison." Her eyes lit up with renewed hope, brightening the dank, dark room. "There's another cave system past this one. None of them ever go back there."

"Reva," Haley said, "even if we could get back there without the guards catching us, the whole place is spelled. We'll never get out."

"Not the whole thing. I'm pretty sure they're only focusing on this cave system. I don't think they even know the other one exists." She told us about a small chamber she'd discovered when she'd been doing her shadowmancy business trying to get that message to Emilio. "It connects to the other system. The only way in is through a super narrow shaft halfway up the wall. It leads into the back chamber, then down another passageway. Eventually, it takes you back outside, way down on the other end of the beach."

"How far down?" I asked.

"Maybe a couple of miles from the pier. Three tops."

"You're sure?"

"I can go out at night," she said, nodding enthusiastically. "Once I get out, I'll find my way to town."

The idea had potential. But it also had a lot of pitfalls.

"Why don't you try to connect with Emilio again?" I asked. "Project, or whatever it is you do."

"There's no time, Ash. It was almost impossible last time. I'm pretty sure he has to be in wolf form to hear me, and even then, it was really hard. I don't know if I got through to him at all."

"I'm betting the Cape is crawling with hunters," Haley said. "Probably fae, too. It's not safe, Reva."

"I know how to avoid them. I'll go straight to the police and ask for the detective's sister."

"I don't like it," Haley said. "What if they catch you? They'll kill you. And they won't do it quickly."

Reva shrugged. "They think I'm a useless kid—not even worth experimenting on. They only reason I'm still alive in here is they've already forgotten about me."

"The so-called useless kid has a very useful point," I said.

"Trust me," she said. "They won't even notice I'm gone."

"You seem pretty sure about that," Haley said.

"I know how to disappear." She shrugged with all the cool confidence of a teenager who'd just gotten away with shoplifting. "I've been doing it my whole life."

Haley blew out a breath, her shoulders slumping. I knew how much she hated the idea—I wasn't too keen on sending Reva out alone, either. But Reva was right—she was small, the only one of us who could slip away undetected and fit through that shaft.

I put a hand on Haley's shoulder. "Hay, we—"

The crack of Dirty Beard's baton shut us up again. McKenna had finally gone silent.

"No more," the bastard snapped. "You all know what's expected of you. We'll be back at oh-six-hundred to start the transport. Any more outbursts, and you'll all be given electroshock treatment."

He shuffled out, the fae turning as one single unit to follow him down the corridor.

"Electroshock treatments?" Haley's eyes blazed. "Fuck this." She turned to Reva. "Okay, Reva. I'm in."

Reva gave me a high-five.

"So now we just need a way to get her out of this cell," Haley said. "We need some kind of—"

"Disturbance? Did somebody call for a disturbance?" I flashed them a big-ass grin.

"What's that look?" Haley asked, swirling her finger in front of my face. "I already don't like that look."

"You aren't supposed to like it."

"What are you thinking?"

"I'm thinking," I said, walking to the front of the chamber and peering out through the bars, "it's time to show these fae-fucking, limp-dick hunters where the big, bad incubus has been hiding."

EIGHTEEN

GRAY

Haley Barnes?

I wasn't even sure I'd heard Deirdre correctly, but the time for questions had passed. We were back in front of Inferno, too close to Sebastian's many spies to continue this conversation so candidly.

"So, that's Las Vegas," Deirdre said loudly, presumably for any of Sebastian's guards in the vicinity. "I'm so glad I got the chance to show you around. I'll take you back inside now."

She grabbed my elbow, steering me toward a service entrance near the back.

"But, what about—"

"There's no time, Gray," she muttered quickly. "Ronan's going to meet us any minute. He asked me to take you to see Darius first."

"Darius?" The idea of finally seeing my vampire and reuniting with Ronan was enough to settle my nerves and hit the pause button on my many questions. "Where is he? Is he okay?"

"He's… stable. The blood overdose is still working its way out of his system, and he—"

"Blood overdose?"

"He attacked and fully drained a demon after he got through the hell portal. I'm sure Ronan will fill you in on everything later. Come on—this way."

Knowing Ronan, he wouldn't fill me in on *anything* later, but what choice did I have but to shut up and follow her? I needed to see Darius, and I didn't know if and when I'd get another opportunity.

We took the service elevators down to the basement level, then followed another long series of hallways until we reached another wooden door. Unlike the last one, this didn't have any glowing runes or codes. Just a big-ass iron bar bolted across it.

Deirdre lifted the bar, then pushed open the door, revealing another dark chamber inside. This one was huge, though, and hot—nothing like Sebastian's little meeting room upstairs.

I stepped into the entry, waiting for my eyes to adjust. The floor was a dull, dirt-colored wood that looked like it hadn't been polished in decades, and the stone walls surrounding us were damp with moisture. Everything beyond the immediate entryway was cloaked in shadow.

Even my breath seemed to echo.

"Your vampire is inside," Deirdre said softly. "All the way in the back. But… a word to the wise? Keep your guard up. He's dangerous, Rayanne, despite the restraints and the hawthorn."

"Restraints?" My eyes welled as I pictured him tied up and sedated. What had they done to him? He'd lost his memories trying to save me, and this was the homecoming they'd given him? "Darius would *never* hurt me."

"But that's just it. This vampire is *not* Darius. You must remember, he's—"

I cut her off with a harsh glare, and she pressed her lips tightly together, as if she had to physically restrain herself from speaking her mind.

Darius had suffered memory loss. That didn't make him less deserving of respect and kindness. It didn't make him broken or some wild, untamed beast that needed to be restrained and beaten.

Deirdre hovered in the doorway a moment longer, as if she were still trying to decide whether to leave me alone with the man I loved. The man who'd saved me in the Shadowrealm. The man whose touch still smoldered on my skin.

"I love him," I informed her, ending the argument before it devolved into something worse. "I'm not leaving here until I know he's okay. Until I see it with my own eyes."

Her eyes softened, and she reached up to touch my cheek. Her palm was warm and soft, her touch kind.

"I understand." She smiled softly, then slipped outside with one final piece of advice trailing in her wake: "Just... don't get too close."

The door closed and bolted behind her, and I stepped deeper into the room, waiting for my eyes to adjust. It seemed the only light came from a sparse collection of electric wall sconces.

Everything about this room felt forgotten.

I turned to the hounds that'd followed me inside. "Sparkle," I whispered. "Sunshine. You two stay here and keep an eye out for me, okay?"

"Ah, there you are, lovely," Darius said. His voice came from the darkness, smooth as silk, sending a ripple of warmth across my skin. "Come closer so I can see your beautiful face."

"Darius," I breathed. Was that recognition I'd heard in his tone?

Or simply the charms of a smooth-talking vampire, just like the one I'd allowed to taste my blood that first time in Black Ruby?

That was the night we'd become blood bound, and it felt like a million years ago now. So much had happened since then. It was a wonder any of us was still alive.

But we are *alive*, I reminded myself. We'd already fought and survived so many battles. This was just one more.

Leaving the hounds at the door, I approached the back of the room cautiously, my heart thumping louder with every footstep.

Slowly, painfully, Darius came into view. He was seated on a long bench, his feet chained and bolted to the floor, his wrists chained and bolted to the wall. A hawthorn stake had been shoved through his left hand;

the skin had partly healed around it, leaving a ring of dark blood.

My stomach twisted. I hated seeing him like this. Bound. Sedated.

I took another step closer, still assessing him.

His clothes were clean and looked new—dark sweatpants and a Vegas Golden Knights hockey jersey I was pretty sure he hadn't picked out from the souvenir shop himself. His face looked gaunt beneath a few days' worth of stubble, his eyes glassy, his brown hair wild and unkempt.

He flashed me a grin as I approached, as smooth and smokey as fine whiskey, but nothing like the real Darius. Nothing like the vampire I'd fallen in love with.

"You're afraid of me, beautiful," he said matter-of-factly. "I can sense it in your heartbeat."

I nodded, but not because it was true, or part of the longstanding joke we'd shared about how much he used to scare me before we'd finally come together.

"You're a very powerful vampire," I said, as if that explained the rapid-fire beat behind my ribcage. Playing the game was easier than admitting that my heart was shattering, sputtering out its last hurrah.

"I suppose I am," he said. His smile was composed, but the glint in his glassy eyes was feral. "I wish I could recall, but in the absence of memory, I'll have to rely on…" He sucked a breath of air through his lips, his tongue darting out to wet them. "…instinct."

I stepped closer, and those golden honey eyes darkened, his nostrils flaring as he scented the air around me.

"What do your instincts tell you about me?" I asked.

"Hmm. Something has changed. The last time we were together," he said, "you were quite a bit less lively. In fact, the demon said something about a missing soul?"

"My soul was trapped in hell, but that's old news. I'm back now." I forced a smile. "Better than ever."

He took another breath, then sighed. "More determined, perhaps. But I sense you've lost something along the way."

More than you could possibly imagine...

"Perhaps you could use a friend?" he asked.

I looked into those eyes, the dark lashes, the beautifully full lips, the face of the man I loved, and I wanted to open up to him, to confess everything that had happened, everything I'd learned. To tell him how scared I truly was.

But I'd be a fool to trust him now.

He was Darius, but... not. The man before me reminded me of an actor, changing his expressions and voice for a role. There was no warmth in his eyes. No recognition. And absolutely no love.

Darius's eyes suddenly darted to the side, and he scented the air again, his lip curling in disgust. Seconds later, I heard the scrape of the iron bar lifting from the door, followed by the click of the hounds' claws against the floor.

"*Demon,*" Darius practically spat. "If I never see or smell or taste another for a thousand years, it will be too soon."

I turned back toward the door as Ronan entered the room.

Anger smoldered in my gut like hot coals as I remembered his most recent devil's bargain, but I couldn't deny I was relieved to see him. Logically I knew he couldn't fix this any more than he could fix the mess he'd made between us, but his presence still comforted me. Ronan had been my best friend long before he'd become my lover. My life.

Nothing was going to change that.

"Why is he like this?" I asked as Ronan approached, hating myself for talking about Darius as if he wasn't in the room with us—wasn't glaring at me with raw, naked lust. But the change that had come over him went deeper than his memory loss. It was hunger, pure and simple. Bloodlust.

As far as I knew, Darius hadn't fed on living beings in decades, and he certainly hadn't overdosed. Yet Deirdre had mentioned something about him attacking and draining a demon?

"Is it just his instincts taking over?" I asked.

"Partly," Ronan said. "For a vampire, feeding on the living is primal. Feeding on donor blood or animals is the conscious choice in the equation."

"One he doesn't remember making." I sighed as the pieces clicked into place. Darius was centuries old. He hadn't come to his choices overnight. They'd been woven into the fabric of his life, shaped by his experiences, reinforced by decades of choices, every decision *not* to kill, *not* to drain the lifeblood of another being inexorably linked to his memory.

Memory that he no longer possessed.

"Well, this is rather enlightening," Darius said. "I don't

recall ever being so thoroughly dissected before. Perhaps next time you might buy me dinner first."

"Gray," Ronan said, and the odd hesitation in his voice set a new flare of panic ablaze in my chest.

"Tell me," I breathed, my voice as fragile as an eggshell. "Just tell me."

"Before we came to the Shadowrealm, he was ambushed by hunters in a motel. They'd intended to kill him, but he... he destroyed them."

"Destroyed?"

"Drained," Ronan said, and the word punched me in the gut. Ronan gave me a moment to process this before continuing. "He fed on both of them, consumed by bloodlust. It was essentially an overdose—way too much, too fast, his system couldn't process it all. Somehow, he made it back to us, and we got him stabilized."

"Speaking of feeding," Darius said. "I don't suppose either of you knows where a vampire like me could get a... bite?"

"But then he attacked a demon?" I asked, ignoring Darius. "Deirdre said something about it."

"I came out of the hell portal with you, but Darius had already gotten through ahead of us. I found him feeding on one of Sebastian's guards."

"Now *that's* something I do remember," Darius said. "I'm not quite sure I'll ever get the taste of that filth out of my mouth." Darius laughed, a sound I'd never heard before. It wasn't *his* laugh. It belonged to some other vampire, some other time, some other place.

It occurred to me then just how fragile everything really was—for each of us. Every day was like walking on the edge of a knife. One misstep...

We had absolutely zero control.

Yet somehow, we kept walking along that blade anyway.

"Let's go." Ronan tugged on my sweatshirt, careful not to touch my skin.

I jerked away from him. Better that he not touch me at all. "We can't leave him here, Ronan. Not like this."

"There's nothing we can do right now," Ronan said, his tone suddenly gentle. This was hurting him just as it was hurting me. I had to remember that. "He doesn't know us anymore, Gray."

Darius scoffed. "The fact that you've detained me against my will, dressed me in these bargain basement atrocities, starved me, and poisoned me with hawthorn tells me *everything* I need to know about you, demon." He turned his gaze back on me, that same cold grin sliding across his face. "*You*, on the other hand..."

Darius closed his eyes and took a deep breath through his nose, inhaling my scent again. Naively, I waited for him to show me his real smile, to look at me with even the faintest glimmer of recognition.

But when he opened his eyes again, there was nothing. Only that icy smile that sent chills to my very core.

"You really are an absolutely lovely creature," he murmured, his deep voice sliding down my spine like a caress.

I felt my body inching toward him, seeking his touch as if by muscle memory. I leaned in close to the wall, right to where his un-staked hand was bound, just close enough for him to graze my face.

Ronan stiffened behind me, but didn't stop me.

Darius flexed his hand, reaching out to stroke my cheek with one elegant finger, his thumb pressing the dip in my bottom lip, and I shivered, my breath catching in my throat.

His touch was so familiar. If I closed my eyes, I could almost believe it was still him. That Darius was still with us. That he'd beaten the odds and regained his memories and—

"Gray." A firm grip on my shoulder, the too-warm touch that quickly led to smoke, and Ronan was easing me backward, out of Darius's reach once again.

Ronan released me.

I stood between them, Ronan at my back, Darius before me, and felt myself waver. Memories seized me, flashing images of our night together at the safe house, Ronan taking me from behind, Darius lying beneath me, touching me, bringing me endless pleasures...

I'd felt so loved, so cared for. So safe. In that moment, I'd known without a doubt that as long as we had each other, nothing bad could ever touch us.

If only I'd known that it was just that—a moment. Here, then gone.

That night, their touch felt like home.

This night, a touch from either of them could kill me.

Darius unleashed a faint moan, his eyes darkening with a look of pure, unadulterated lust.

"Whatever you're thinking about," Ronan told me, "whatever you're feeling, he's picking up on it."

I felt my cheeks flame and forced myself to look away.

"Deirdre said she'll brew something to ease his suffering," Ronan said. "It should help neutralize the effects of the overdose and diminish the bloodlust—Emilio's sister did the same thing before. But I'm afraid neither of them can do anything about his memories."

"Have they even tried?"

"What's to try? Those beasts that attacked us in the Shadowrealm weren't called memory borrowers or memory misplacers or temporary memory blockers. They're memory eaters, Gray. They destroyed his mind. I want to believe there's a way, but I just..." Ronan sighed. "Maybe there's no coming back from something like that."

Darius had no response to this. When I turned to look at him again, I saw his head hanging limply, his hair falling in front of his eyes. He'd gone still.

"He'll be okay, though, won't he?" I asked.

After all the secrets, the deceit, the misdirections, the cover-ups, all I wanted now was one more lie. I wanted Ronan to look me in the eye and tell me that Darius would pull through this. That we'd all pull through this.

But Ronan shook his head. "I don't know, Gray."

It was just as well. Lies never really fixed anything, anyway. They just prolonged the breaking.

"Did you know I was the Silversbane heir?" I asked

Ronan. Emotionless. Cold. A throwaway question I didn't really expect him to answer.

"No," he said. "But I always suspected it."

I looked up into his eyes, searching them for some sign of hope. Something flickered there—a spark, maybe, and then it was gone.

"You were always destined for greatness," he said, leaning in close. "I never doubted that."

His smile reappeared, and for one brief instant, I thought he might actually try to kiss me again. But then he pulled back, shoving a hand through his hair.

"We... We need to find Asher," I blurted out. I wasn't sure why—it's not like finding Asher could do anything to bring back Darius's memories or break the chains Sebastian had put on my relationship with Ronan. But I had to stay focused on something—a mission with a definite end goal. Something we actually stood a chance at achieving.

"We will," Ronan said firmly. Definitively. Then, in a softer voice, "That's a promise, Gray."

I shook my head, biting back a snarky retort. There was a time when I believed Ronan's promises without question. When that firm, no-nonsense, no-bullshit tone had the power to pull me from the darkest depths of worry and fear. When one touch of his palm against my cheek could soothe the deepest ache in the darkest parts of my soul.

But he wasn't allowed to touch me now, and the ache bloomed unchecked, blackening me from the inside out.

I turned my back on both of them—my demon and my

vampire, the men whose claims on my heart were burned into me like brands—and walked to collect my hounds.

Right now, our priority was Asher. He needed me to stay strong.

And I needed him to be... No, that was it. No more words necessary. I needed him to be. To just *be*.

NINETEEN

GRAY

"How soon can we get back to Raven's Cape?" I paced the hotel room, wishing I had a suitcase to pack or papers to shuffle or *anything* to distract me from the black hole eating away at my heart.

I was the fucking heir to the Silversbane legacy. The prophesied witch born with the power to unite the covens and bring order to the chaos and blah, blah, blah.

So why couldn't I save the men I loved?

Why did I grow up alone, isolated from my three sisters?

How did my parents actually die?

How did Deirdre end up in Sebastian's company?

Where were my sisters now? Did they know about me?

Who signed my original contract with Sebastian?

How much, if anything, had Calla known?

What did Sebastian want with my ancestors if he

already knew I was the prophesied witch? Was it just my sisters he was after, so he could have the complete set?

I looked around at the hotel room, at Ronan, at the hounds pacing their own circles at the end of the bed. How had all of this come to be?

So many questions. So many impossible answers. And they just kept on coming, one leading to another to the next, each one more thorny than the last.

Destiny was cruel. That was the only answer. The only one I kept running up against, time and again.

Liam had once told me that destiny and choice were not mutually exclusive. *"But there are things about your path you must learn, must accept, no matter how difficult."* I wondered now if this was what he'd meant. The Silversbane legacy. Or my enslavement to Sebastian. Or something else entirely —something we'd yet to encounter.

How much of my current predicament had he already seen as one of his infinite possibilities? And if possibilities were, in fact, infinite, didn't it stand to reason that there were other paths we might still take? Other choices we just yet hadn't considered?

I pressed my fingertips to my temples, massaging my head. When this was all over, I'd eat and cry myself into a week-long coma with a few gallons of ice cream and a pan of Emilio's brownies, all of it topped off with a bottle of Darius's fancy wine. But for now, we had to keep moving.

"So Sebastian's letting you go?" Ronan asked. "Just like that?"

"For now."

"But how did that even happen? He doesn't—"

I held up my hand. "Ronan, it's a really long story, and I'll tell you all about it once we're on the plane. Okay? Right now, I just want to focus on getting the hell out of this city."

"We can't leave yet," Ronan said. "We need to find a safer situation for Darius. I'm not familiar with the vampire families in town, and we can't just leave him at Inferno. I don't trust Sebastian to—"

"Wait, *what*?" I spun on my heel to face him, my eyes wide. "Leave him at Inferno? Are you kidding me? We're not leaving him anywhere. We're *all* going back to the Cape. Together."

"Gray, he's not..." Ronan shoved a hand through his hair and blew out a frustrated breath. "He doesn't even know he's part of us. All he knows now is the taste of blood, and the fact that he's not getting it. It's driving him mad. Taking him back to the Cape in this state—likely against his will—is beyond dangerous. It's flat-out stupid."

"Then we'll take precautions. We're not splitting up again, Ronan. The three of us need to get back to the Cape, back to Emilio. Then we need to help Asher."

Ronan crossed the room, reaching for my shoulders but stopping just short. I flinched away from him anyway.

He didn't even bother hiding the pain in his eyes.

"You think I *want* to leave him?" he snapped, making Sunshine yelp. "You think I wanted any of this to happen?"

I didn't need to answer that. Of course he didn't want this to happen. But it *did* happen.

I fell back onto the bed. My heart broke as much for

Ronan as it did for me. Deep down I knew the truth, no matter what Sebastian wanted me to believe.

Ronan loved me. And it was killing him that he couldn't do anything about it. Ronan cared a great deal for Darius, too, and now he'd lost a friend. A brother.

"I'm sorry, Gray," Ronan said now, sitting next to me on the bed. "I'm so, so fucking sorry."

"Don't." I sat up next to him, careful not to get too close. "Look. I know that you're not allowed to love me, and Darius can't remember that he ever did. I know that Asher is still trapped inside that hellhole. And Emilio is probably going out of his mind trying to solve this case, and I have no idea how to help him once we get back." I turned to look into his eyes, and when I saw the love there, blazing as it always had, I took a risk, brushing my hand through the hair falling across his forehead. There was a second where it didn't hurt, didn't burn, but then the smoke came, and I pulled back.

In a much softer voice, I said, "But I *do* know that we all belong together. No matter what the circumstances. We're stronger together, Ronan. You know it. We need to get back there."

He watched me a moment longer, then finally nodded. "I know. You're right. I know."

"I don't want to split up again. Not if we can help it. The five of us are… We're a family, Ronan. No one can take that away from us. Not even Sebastian."

"And Liam?" he asked. "Where does he fit into all this?"

I forced a casual shrug, swallowing past the lump in my

throat. "I don't know yet. Liam and I... We have a few things to figure out."

"It seemed like you were figuring things out pretty well in the Shadowrealm. I saw the way you were looking at each other." He shrugged, all of this said without jealousy. Without disapproval.

Ronan had always made it clear that he wanted me to be happy—that he understood there was room in the human heart for the love of more than just one other being, and he'd never been jealous. Not of Darius, with whom he'd happily shared me. Not of Asher. Not of Emilio, who was just beginning to find his way into my heart. Ronan considered them all brothers. They all felt that way about each other.

But Liam was different. He'd always been just a little... outside of things. From the moment he'd arrived in Sophie's bedroom the night of her murder, he and Ronan had butted heads. They'd worked through some of their differences since then, but I wasn't sure Ronan was ready to hear the full story of me and Liam. And if he knew that Liam had made a bargain with Sebastian for my soul long before any of this had ever started...

My heart squeezed, tears springing to my eyes. I blinked them away, hoping Ronan hadn't noticed.

"Do you remember when I told you there was nothing I wouldn't do for you?" he asked. "I meant it, Gray. I want you to feel like you can be open with me about anything. Your feelings for Liam included. If you—"

"Why?" I whispered, fresh tears spilling, and in that one

word—*why?*—he knew I wasn't talking about Liam or anyone else for that matter.

I was talking about Ronan. About what he'd done to get me out of the Shadowrealm.

It was a long time before he found the words to respond.

"This... this was one of those things, too," he said. "I said there's nothing I wouldn't do for you. That includes giving you up to keep you safe."

"There might've been another—"

"There wasn't. You were trapped in the Shadowrealm. Even Liam couldn't get you out. The thought of you there alone, facing those demons... I couldn't let it happen. Darius and I had to get to you, and the only way we could was through the hell portal. Sebastian never does anything without a price, and he knew I'd pay any price for you. So yeah, I gave you up. I did it because I wanted you to live. To love. To be that crazy, stubborn, beautiful witch you've always been." He offered me a sad smile. "As long as I know you're out there living your life, I... I have to be okay with that."

"But I'm *not* out there. I'm here. Trying to find a permanent way out of this bullshit deal with Sebastian. If I don't, there is no living my life, with you or without you."

"Don't say that," he whispered, his lips so close to mine I could already taste his kiss. "You're young, smart, passionate, powerful, beautiful... There's so much more you—"

I shook my head, cutting him off. All I could think about was his kiss. How long until I forgot the feel of his lips? The warmth of his breath? The soft velvet of his tongue? The intensity in his gaze as we...

I closed my eyes—the only thing I could do to break the connection.

"You have taken a piece of my heart, Ronan," I said. "Carved it right out and set it on fire. I'm so in love with you I can't even breathe to think of a life without you. Now you're asking me to accept this? To stand by and watch everything we are to each other burn to ashes?"

"Look at me, Gray. Please."

I opened my eyes. His own were red and glassy, heart-break written on his face. The sight of his pain made my heart stop.

"There's nothing else we can do," he said. "It's over. It's just over."

My heart started up again with a painful sputter. And this time when it beat, it fell out of step, missing its twin. Missing my best friend.

"I will *never* stop loving you," I whispered, taking his face into my hands. It hurt to touch him, my skin burning with an ache I would never be able to ease. Not with words and promises. Not with dreams of a better future. Not with kisses.

"This isn't—"

"I love you, Ronan Vacarro. So, so much." I looked deep into his eyes and waited for him to say it. That he loved me, too. That nothing Sebastian said or did would ever change that, even if he couldn't act on it.

"Gray, I..."

Say it, Ronan. Just say it…

"You should… get some rest," he finally said, standing up unceremoniously from the bed. All traces of regret, of love, of friendship were gone in a flash. "I need to make arrangements to transport Darius. I'll come get you when it's time to go."

"That's *it*?" I stood from the bed and followed him to the door, shouting at his back. "That's all you're going to say?"

"What do you *want* me to say, Gray?"

I grabbed his shoulders and spun him around, ignoring the smoke. "I want you to look me in the eye and tell me you don't love me. Tell me this is really over between us."

I placed my hand on his chest, seeking the familiar drum-beat of his heart. It pounded behind his ribcage, harder and harder with every breath, even as my touch burned through his T-shirt.

He leaned in close, so close I could count his eyelashes. His breath came in short staccato bursts, each one kissing my lips.

"Say it again," I whispered. "Tell me again that it's over."

He clenched his teeth, grounding out every word. "This. Is. Over. We're done."

He pulled back and cleared his throat, shifting his gaze to a spot just above my eye. His face was neutral once again. Cold. "From now on, we are guardian and demon sworn. Nothing more."

"I'm never giving up on you," I said. "No matter what

you say. No matter what Sebastian does. And I *know* you won't give up on me, either." I said it with all the confidence I could muster, needing to believe it for myself.

"It's too late, Gray." He turned away from me and wrenched open the door. "I already have."

TWENTY

GRAY

After another long and brutal argument, Ronan finally agreed to ask Deirdre for help in transporting Darius. In a moment of sheer brilliance, she'd concocted an IV solution using essence of hawthorn, and with that, we were able to fully sedate him and get him on the plane without incident.

The plane wasn't Darius's private jet—one of the few things Ronan and I agreed on was that Darius's memory loss needed to be kept secret from the larger vampire community for as long as possible, including his pilots and other associates. So instead, we'd taken an aircraft on loan from Sebastian, no doubt a grand gesture designed to lull us into thinking he could be a friend. After all, Sebastian always had a price.

Ronan and I hadn't exchanged a single word since boarding the plane. By some miracle, I managed to hold it together for the entire flight, as well as the drive from the airport to Emilio's sister's house in Raven's Cape.

But the moment Emilio opened the front door and bounded down the front steps to greet us, I lost it.

"Gray?" He looked at me like he hadn't seen me in a hundred years and wasn't sure he could trust his own eyes.

I nodded, tears spilling freely, and collapsed into his arms, burying my face against his chest. His familiar scent enveloped me like a hug, all forest and sunshine and vanilla, and I slid my arms up inside the back of his jacket, soaking up his warmth. His strength.

Sparkle and Sunshine, my ever-present companions, ran circles around us both.

"I missed you so much," I breathed.

"You, too, *mi querida*. More than you can imagine." He wrapped his big arms around me tighter, holding me close, his hand cupping the back of my head. His thumb stroked behind my ear, the touch immediately soothing my jagged nerves.

"I see you brought... these guys," he said, not quite hiding his grimace as the hounds nipped at the hem of his jacket. He reached down to pat Sparkle on the head, and Sunshine nosed her way in for some loving, too.

"Sparkle and Sunshine." I pointed each one out. "Courtesy of Sebastian."

Ronan had given Emilio some of the details over the phone before we took off from Vegas, so news of my new arrangement didn't come as a complete surprise. But Emilio still winced when I told him about it—the meeting, the temporary stay Sebastian had finally agreed to. And of course, the hounds.

"You… named them?" he asked.

"I figured it was the only humane thing to do. Apparently, we're going to be spending a lot of time in each other's company. And by a lot, I mean an eternity." I smiled, trying to keep the mood light, but failed miserably. My face crumpled once again.

"Did Sebastian say how long you had?" Emilio asked gently.

"We left it kind of open ended. I'm hoping I can figure out another loophole in the interim."

"We will, Gray. That's not even a question." He put his arm around me and pulled me close again, big and protective and comforting, exactly what I needed. I let out a breath, some of my stress evaporating. Emilio had always had that effect on me.

Behind him, two men headed down the front steps from the house—shifters, I thought. Probably wolves. Jael came next—Emilio had told us he'd been staying with them, helping out. Then, bringing up the rear, a woman who could only be Emilio's sister, Elena.

I pulled out of Emilio's embrace and attempted to wipe away my tears and smooth out my hair, but I was probably making everything worse. I was still wearing Ronan's sweatshirt and the clothes I'd woken up with at the hotel, and I felt like my entire body was covered in a layer of grease from Sebastian's mere presence.

Clearly not my personal best, but Emilio's sister offered a warm, genuine smile anyway.

"Welcome to Raven's Cape," she said, introducing

herself and leaning in to kiss my cheek. "I only wish you'd come here for a happier reason."

Her accent reminded me of Emilio's, and I wondered what else they had in common, what their childhood had been like, how long it had been since they'd seen each other before this. Emilio had never said much about her, but now I sensed a distance between them, a tension lingering just beneath the surface of their smiles. I wondered if she was the reason for the sadness I sometimes saw in his eyes. The regret.

I thought about his words back at the safe house the night I'd grilled Fiona Brentwood.

People do all sorts of misguided things when they're trying to protect the ones they love, querida. Let's just say I know something about that.

Maybe he'd been talking about his sister.

"Those are my guys," she said, bringing me back to the moment. She nodded to the shifters that were now speaking with Ronan and Jael at the car. "Detectives Aiden Hobb and Russel Lansky."

"They're helping with the case," Emilio said.

"Right now, they're helping with your vampire," Elena said. "But there's plenty of room in the house for everyone, so no worries. Even the... the dogs."

"They're not dogs, Elena." Emilio rolled his eyes playfully. "They're—"

"Shh!" She put her hands over her ears. "I have to tell myself they're dogs, or we're going to have a serious problem."

Emilio laughed. "Whatever you say."

"It *is* whatever I say. It's my house. Also, my jurisdiction." She turned back to me with a real smile. "You can set up in the spare room on the right, straight back from the front. There's a bathroom in there too if you want to shower. Once you're all settled in, I'll make us all a snack. Yes?"

"Thank you," I said. "That sounds great. Especially the shower and snack."

"By *snack*," Emilio said, "she means a seven-course meal, complete with appetizers and dessert."

I beamed. "Even better."

Elena went to help the others get Darius situated. Emilio told me they'd set up a room in the basement for him, trying to make sure he'd be as comfortable as possible.

"No stone benches," he promised me. "But we do need to keep him sedated and bound for now. Just until we can assess the situation and figure out how to best help him. Okay?"

"There has to be something else we can do," I said, my stomach knotting up again just thinking about Darius being... handled. That was the word for it. They were handling him, shuffling him from the car to the house, down into the basement, talking about him as if he were a stranger. A prisoner. "Emilio, it's *Darius*."

"Oh, *querida*," he said, his voice soft and reassuring. "This isn't right. I know it isn't. But it's the best we can do right now." He cupped my cheeks, his thumbs brushing away the last of my tears.

I wrapped my hands around his wrists and sighed, grateful for the contact. For a touch that didn't turn into smoke. When I looked up and met his gaze, Emilio was openly staring at me, his soulful eyes searching my face.

"What is it?" I whispered, suddenly shy. I didn't even want to *think* about how horrible I looked right now, but Emilio seemed completely captivated. "You're freaking me out, *El Lobo*."

"I'm sorry. It's just... it's really good to see you, *brujita bonita*. When they told me what you'd done in that prison, what it meant..." He closed his eyes and swallowed hard. When he spoke again, his voice was ragged. "I thought I'd never hold you again. How did you even survive that place? And then you got stuck in *hell*?"

"That's... a really long story." I felt like I'd been saying that a lot lately, and I'm sure the other guys had their own tales to tell, too. We'd all been away from each other for so long, it seemed like it'd been years since we'd last shared a meal together, let alone talked. Really, really talked.

"I guess we have a lot to catch up on," he said.

"We will," I promised him. "After dinner, though. You got me all excited for Elena's seven-course meal."

Emilio nodded, lowering his hands from my face. I missed the contact immediately, but forgave him when he reached into his jacket pocket and pulled out a small box, gift-wrapped in pale turquoise paper and tied with a red ribbon.

"Is that for me?" I asked.

Emilio smiled. "Just a little something I saw and thought you might like."

A bubble of giddiness floated up inside, and I bounced on my toes, eagerly tearing open the paper. After so much darkness, so much insanity, it felt good to find the simple joy in something like a present.

The paper fell away, revealing a deck of Tarot cards.

And I gasped, tears blurring the colors and designs together.

I'd been mesmerized by this deck since I was a little girl.

"Are they... do you like them?" He asked. "I know you like to use Sophie's cards for your readings, but everything was so chaotic when we left the safe house, I didn't think to grab any of your things. When I saw this deck, I... I just got this image of you holding the cards. *These* cards. I felt like you belonged together. Does that sound nuts?"

"Emilio," I finally breathed. "It's not nuts. They're perfect."

"Are you sure? Because if you don't like them, I bet we can exchange them. There were at least a hundred different decks at the shop, and—"

"It's not that. It's...." I took a deep breath, the shock of it still washing over me. "This is the deck Calla used to use."

It was her favorite deck. The only card I had left from it was the High Priestess—I'd found it inexplicably tucked into my book of shadows the night we'd dug the book up out of my backyard. At the time, it'd felt like a message from Calla. An infusion of strength and wisdom and encouragement. Now, it felt like she was looking down on me again, wrapping me up in a gentle hug, reminding me that she was still with me.

"There was a time I'd be surprised to hear that," Emilio said, "but if I've learned anything from you, it's that there are no coincidences."

"No, there really aren't."

"You were meant to have those cards, Gray. I felt it from the moment I saw them in the case."

I nodded, unable to express how touched I really was.

When I finally looked up from the cards, Emilio offered me a shy smile. The sight of it filled me with so much warmth, it felt like the sun had finally found me again, thawing out my bones from a deep freeze.

There was so much going wrong. So much falling apart.

But here in Emilio's embrace, I'd found a moment of pure peace.

"You're trembling, *mi querida.*" He rubbed my back, as if I needed warming up. As if I could ever be any warmer than I was right here in his arms. "Are you okay?"

"More than okay." I pulled back and looked up into those soulful brown eyes again, my heart fuller and lighter than it'd been in weeks. "You make me believe we're strong enough to—"

He cut off my words with a kiss. A quick one, soft and pure, just this side of friendly, but a kiss nevertheless. There was a promise of more to come in a kiss like that—so much more—and for now I tucked it away for later, knowing that in the midst of all this chaos, there was at least one good, pure, beautiful thing waiting for me on the near horizon.

"Whatever you were going to say," he said, pressing his forehead to mine and closing his eyes, "it's true. We *are* strong enough. For whatever's coming our way. For whatever we need to do to fix this. For whatever we need to do to protect our pack."

* * *

Elena's dinner was amazing, and despite the challenges we were all facing, we still managed to laugh. To enjoy Elena's cooking, trading a few stories from their mutually trouble-making childhoods in Argentina. I learned that Emilio liked to chase away the chickens that his mother had meant to cook, and Elena had a knack for growing what she called a "very special medicinal herb of the smokable variety." Everyone got a good laugh at that.

Through all the laughs and the good food and the endless wine, there was only one thing missing. One thing that Ronan and Emilio both had deemed too dangerous to bring to the table.

My vampire.

TWENTY-ONE

GRAY

"Good evening, love."

Darius called to me before I'd even reached the bottom of the basement stairs, and I closed my eyes and stopped, hoping he couldn't sense the skip in my heartbeat at the sound of his voice.

Love. The sweetness of that word on his lips made my chest hurt. How many times had he called me that? Had he whispered it into my ear, his lips brushing my skin?

"I was hoping you might visit me," he said again. "It's dreadfully dull in this establishment. And the menu leaves *much* to be desired."

Thanks to Deirdre's potion, Darius had remained in a heavily sedated state for the entire trip home from Las Vegas. He'd been down here ever since, fed a steady IV drip of some kind of hawthorn-infused herbal tonic Elena had fixed up—just enough to keep him calm and slightly lethargic, but not totally immobilized.

In his current state, Ronan and Emilio said, he could still attack us. Even me. They said we had to be careful.

That didn't mean we had to be cruel.

The basement was finished, with warm yellow walls, and plush beige carpeting. Darius was seated on the couch, his legs free, but his upper body wrapped impossibly tight in what looked like a souped-up straitjacket. The IV was taped to his neck, the tonic in a clear IV bag hanging from a pole at the end of the couch.

I gasped, horrified. I didn't know what was worse—the chains at Inferno, or this?

"I'm sorry," I whispered.

He took in my appearance, his eyes drinking me in slowly, lazily. Elena kept her house warm, and after my shower, I'd pulled my hair into a messy bun and changed into the clothes she'd left out for me—a pair of soft cotton shorts and a black Dead Weather T-shirt, Ronan's sweatshirt tied around my waist. It wasn't especially glamorous, but Darius seemed to appreciate the outfit.

My cheeks heated under his gaze.

"Don't be," he said, a teasing smile tugging his lips. "I'm sure I've been in worse scrapes. Haven't I?"

I nodded, thinking of the time we were attacked at the morgue. The time we fought off those vamps at Norah's place. The time we battled memory eater demons in the Shadowrealm...

Darius had been through so much. This wasn't fair. It wasn't right.

I knelt on the carpet before him, resting my cheek on his

knee and closing my eyes. The familiar scent of his skin emanated through the fabric of his borrowed sweats—whiskey and leather and something inexplicably his.

"Are you sure you want to do that?" he mused. "I'm quite dangerous, if popular opinion is to be believed."

I lifted my face, forcing myself to open my eyes and stare into his. He held my gaze, unblinking, studying me as I studied him.

"Whatever are you looking for, love?"

The tenderness in his voice was like a scalpel, so clear and sharp I could almost tell myself I didn't really feel it slicing through my heart.

But that would be a lie. Every moment Darius spent tied up here, his memories lost or locked away or entirely eradicated, hurt me in ways I couldn't pretend *not* to feel. I felt every bit of it. For him. For me. For all of us.

Tears escaped, despite my efforts to keep them prisoner.

"There, there." Darius ducked his head, offering a warm smile. "It can't be as bad as all that, can it?"

"It's *worse* than all that," I said.

"Tell me what's troubling you. Maybe I can help." He tried to shrug, but his movements were limited by the straitjacket. "Well, not *help*, exactly. But I can certainly listen. I'm an excellent listener."

That got a smile out of me. Darius had always been a good listener.

I untied the sweatshirt from my waist, setting it on the floor as I rose up on my knees, my hands sliding up his thighs. He opened his legs to allow me to get closer, and I did—as close as I dared. We were at eye level now, and I had no idea what would come next. There was no plan, no projection. Only instinct. And right now, my instincts were telling me that this was okay. That it was right.

"Darius, do you remember me at *all*?" I asked.

His face changed then, the teasing smile gone, his eyes smoldering as he stared deeply into mine, searching. I held my breath, waiting for the flicker of recognition to come. A smile. A word. A joke. A look that only Darius could give me.

But after another moment of searching, his face fell, his eyes filling not with recognition, but sorrow. Disappointment.

"For what it's worth," he said gently, "I truly wish I could. I'm so sorry, love."

He looked utterly pained by the admission.

I nodded, but I had to believe he was still in there. That his memories hadn't been erased, only misplaced, locked away behind a wall. We just had to figure out how to knock that wall down.

I took a deep breath and got to my feet, still standing between his knees.

Sliding my hands over his shoulders, I reached behind him for the straps of the jacket.

"Lean forward," I said.

"Gray, is this really the best course of action?" he asked.

"Don't you want to get out of this contraption?"

"More than you know. But the others… they think I'm a threat to you. Perhaps there's some truth to that."

"You would never hurt me," I said, needing him to believe it as much as I did. "You... you might not remember it now, but you care for me a great deal."

We're blood bound, I wanted to say, but held back. In his eyes, my words wouldn't make it so. Darius would need to remember that bond on his own, or it wouldn't matter to him.

"That very well may be, but I'm also not..." His eyes darted toward the IV bag. "I'm not in the best physical condition right now. I'm not sure that I could restrain myself. If I hurt you, even inadvertently..."

His eyes were pained. The thought of hurting me had upset him.

Hope surged inside me. Since I'd last spoken with him in the basement of Inferno, he'd clearly regained some of his awareness. His humanity. The fact that he was even thinking about my safety rather than trying to talk me into freeing him was a good sign.

"Lean forward," I said again, and he finally obeyed.

With new urgency, I worked at the locks and buckles and hinges at the back of the straitjacket until I'd gotten them all undone.

I pulled the jacket off, revealing his bare arms and chest, freeing him from the confines of this monstrous form of torture. It was as heavy as a bulletproof vest. I had no idea what it was made out of.

I tossed it to the floor. As long as I had a say in this, he'd never be forced into that thing again.

Darius kept his arms at his sides on the couch, slowly

flexing his muscles. His pale skin began to regain some of its color. "That's... better," he sighed.

"We're not done yet." I reached up to unhook the IV, pressing my fingers against the skin of his neck. At my touch, he shivered, his thighs tightening around my legs.

Without the straitjacket, the IV was the last thing keeping him even remotely restrained. Once I disconnected it, the hawthorn would wear off quickly, and he'd regain his full strength.

If he decided to hurt me...

My hands trembled, but there was no going back now. He needed to know I believed in him. Trusted him. I *did* trust him.

Gently, slowly, I slid out the needle. A trickle of blood ran down to his collarbone.

And he was totally free.

"Brave move," he whispered through a smile. "Or maybe reckless. Either way... Thank you, little brawler."

"Darius!" I leaned forward and cupped his face, my heart ready to burst. "You remembered something!"

"I... did?"

"Little brawler! That's what you call me." I lowered my mouth to his, pressing a soft kiss to his lips. He hesitated only a moment before parting his lips, allowing me to deepen our kiss. Darius sighed into my mouth, a low moan rising from his chest.

I pulled back, searching his face. When our eyes met, something sparked in his. He was coming back to me. I could feel it.

"That's right," I urged, willing that spark to ignite into a flame. A fire. "You know me, Darius Beaumont. In every way that counts. Every way that means something, you *know* me."

"I..." Slowly, he lifted a hand to my face, tracing my brow bone with his fingertips. His touch was soft and gentle, a caress, a whisper.

His touch was all Darius.

I climbed into his lap, straddling him, sliding my hands into his silky dark hair. It'd gotten longer since we'd first met, almost to his shoulders now, and I tangled my fingers into it, drawing him closer.

His eyes darkened with a desire that bordered on pure, primal hunger, but he was no longer cold. No longer distant.

"I miss you," I said, emotion breaking my voice. It had only been days since we'd held each other in that cabin in the Shadowrealm, but even that had been too long, especially after nearly losing him.

"I'm right here, love." His gaze swept down my face, lowering to the pulse point on my neck. Beneath me, his cock stiffened under the thin sweatpants, already teasing me, making me wet.

I clenched my thighs to stave off the ache, and another low moan escaped his lips, his eyes fluttering closed.

"I'm yours," I whispered, rocking forward against his hard length. "Always."

Darius brought his mouth to my neck, his hands sliding

up the back of my shirt. His touch set me on fire, every movement agonizingly slow, devastatingly perfect.

He kissed a line down my neck, across my collarbone, the points of his fangs grazing my flesh, but never breaking it. With each kiss, his tongue swirled over my skin, making me desperate for more.

In a move so fast I didn't even see it happen, he reached up and whipped off my T-shirt, tossing it to the floor. My bare breasts brushed against his chest, and he cupped them both, running his nose along the top curves, inhaling the scent of my skin.

I let out a whimper of pleasure, rolling my head back, arching closer.

Teasing my nipple between his thumb and forefinger, Darius captured the other in his mouth, flicking it with his tongue. The scrape of his fangs sent a jolt of white-hot pleasure to my core, and I gasped, losing myself in the warmth of his mouth.

He continued to tease me with his tongue, expertly swirling and sucking as I rocked against him, the friction building between my thighs.

"Mmm. Are you hungry, little brawler," he teased between kisses, sliding his hands inside the bottom of my shorts and underwear to cup my ass. His fingers dipped between my thighs, seeking my wet heat, teasing my entrance.

Warmth gathered, my core pulsing with a deep ache that could only be soothed by one thing.

"Starving," I whispered, reaching down the front of his

sweatpants and fisting his cock. It was hot and velvet-smooth and as hard as steel, growing even harder at my touch.

"Fuck," he breathed, rolling his hips as I stroked him, teasing the head with my thumb. "That's..."

"*Mine*." Something came over me then, a fierce posses-siveness driving me wild with need. I needed him to kiss me. I needed him inside me. I *needed* to make him come.

I kissed him again, nipping at his lower lip.

Darius nipped me back, sucking my lip into his mouth, drawing blood.

He ran his tongue along the edge, growling at the taste of my blood, and in a blur of movement and strength, we were off the couch. He held me against his chest with one arm, my legs winding around his hips as he slammed my back against the wall.

Shoving a hand between us, he slid his fingers down the front of my shorts, pushing inside me, stroking me as I'd stroked him—fast and hard and faster still and oh my fucking *God* I'd never felt anything so hot.

My thighs trembled, my body tightening around his slick fingers...

"Is this what you want?" he growled, bringing me closer to the edge with every thrust. The question sounded like a threat. A promise. Danger and devastation wrapped in a silk scarf, and I nodded mutely, my eyes silently begging him for it.

And you will beg *me for it...*

His old words echoed in my memory.

"Say it," he demanded.

"This is what I want."

"Beg me, little brawler."

I was so turned on I could barely make words, but somehow, I forced them out.

"Please, Darius," I moaned against his lips. "I want you inside me. Fucking me." I grabbed the back of his head, fisting his hair and tugging hard. "Make me *feel* it."

A surge of wild, unrestrained need flooded his eyes, and without another word, he yanked the bottom edge of my shorts and underwear to the side and slid his cock inside me, thrusting deep. Hard. Banging me against the butter-yellow basement wall as I urged him to keep going, harder, faster, deeper, more, raking my nails along his back, biting down on his shoulder until we both came, hard and fast and shuddering, and I tasted the rich, coppery silk of his blood in my mouth.

* * *

He pulled away slowly, gently lowering me back to my feet. His eyes were wild, his hair knotted, his skin slick with sweat.

He pulled his sweatpants back up and tucked himself inside, and I did my best to clean up and straighten out my shorts. I was pretty sure the underwear was a lost cause— I'd heard them tear at one point, and now I felt the coolness of the air where the fabric should've been.

I was definitely going to wake up sore. I could already

feel it starting—the ache in my thighs, the swollen mouth, the burns.

Darius flashed me a devious smile, and a fresh pulse of desire surged through my blood.

"Better be careful, little brawler," he teased. "Bite me one more time and you might turn into a vampire."

I rolled my eyes. "I'd have to bite you a lot more than once to turn into a vampire."

"That could be arranged." He held my gaze, his lush lips swollen, his smile light and content.

A flood of gratitude surged inside me. "I knew you'd come back," I whispered, pressing my palm to his cheek.

He watched me a moment longer, confusion drawing his brows together, and I waited for the gentleness to return to his eyes. The warmth.

The sex had been rough and wild and searingly hot—I was all for doing that again sometime. But suddenly I longed for a glimpse of the tenderness he'd shown me in the cabin in the Shadowrealm the first time we'd been together.

"Darius?" I asked.

"Hmm?" He cocked his head, still watching me with those honey-gold eyes, but where once there was friendship and familiarity and love, now there was only a mild amusement. The coldness had slid back into his gaze, a chill that went straight to the softest part of my heart and froze it.

"Vampire or not," he said with a low chuckle, "any man would come back for *that*, love."

I felt the blood leak instantly from my heart, pierced by

the sharp arrow of that one word. *Love.* Where before it'd given me hope, somehow he'd managed to twist and mangle it into something cheap.

"Same time tomorrow, then?" he asked. "Perhaps I'll let you tie me back up. But not before I've had a chance to feed on something other than the shite they serve here."

I couldn't answer.

I felt dizzy. Lost. Darius and I were bound, yet even the taste of my blood hadn't been enough to bring him back to me. To heal him.

I grabbed my shirt from the floor and slowly dressed, the once-pleasurable burn of my muscles cooling into a stiff, bitter pain.

I wouldn't let him see it. Wouldn't let him know he'd broken me.

And I wouldn't let him out of this room.

I picked up Ronan's sweatshirt, holding it close as I approached Darius again.

"Whatever you want, bloodsucker." Pasting on a mischievous smile, I stretched up on my toes, capturing him in a deeply sensual kiss. He moaned softly, drinking me in.

It seemed Darius wasn't the only actor in the room.

Certain my devious mouth had captured his full attention, I pulled out the hawthorn stake I'd stashed in Ronan's sweatshirt and jammed it into the tender flesh beneath his ribcage, hating that Ronan and Emilio had been right.

Hating that I'd doubted Darius enough to bring the stake with me in the first place.

TWENTY-TWO

DARIUS

Intoxicating.

It was the closest word I could think of to capture her effect on me, yet it still felt woefully inadequate. The demon had told me she was a witch, and now I knew it must be true, for I was thoroughly bespelled.

I let her guide me back to the couch, where I promptly collapsed into my former position, my muscles turning numb from the effects of the hawthorn. Unlike the watered-down intravenous version, the stake was undiluted, its potency unmatched.

She'd chosen a big one, too.

"You wound me." I managed a weak smile, my words slurring. "And here I thought we had a real connection."

"We do," she whispered. "You just don't remember it."

"I could have killed you, love."

Her eyes shone with tears—tears I didn't deserve. After a deep, shuddering breath, she turned away from me, saying nothing more, disappearing up the stairs the way she'd come down.

Though she hadn't said the words, I felt them lingering in the wake of her exit.

You already have.

I realized then, with a sickening twist in my stomach, that she'd thought I'd remembered her. That she'd given herself so freely, so intensely, so... erotically, because she'd trusted me. Trusted the connection we were supposed to have had.

I wished things could've been different.

There was something so intensely familiar about her, but try as I might to find her in the dark recesses of memory, I couldn't recall ever having met her. I don't know how I'd managed to recall the nickname I'd supposedly given her. And though the brief taste of her blood had stirred something deep within me—something that spoke of a much more intimate history than she'd let on—it hadn't awakened any dormant memories.

Despite what she and the demon had told me about our relationship—that we'd even had one at all, that my memories of it had been stolen by some sort of shadow creatures in another realm—I looked into her eyes and saw nothing. Knew nothing.

Well, that wasn't entirely true. I knew she was going to stake me—perhaps even before she'd known it. Despite the pain and immobility it would bring, I'd let her do it anyway, almost welcoming the sharp pierce in my flesh.

It was better this way. She needed to understand I

wasn't the man she'd fallen in love with before. I was a vampire. A hungry one. And being with her like that… I closed my eyes, still scenting her desire in the air. Remembering her now, the soft curve of her mouth, the heat of her breath as she moaned beneath my touch…

She'd nearly undone me.

And I'd wanted so, so badly to devour her. To sink my fangs into her throat and drain every last drop of that sweet, silky blood.

Shame burned inside me, but that was the truth of it.

Though I'd sworn we'd only just become acquainted, something about that final look in her eyes said I'd hurt her. Not physically, but in a way that was so much worse. A way that only someone who cared about you could manage.

An ache opened up in my chest, the bright pulse of it outrunning even the hawthorn working its way through my system.

Nothing the demon had said had affected me like this. Nothing the old witch had whispered as she'd plied me with her brew even came close.

But now, as I recalled the intense blue of Gray's eyes, the pain in them that I'd caused, I felt it.

For the first time since I'd arrived in this ocean-washed city, I felt the sting of something hot and fresh in my gut, the bitter taste of it coating my tongue like the very salt that coated the streets outside.

Regret.

TWENTY-THREE

GRAY

The wind gusted, whipping the ocean into frothy white peaks and threatening to steal the breath from my lungs. Unperturbed by the cold, Sparkle and Sunshine bounded along the shore, chasing the receding tide and running from the surge like twin puppies.

Personally, I would've rather met Deirdre in a cozy little café in town, where we could sip hot mochas by a crackling fire. But it was better this way. Safer. We had a lot of ground to cover, and we couldn't risk being overheard.

I needed to know about the Silversbane legacy. My blood magic. If my blood was powerful enough to call my ancestors out of their eternal rest, surely it was powerful enough for other magic, too.

Like restoring Darius's memories.

It sounded crazy. Impossible. But after my disastrous reunion with Darius last night, I couldn't stop thinking about it. He'd remembered my nickname, and when he bit my lip, the taste of my blood had affected him deeply. Not in any way I could put into words. Just in a way I could feel, right down to my soul.

Darius and I were blood bound. Deeply connected. Mated, for all intents and purposes. And that connection hadn't broken. How could it? It wasn't linked to memory, but to blood—something he hadn't lost at all. I wanted him to remember our bond for my own emotional reasons, but physically, that bond still existed. I'd felt it drawing us close last night. I'd seen it in his eyes, even if it wasn't there in his mind.

When he'd healed me with his blood in the Shadowrealm, I'd connected to his past, sensing the memories of his former life, seeing them play out before me like a dream. It was as if he'd transferred them to me through the blood bond.

I didn't know what that meant, or how—if at all—that could help now. But there was something to it. I could feel it.

The memory eater demons had stolen the memories from Darius's mind. But maybe they weren't *gone*. Maybe there was a backup copy.

My blood was the key—I was sure of it. I just couldn't figure out how. The solution was there though, like a dream you try to chase into the waking hours, losing it at dawn only to get it back in flashes later on.

Right now, I was pinning my hopes on Deirdre. On my so-called super special Silversbane magic.

"Thank you for meeting me," I said when she finally

crested the dune at the edge of the parking lot and joined me on the beach. "I didn't know who else to call."

Deirdre pulled her jacket close around her throat, the wind ruffling her short gray hair. Her eyes held the same grandmotherly warmth she'd showed me in Vegas. "I'm glad you called me, Rayanne. There's still so much I want to tell you. So much you need to know."

"How did you manage to slip away?" I asked her.

"Oh, I'm not really his prisoner." She lowered her eyes, her cheeks coloring. "Sebastian and I have an odd arrangement that dates back many years. I belong to him, and can never truly leave, but I'm not chained to him. I come and go, largely as I please."

"Do you *want* to leave him?"

She looked taken aback, as though no one had ever asked her the question before. Maybe they hadn't. I wasn't even sure what possessed me to ask, other than the fact that I was still trying to get a handle on how Sebastian operated. On whether I'd ever have a chance at truly leaving him after this momentary reprieve was over.

"No," she finally said, linking our arms and leading me further down the beach, Sparkle and Sunshine trailing behind us. "I made my choices. It's not always perfect, but this is my life now, and has been for a long time. *He* is my life."

"Are you... in love with him?" I did my best to keep the judgment from my tone, but I wasn't sure I succeeded.

To her credit, Deirdre didn't flinch.

"No," she said plainly. "Sebastian believes he's in love

with me, but like many men before him, he confuses love with obsession, and that obsession has driven him to madness. His focus is single-minded, and when he fixates on something..."

She stopped along the shore, gazing out at the foamy sea. Far out on the horizon, the sun was struggling to peek through the clouds, but the clouds were winning that particular battle. Such was life on the Pacific coast.

When she turned to face me again, it looked like she'd aged a decade.

"So what is it you want to know about blood magic?" she asked, dropping the subject of Sebastian altogether. "I thought you didn't want to summon your ancestors until after you'd dealt with the conflicts facing your people here."

"I don't." I pulled my jacket sleeves down over my hands, blowing into them for warmth as we continued our walk. Elena had picked up a bunch of new clothes for me, but I forgot to ask for gloves. "I need to know how blood is linked to memory."

"To memory?" She narrowed her eyes, scrutinizing my face. "Is this related to the situation with Darius?"

Nodding, I took a deep breath of salty air, trying to put my jumbled thoughts into words.

Doing my best not to sound like a mad scientist, I told Deirdre about what'd happened in the Shadowrealm, and my tissue-paper-thin theory about a possible backup copy of Darius's memories.

It sounded crazy saying it all out loud. But if there was

even a chance that my blood could heal him, could restore even a fraction of Darius's memories, I wanted to know how to try.

"Your relationship with Darius is unique," she said, stopping to pick up a piece of driftwood and throwing it down the shore for Sparkle. The hound bolted after it, chasing it into the surf, then promptly forgetting about it. "What you're trying to do… Well, to be perfectly honest, I've never heard of something like it before. But that doesn't mean it's not possible. A vampire blood bond is a deep, deep connection. You and Darius have that link. And yes, that link could store some residual memories."

Hope warmed my insides, and I let loose a smile—the first one of the day. "Do you think it's possible I could somehow transfer them back? Magically?"

"Possible, yes. Anything is possible. The fact that you're here instead of locked away in Sebastian's realm shows you that much. The problem is that it's too risky, Rayanne. If you attempt a blood spell, you may end up summoning your ancestors after all."

"But I wouldn't do a summoning spell. This would be something else."

"We don't know what this 'something else' would entail. It might be very much like a summoning spell." She shook her head, dashing my hopes. "I'm sorry. I have to advise against it."

"So what you're telling me is the only thing this Silversbane blood is good for is doing Sebastian's dirty work?"

"Don't say that," she said. "Blood as powerful as yours is a gift."

"My blood is a curse." I kicked at the rocky shoreline. If I couldn't use my blood or my magic to help the man I loved, what was the point? "And Sebastian wants to weaponize it against my ancestors."

Deirdre stiffened. "Rayanne—"

"Gray. I go by Gray now." Rayanne was a remnant of a past too painful to remember. The only other person who still called me by that name was Jonathan, and he wasn't even a person anymore.

"*Gray*," she said, though I could tell she wasn't fond of the name. "He's not interested in your deceased ancestors. He's interested in your mother."

"Calla?" I asked, alarmed.

Deirdre shook her head. "Your biological mother. My daughter-in-law."

"Doesn't she count as a deceased ancestor?"

"Oh, child. There is so much..." Deirdre's face paled, her mouth pulling into a deep frown. The wind stilled. The hounds stopped chasing each other up ahead. Even the waves hushed, as if they, too, were waiting to hear her next confession.

"I'm afraid your mother isn't dead, Gray. A fugitive from hell, but very much alive."

TWENTY-FOUR

GRAY

Your mother isn't dead... A fugitive from hell... Very much alive...

Deirdre's words slammed into my chest, forcing all the air out of my lungs. She didn't even give me a chance to catch my breath before she continued, her sentences blurring together, each one another blow from which I didn't think I could recover.

"Trinity," she was saying now. "That was her name."

Trinity. I reached back in my mind, but found nothing. No connection. No recognition.

"When she became pregnant with you, she'd already had two of your three sisters—Serena, the oldest, and Adele, a year younger. But you, she insisted, were different. Special."

"Wait. Did I... Did I have another name? Before Rayanne?"

223

"Morgan Susanna," Deirdre said with a soft smile. "Your name was changed before your adoption to protect you."

"Morgan Susanna." I said it out loud, trying it on for size. It didn't fit. Not at all. Like Rayanne, it felt like someone else's name now. "I think I'll stick with Gray."

"If you must." Deirdre winked. "Anyway, around the twenty-fourth week of your pregnancy, Trinity began to have visions of a fourth daughter, and believed that you and your sisters would become great witches, one day uniting covens in war against supernaturals in a battle for magical dominion on earth."

"Like the prophecy," I said. But it wasn't. Not really. The prophecy never said anything about a battle for magical dominion. Not specifically.

"Partially," Deirdre said. "But your mother was convinced. You four were the foretold witches, which must also mean she herself was an heir of Silversbane.

"The following year, your sister Georgie—the foreseen fourth daughter—came into being. One month later, your father..." She paused, pressing her hand to her heart. When she spoke again, her voice was thick with emotion. "My son, Thomas Derrick Olivante, disappeared."

Thomas Derrick Olivante.

The name echoed between us. My father.

"Disappeared?" I asked. "What do you mean?"

"The police suspected an affair, possibly a deadbeat dad situation. But I knew better. Your father adored you. He devoted his life to his wife and daughters, and no matter

224

how unhappy or nasty your mother became, he never gave up hope. Never once complained about taking on the burdens of housework or meals or bedtime routines in addition to his regular work, all so your mother could have her endless 'free time.'"

"So what do you think happened to him?"

Her eyes grew cold. "Your mother murdered him, Gray. I was never able to prove that, but my son was not missing. He was dead. A mother knows. I felt the departure of his soul from this realm."

The wind whipped my hair into my face, stinging my eyes. I blinked back my own tears, snuggling deeper into my jacket. "What happened next?"

"Even without your father, you girls were thriving. It quickly became apparent that you were *extremely* powerful witches. Even as babies, you could heal each other's injuries, make flowers grow on barren dirt, find lost objects, predict the future."

Sunshine nipped at my hand, eager for another stick to throw, but I nudged her away, riveted by my grandmother's story.

"Everyone loved the four magical babies of Blackmoon Bay," she said, "but Trinity—"

"Wait. Blackmoon Bay?"

Deirdre nodded. "You four were born there, Gray."

"How is that even possible? I grew up on the east coast, and after Calla died, I just sort of… ended up everywhere else. Including the Bay."

"Yes, and you stopped ending up *anywhere* else once you

reached the Bay."

"Because I met Ronan, and he helped me get set up."

"He did. But he would've done that anywhere. You stayed in Blackmoon Bay because the city is part of your soul. It called you home, Gray. Just like it called Haley home. And eventually, it will call your other sisters home, too."

"But Ronan already had a life in the Bay before I came along. Friends. A job."

"He did."

"Don't you think that's kind of a crazy coincidence?" I asked. But then I said, at the same time she did, "There are no coincidences."

We shared a laugh, breaking the tension just a bit.

As we walked a little further down the shore, I linked my arm into hers, suddenly wanting to feel connected to her. Grounded.

Deirdre tucked in closer, too.

"Trinity was a jealous woman," she continued. "Her own mother was quite powerful, too, yet she'd never inherited the gift. Trinity's witchcraft was mediocre at best, relying heavily on tricks and sleight of hand. The idea that her infant and toddler daughters possessed so much power, when she herself had virtually none, finally drove her mad.

"Desperate to claim your power for herself, she tried all kinds of magical experiments and spells on you and your sisters, but nothing worked—largely because she didn't have the skill, but also because it was against the natural order. Stealing another witch's power... It's an abomination. No force or entity or energy outside of her own greed would've aided in something so sinister. So, Trinity remained as weak as ever, while her daughters continued to grow in power. Finally, in a last act of desperation—"

"Oh, no." I closed my eyes, swallowing hard. "Don't tell me. This is the part where the evil villainess gathers up a bottle of blood and a box of chicken bones and heads down to the crossroads…"

"Yes, Gray," she said, her tone grim again. "Your mother made a crossroads deal—no bones or blood necessary. Sebastian, as you know, trades in souls."

A shiver ran through me, making my teeth chatter. Was my mother the one who'd sold me out to Sebastian in the first place? How could she have done such a thing?

I opened my mouth to ask, but Deirdre was already speaking again.

"The terms were simple: her daughters' magic in exchange for her own mortal soul, to be collected in ten years' time."

I sighed in relief. Something told me this story had a terrible ending, but at least my mother hadn't sold my soul. A dim light in a room full of darkness, but a light never-theless.

"But like most people in their hour of utter desperation," she said, "Trinity neglected to read the fine print. She got her daughters' magic, sure, but not in the way she intended."

"What do you mean?"

"Well, from you, she got the ability to bring the dead

back to life—so long as the deceased was a plant in need of some water and sunlight. From Serena, she got the power to summon spirits with a drop of her blood—but only the spirits of her long-dead childhood cats, Maise and Matilda. Adele's gift of foresight allowed her to see into the future— by fifteen seconds. And thanks to Georgie, who'd go on to become a talented herbalist by age three, your mother became adept at brewing tea."

"That's... it? That sounds like a practical joke."

"Oh, it was no joke. She'd asked for her daughters' magic, and that's what she got. She just wasn't specific."

"I'm assuming she didn't just let it go at that," I said. "Chalk it up to a lesson learned."

"No. She didn't." Deirdre shook her head, her eyes clouding with some ancient sadness I could only guess at. "Your mother wasn't well. Not by any definition."

An icy chill slid across my skin, my whole body erupting in goosebumps. Something dark and malicious slithered out of my memory, seeping into my mind, bringing with it flashes of something it'd long since tried to bury.

It was part of the same memory I'd recalled when Deirdre had first mentioned the name Silversbane in our meeting with Sebastian—the dark-haired woman at the creek, frantic, manic, forcing me into the water. Holding my head under, even as I fought for my last breath.

"*I am Silversbane! This magic is* my *legacy. Mine! Why should you have it when it was promised to me? My birthright! You have stolen it, Shadowborn filth!*"

New memories rushed in, filling in the gaps. My mother had promised to take us for a walk in the woods. She'd bundled us up in winter coats and hats, even Georgie, who still needed to be put in a carrier.

But she hadn't bothered with our socks or boots. She marched us into the winter woods, our feet freezing. All of us were crying.

"No, mama!" Serena cried. "Don't put Delly in there. She can't swim!"

Delly. Adele. My mother pushed her into the creek first, then me. Delly crawled out on her own. My mother held me under, waiting for the cold water to press the breath from my lungs.

"Stay down! Stop squirming, little bitch!"

"Mama, stop!"

The pain in my skull had been unbearable. The blackness closing in faster than I could fight...

"It was her," I gasped, the images finally receding. "At the creek in the woods behind our house."

Deirdre frowned. I waited for her to deny it. To provide some other explanation. But all she said was, "I'd always hoped you girls were too young to remember. But darkness like that makes an impression on your very soul. It never leaves you."

"My mother tried to drown us," I said, needing to hear the words spoken out loud, even if Deirdre herself couldn't say them. Even if they tore up my insides on the way out.

"Yes," she said. "All four of you."

"My mother tried to murder her babies," I said again, as

if it would make any more sense the second time around. It didn't; this was a tale that only got more horrifying in the telling.

"I had long since suspected your mother in your father's disappearance, but without proof, there wasn't much I could do. She never prevented me from seeing you four girls, so I did what I could to protect you—charms, spells of protection, amulets sewn into the hems of your clothing. I visited as often as I could. It wasn't enough."

"So that's how we survived that day? Protective charms?"

"That may have been part of it. But there was also a neighbor walking his dog in the woods behind his property. He heard your sister screaming for help, and ran down to the creek to find out what was going on. He told us later that your mother had insisted she was trying to save you— that Serena and Adele had snuck you and Georgie out of the house while she was in the shower, knowing that you weren't permitted in the woods alone. She'd chased after you as soon as she'd noticed you missing. She said you and Adele had fallen in the water. He called me as soon as he got your mother and you girls back to the house. She was refusing to seek medical attention for you.

"That night," Deirdre continued, "I called on the help of my coven sisters. We cast a powerful spell to put your mother to sleep and to fully open her to the power of suggestion. While the sisters took the four of you out of the house, I worked to manipulate your mother's memory, making her believe she'd succeeded in killing you. The coven and I saw to your adoptions, ensuring your mother never knew what had truly happened."

Tears that had nothing to do with the bitter wind slid down my cheeks, as salty as the sea before us. My chest hurt, the pain of that day fresh in my lungs. In my skull. I didn't know what hurt worse—nearly drowning in icy water, or learning years later that your own mother had tried to murder you. Sunshine and Sparkle pressed against my legs, stopping me from walking. Absently I reached down to pet Sunshine's head, rubbing the notched edge of her ear. She nuzzled my hand, and the pain in my chest receded, just a little.

Wiping the tears from my eyes, I turned my attention back to Deirdre, searching for the right question to ask next. This, I sensed, was only the beginning of a much longer, much more sinister story, and I needed to tread carefully.

I didn't know what other memories might be unlocked.

"How did she—" I began, but before I could finish the question, Deirdre's face paled, her eyes widening in fear.

The hounds yelped, taking off down the shore, and Deirdre raised her hands in front of her chest.

Magic, I thought.

"Down," she ordered. "Now!"

I didn't hesitate. Just dropped to the rocky shore and covered my head, barely ducking the blast of Deirdre's magic. Beams of bright, yellow-orange light shot out from her hands, and I twisted around to see the magic slam into a man charging toward us, gun drawn. The attack knocked him on his ass, unconscious, but more men followed in his wake, at least half a dozen goons not far behind. They rushed at us, even as the hounds bounded right for them.

"Hunters," she deadpanned.

"Where did they come from?" I got to my feet, bringing my hands to my chest, palms out. I hadn't used my magic since the battle with the memory eaters in the Shadowrealm, but it came to me easy now, blue flame sparking to life in my hands.

Still, it wasn't enough. I could feel it. I was out of practice, and the hunters were closing in fast.

"I don't know," she said, "but we're about to get up close and personal with a couple more."

Closing my eyes and calling on the magic of the earth, I drew more power into my core, pushing it out through my limbs, charging my entire body.

"Now!" Deirdre shouted, and I opened my eyes and sent a blast of energy outward right alongside hers just as two hunters drew their guns on us. Deirdre and I hit them at the same time. Her man went down, unconscious like the last. Mine only stumbled and gasped.

Ten feet away, Sunshine let out a primal growl that made the hairs on the back of my neck stand up. I saw her lunge at someone, knocking him into the water. Sparkle was still running down the beach—chasing after another hunter who'd turned tail.

Where had these assholes come from? Were they part of Jonathan's group? Part of the prison hunters?

"You're up again, Gray," Deirdre said, queuing up another blast as my guy righted himself and another one charged at Deirdre.

I took a deep breath and tried again, drawing in power as a spell took shape in my mind:

> Goddess of the earth, Goddess of the sea
> In this battle, I call upon thee
> Lend me your strength, avail me of your power
> Before this magic, make my enemies cower

Channeling my intentions into the words, I repeated the spell out loud, forcing the magic out through my palms.

The force of my attack was so strong, so unexpected, I had to fight to stay on my feet. It slammed into both hunters, simultaneously knocking them backward, dashing their heads against a sharp, rocky outcropping at the water's edge.

The tide surged forward, staining the beach with their blood.

"Oh, shit," Deirdre whispered. "That's... not good."

"We need to call Emilio," I said as the rest of the hunters took off, disappearing down the shore the way they'd come. "They might be part of the group he's looking for."

We jogged to catch up with the hounds. Sparkle had dragged her quarry back to Sunshine, and now the two feasted on his body.

His face was mangled beyond recognition.

"Sparkle," I called. "Sunshine. Come."

They stopped their gorging and stood at attention, wagging their massive tails, panting, tongues lolling, blood and flesh dripping from their razor-sharp fangs as they padded over to me.

They were a goddamn nightmare, and if I'd eaten lunch, I'd be spewing it all over the beach. Yet when I looked at them now, all I could feel was gratitude.

"So," Deirdre said, placing a tired hand on my back as she tried to catch her breath, "next time we plan a grandma-granddaughter outing, maybe we could try something a little more traditional? Knitting club, perhaps? Checkers?"

The leftover energy from the magic and the fight made me jittery, and I let out a nervous laugh, grateful for the small release. "Something tells me you're not the knitting and checkers type, Grams."

"No, child. I suppose I'm not." She let out a sigh, pulling her coat tight around her neck. There were so many words in that sigh, so many things still unsaid between us. But for now, she shook her head, looking at me with tired, knowing eyes. "And I'm sorry to tell you, neither are you."

I looked down at my palms, the center spot where my magic had emanated from. Two men had died by my hands, yet my hands were clean, the skin smooth and unmarred.

Inside, the magic stirred. Warming me. Comforting me. Reminding me that like Deirdre, I wasn't born to have a normal life. I could pretend otherwise, I could fight that fact as hard as I'd fought my mother when she'd held my head under that freezing water.

But in the end, the only choice I really had was acceptance.

I was a Silversbane witch. The witch of the prophecy. And my work was just beginning.

TWENTY-FIVE

GRAY

Vita mutatur, non tollitur.

The words were printed on the Tarot card I'd drawn, and I repeated them out loud, tracing my finger over each one.

Life is changed, not taken away.

Emilio, Elena, and the RCPD shifter squad had arrived on the beach minutes after Deirdre's call. Emilio took our statements, then ordered Hobb to bring me and the hounds back to the house. Not wanting to leave town after the attack on my life, Deirdre checked herself into a hotel in the city.

Ronan and Darius were gone when I got back. Now I was alone on Elena's couch, looking for guidance from the universe.

Be careful what you wish for.

It was the first time I'd used my new deck, and I'd drawn—of course—the Death card. Unlike the ominous

Death card in Sophie's deck, this one was more peaceful, featuring a pale, nude woman lying on a moss-covered rock in a serene forest. The angel of Death stood behind her in his black cloak, come to claim her soul. Butterflies danced in the rays of light that illuminated her body, and lilies grew in the moss at the base of the rock.

Carved in stone were those words, Death's ultimate message:

Vita mutatur, non tollitur.

Life is changed, not taken away.

It appeared to me now, the card and the message, reminding me that I was in the midst of my own inevitable change. That even as one life died, another was just beginning.

I'd asked Sebastian for an extension on my contract— enough time to save my friends and deal with the threats facing us.

Fighting, learning to grow and strengthen my magic, training, backing up my rebels—all of those things were important. But if I was truly the Silversbane heir—truly the witch of prophecy—then I needed to learn how to lead. How to inspire. How to save and protect the witches I loved as well as the witches I'd never even met.

I needed to find a way to bring us all together—witches and supernaturals alike—uniting us against the mounting threats facing our communities.

Was I ready for all that?

For so long, I'd lived in the shadows, hiding my witch-craft, denying my magical heritage, pretending to be anything but who I really was. Eventually, destiny caught up with me. And now I was doing my best to keep up with *it*.

Was I even worthy of the Silversbane legacy?

I closed my eyes, pressing the Death card to my chest. I wanted so, so badly to talk to Liam. This was exactly the kind of philosophical dilemma he loved to talk about, and his words of wisdom had never failed to open my eyes to new perspectives, new possibilities.

I was still so angry with him. But I also needed him. Wanted him. Wanted his companionship, his hopelessly confusing explanations about the natural order, his jokes, his sweet kisses.

Yet he'd betrayed me. How could I reconcile the two? How could I hate a man I still cared so deeply for?

I couldn't. That was the answer. I couldn't hate Liam any more than I could deny I was Silversbane.

Maybe that was part of what I needed to accept, too. That people made mistakes. That even Death made mistakes.

Oh, Liam. Where are you?

Ever since he'd confessed to me about his deal with Sebastian, I'd assumed that was the betrayal I'd dreamed about, the one the Three of Swords card had warned about in Sophie's book of shadows. But sitting here now, holding the Death card and reflecting on all the things Deirdre had shared today, I wasn't so sure anymore.

My heart felt like it'd been run through with so many swords. Liam's confessions, Ronan's deal that would forever keep us apart, my own mother trying to drown me. In light of the last one, how could I hold any anger toward Liam? He'd never meant for me to die. He'd never even meant to hurt me. And though it was the ultimate outcome, sending my soul to Sebastian had never been his intention —he'd honestly thought I'd be honored to become Death, just as he was. And at that time, he wasn't even human— not in the way I thought of him now.

My own mother had tried to drown me and my sisters. Her babies. And she likely killed my father, too.

"Things are not always what they seem," came a voice in my mind, warm and bubbly and belonging only to one person: my Sophie. She'd said those very words to me in my magic realm, right after I'd read about the Three of Swords in her book of shadows.

I didn't dare open my eyes, didn't dare break the vision.

"Do you think I should forgive him?" I asked.

"Liam? I think you already have."

I shook my head, still resisting the idea. Could forgiveness really come that easily? *Should* it?

"Open your eyes, girl," she said, and even though I didn't want to lose her, I did as she asked. Sophie never led me astray.

The Death card came back into view, but when I looked up, I was no longer on the couch in Elena's living room, wrapped up in a blanket dotted with lighthouses. Instead, I found myself sitting on a carpet of velvety green grass in a meadow I'd missed for far too long.

My realm. The source of my magic. A place I hadn't seen since Jonathan had taken me hostage.

"You shouldn't be here," a deep voice bellowed. "It isn't safe."

"Liam?" I looked up and met his gaze, startled at the force of what I saw there. Happiness. Longing. Sorrow. Regret. Love. All of it flickering through his ancient blue eyes, completely disarming me.

He was back in his shadow form, an uncanny reminder of the angel of Death in the Tarot card, but he was still Liam. I saw the humanity in his eyes—a depth and nuance that wasn't there when I'd first met him in this form. I wondered if he'd always carry Liam with him. Always carry our time together.

He sat down in the grass next to me, not too close. He was giving me space. Testing the waters.

"I haven't captured Jonathan yet," he said. "He's eluded me at every turn. If he attacked you here, I..." He trailed off, gazing out across the meadow, no longer looking at me.

"You're... still tracking him?" I wasn't sure why that surprised me, but it did.

"I've been hunting him since I returned from burning your scroll at the Great Hall of Records, Gray. This is your realm, and Sebastian has granted you temporary freedom. You shouldn't be kept away by the threats of a madman, or by anyone—or anything—else."

"I agree, but you didn't have to—"

"I wanted to. I *want* to."

We sat in companionable silence, the breeze caressing

my skin. After my day at the beach, this felt warm and pleasurable, like the very end of summer when it's no longer hot and humid, but before the air turns chilly. The scents of lavender and lilacs filled the air, as sweet and clean as I remembered.

"I miss it," I said. "Being here. Back before I knew about... well, anything, really."

"That's the thing about knowledge," he said. "Once you know a thing, you can't unknow it. Unless, of course..."

He trailed off, and I knew he was thinking of Darius. The memory eaters.

I ran my hand over the grass beside me, the soft blades tickling my palm. "Well, here's something I now know. I have three sisters. Also, I'm the witch of prophecy. And my mother tried to murder us when we were babies."

Liam didn't say anything.

"I suppose you already knew all that," I said.

He nodded. I wasn't surprised, but it still stung. He'd kept so much from me. Not just as Death, but as Liam. As my friend. As a man I was starting to love. He was *still* keeping things from me. Things about my future. About all the possibilities. Things about my past.

But maybe that was part of what it meant to love someone, too—shielding them from the painful truths. It wasn't always the best policy, but sometimes, you carried their pain so they wouldn't have to.

My heart hurt. Being this close to him... I wanted him back in my life. Back in my world. But that could never happen now. He'd failed to pass on the Death mantle to me. Now, that was his eternal calling. His prison.

"Will you seek them?" he asked.

"I already know about Haley," I said. "But as for the others... How could I not? We're supposed to band together and unify the covens." I drew my knees up to my chest. "I don't know what that means. I don't know what that would look like. I don't even know where to start."

"You've already begun, little witch." Liam smiled, his eyes shining with pride. "You've managed to get the upper hand with the Prince of Hell. I'd say that's a very good start."

I wasn't so sure about that. Sebastian had given me an extension, but he could call it back whenever he felt like it. For all intents and purposes, I was living on borrowed time, and a loan from the Prince of Hell came with the highest interest rates around.

"I need to ask you something," I said. "The woman whose soul you were supposed to bring Sebastian—the one who'd bailed on her contract. It was my mother, wasn't it?"

Liam met my eyes again, his smile fading. If he was uncomfortable with this line of questioning, though, he didn't show it, and I knew that whatever he said next would be the truth. I couldn't explain why, but in that moment, it felt like we'd come to a new understanding.

Liam wouldn't lie to me about this. I knew it in my bones.

"It was," he finally said. "She made a deal with him

many years ago, but when it came time to collect, she vanished."

"My grandmother says she's still alive. A fugitive from hell."

"Oh, Trinity is very much alive. Undetectable, though I'm fairly certain she's still on the material plane. It's likely she has powerful allies protecting her."

"Powerful allies, like who? Who could be that powerful —or that stupid—to harbor a fugitive of hell?"

"If we knew, I'm certain Sebastian would've found her by now. There are many factions, Gray. Many groups and subgroups and beings who believe things should be different, and any one of those groups may have been sympathetic to your mother's cause, especially if they believed she could eventually connect them with the Silversbane heirs."

"She supposedly thinks we're dead."

"Yes. Let's hope it stays that way." On that ominous note, Liam rose from the grass, offering a hand to help me up. I took it, standing up and tilting my face up to meet his gaze once more.

"Where will you go after this?" I asked.

"I have been ordered to resume my duties, as I knew I must." The finality in his words pressed down on me like a physical weight, tightening my chest, making it difficult to breathe.

"Will I see you again?" I asked, fighting to keep the tremor from my voice.

"This is not goodbye for us, Gray. I assure you. But it may be some time before we see each other again."

"But… I don't understand. Can't you visit as Liam? Like you used to?"

"Not as Liam, I'm afraid. If I return to you on the material plane at all, it shall be in my raven form." He cupped my cheeks, his black gloves like spider webs against my skin. "Pray that I do not return, for if you see my raven by your side, know that I am there only to escort the departed soul of someone you love."

"I don't want to go back without you," I breathed, my eyes falling closed over tears. I was losing him all over again. "I'm not done being mad at you yet. And I'm not done forgiving you."

"Your words have given me more hope than you can imagine."

"Then why do I feel like this *is* goodbye? Why does it feel like… like you're dying?"

"*Vita mutatur, non tollitur.*" He lowered his mouth to mine, pressing a soft kiss to my lips that unleashed a shower of sparks between us.

"Please don't go," I whispered when he pulled away.

"I must." He stroked my cheeks, a few remaining sparks still lingering. "Though I didn't understand it at the time, this was always the only possible outcome for me, Gray. But your story has many, many volumes before you reach your final outcome, and most of them have not yet been written."

I nodded, and he released my face, the bright blue of his eyes fading as I slowly drifted back to consciousness.

When I opened my eyes again, I was back on Elena's couch, still clutching the Tarot card to my chest.

This one wasn't the Death card, though.

It was the Star. A card of healing and renewal.

A card of hope.

TWENTY-SIX

EMILIO

If ever there was a sight for sore eyes, it was her.

The moment I walked in the door and spotted her on Elena's couch, curled up with her new Tarot cards and a mug of tea, her legs wrapped in a blanket, my heart nearly stopped.

She was beautiful. She was here. She was whole.

Ever since she'd been taken from us at the safe house, I'd dreamed of this moment. Having her back. Safe. She'd been in Raven's Cape for days, back in my care, but I still couldn't get used to it.

And after today, when I saw the carnage on the beach and thought she'd been hurt...

I clenched my fists, wishing I could have torn those hunters apart myself. It was a wonder I let the ones we'd captured live.

If we hadn't needed their intel, I don't think I would have.

Gray sipped her tea, thumbing to a new card in her deck. She hadn't heard me yet, and I took a minute to watch her, to soak it all in, memorizing the image.

I could come home to this every night for a thousand years and never get tired of it...

When she finally sensed my presence and turned her face toward me, a smile stretched across her lips, lighting me up from the inside.

"Emilio," she breathed. She set down her cards and mug, fighting her way out of the lighthouse blanket that'd tangled around her legs.

"Don't get up. I'll come to you." I took off my coat and my holster, then joined her on the couch, pulling her legs into my lap. She snuggled in closer, tucking her head beneath my chin. Her hair tickled my neck, and I breathed in her sweet scent, wrapping my arms around her, holding her close.

If I had my way, I'd never let her go.

"Tell me the update," she said.

"Do I have to? I'd much rather pretend we're here on vacation, taking a break from a long day of... well, whatever it is people do on vacation."

"That sounds nice," she said dreamily, letting us both live in the fantasy a little longer. I pressed my lips to the top of her head, kissing her hair.

She sighed contentedly, but despite her outward calmness, I felt the anxiety spike in her energy. She needed to know where we were at with the hunters.

Blowing out a breath, I said, "The guys Deirdre knocked

out? We brought them in for questioning once they regained consciousness."

Gray swallowed hard. "And the… others?"

"After our investigation, we concluded they killed each other during an argument," I said firmly. If Gray thought I'd let her take the fall for killing the men whose sole mission had been to kill *her*, she was crazy. "Case closed."

"Any sign of the prison?" she asked.

"Jael picked up the signature of fae spellwork near the sight, but he said it was an inactive spell, already fading. There were no signs of any cave entrances or activity in the area. No footprints, no litter, no disturbed plant life. None of the things we usually see when we've got activity in an area near the beach. Ronan and Darius are still combing the shoreline, looking to see if we missed anything."

She arched an eyebrow. "So Ronan let Darius out on good behavior?"

"He seems to have mellowed out a bit since your… encounter."

She lowered her eyes, her cheeks darkening. The scent of her desire drifted on the air, threatening to send me into a frenzy. God, she was beautiful.

"Did the hunters give you anything to go on?" she asked, shifting so she could look up at me. The movement of her legs made my cock stand up and take notice.

Not a good time, bud.

"Not… especially." I shifted, trying to steer my wayward thoughts back to the topic at hand. The case, not the gorgeous witch sitting in my lap. "Lansky and I did the good cop, bad cop routine for hours, but all we managed to learn was that Jonathan has gone missing, and no one knows what the hell they're supposed to do now."

"I'm pretty sure he's still trapped in my realm," she said. "I... connected with Liam earlier, and he said he's been tracking him there, trying to make sure he doesn't get out. Even if he does, though, I doubt his men would even recognize him anymore." She shuddered against me, undoubtedly remembering her encounters with the deformed creature formerly known as Jonathan in the Shadowrealm.

I ran my hand down her back, calming her.

"It's hard to differentiate fact from fiction with these assholes," I said, "but from what we've gathered so far, it sounds like there's a separate faction of hunters that splintered off from Jonathan's group, and they're working more closely with the Darkwinter fae."

"So, Jonathan *wasn't* working with fae?"

"He may have been, but for whatever reason, others have moved in on his territory. Like I said, these guys are pretty tight-lipped, and half of what they're feeding us is probably bullshit, but it's starting to sound more like a coup."

"The ones you picked up from the beach—those were definitely Jonathan's guys?"

"Yes. They had brands on their arms that matched the ones Darius saw on the hunters who attacked him in the hotel room, as well as the markings we found on—"

"Sophie and the other witches." She shuddered again.

"We still don't know what the markings mean, if anything."

"Probably some kind of sigil magic. Jonathan was so desperate, trying any combination of magic he could get his hands on, cherry-picking his way across all kinds of traditions and lore."

"What worries me is that this other group may have better resources. More capabilities." I pulled the blanket up around her shoulder, holding her close again. "It happens in the business world all the time. The little fish invents something useful, but doesn't quite know how to manage or market it. Big fish comes in and gobbles up the company, expanding on it, branching out. Taking it global."

We'd talked a little bit after dinner the other night about the situation in the Bay, and our theories about the wider implications of Darkwinter's involvement and the Council's treachery. We still hadn't put together the whole story, but we were getting closer, piece by painstaking piece. And the picture all these clues were starting to paint did *not* look good.

"So what happens now?" she asked.

"My sister and Hobb are taking a crack at the interrogation, trying to get more info out of these guys. But we can't hold them much longer without charging them. And without physical evidence of a crime—"

"They attacked me and my grandmother," she said, pulling out of my embrace to shoot me an incredulous look.

I shrugged. "And they're witnesses to the fact that you and your hounds killed four of their friends—something we *definitely* don't want getting out, especially to the human cops on the force. On the record, those assholes killed each other. And right now, the hunters left standing aren't going to push the issue because they believe we're getting too close to the truth as it is, and they're still loyal to Jonathan. They don't want to draw any more police attention than they already have. But if we start charging them with a crime, digging in deeper, they're gonna fight back like caged animals."

"This is... I'm so... God, I feel like tearing my hair out. Literally." She rose from the couch, fisting her hair and pulling tight, her eyes squeezing shut. "Maybe I should go down to the station, see if your sister can use me for anything."

"Elena and her team are handling things at the station," I said. "There's nothing you can do for her right now."

"But I need to do... *something*." She opened her eyes, piercing me with her fiery gaze. "I'm going crazy here, Emilio!"

"You need to take a hot bath and relax. You should take advantage now—no one else is here."

"But—"

"The case will still be waiting for us in the morning," I said. "I promise we'll all regroup and go over everything with fresh eyes and a big breakfast. Okay?"

She opened her mouth to protest, but then closed it, letting out a soft sigh.

"A hot bath does sound kind of heavenly right now."

She smiled again, her eyes lighting up, the tension already lifting from her shoulders. "Okay, *El Lobo.* You win."

"Good. I'm glad you're going willingly. Now I don't have to strip you down and throw you into that tub myself."

She raised an eyebrow. "Was that an option? You didn't mention that in your initial pitch."

"I... uh..." *Oh, Gray. What are you* doing *to me?* I rose from the couch, turning away from her sexy, mischievous smile. "I'll... go find you a towel. And some bubbles. And candles."

And a cold shower for myself, thank you.

"You've thought of everything," she teased.

"Trust me, *mi brujita bonita.* You have *no* idea what I'm thinking."

TWENTY-SEVEN

GRAY

If thoughtful gestures and all-around sweetness were Olympic sports, Emilio would take the gold every time. He'd drawn the bath for me, filling it with lavender bubbles and lining the window ledge with candles, giving me a little spa retreat in the midst of the chaos. There was also a generous glass of white wine on the edge of the tub and a fluffy white bathrobe hanging on the hook behind the door.

He truly had thought of everything.

Stepping into the tub was pure decadence, my muscles instantly relaxing in the heat. I could've stayed there all night, waiting for my skin to prune. But despite the pleasure of the bath, all I really wanted to do was get back to Emilio.

Hoping he wouldn't mind too much, I cut my spa night a little shorter than I'd planned, wrapping myself in the fluffy robe and heading out into the living room. The warm, healing scent of fresh-baked brownies drifted on the air, making my mouth water.

I found Emilio on the couch, sitting before an untouched pan of brownies and two big glasses of cold, frothy milk on the coffee table.

I didn't even try to hide my goofy grin.

You crazy wolf. What would I do without you?

"Feeling better?" he asked.

"How could I not be? I just had a hot bubble bath and a glass of wine, and now I come out here to discover that a really cute guy made me brownies."

Emilio made a show of looking around. "What guy? I'll kill him."

Laughing, I took a seat next to him on the couch.

"And how do you know these brownies are for you?" he teased.

"Because torture isn't your style. You're too good to me to withhold such vital goodness." Not waiting for permission, I grabbed a spoon, then dug into the pan. It was, I'd learned, the best way to eat Emilio's sweet-and-spicy triple-chocolate brownies.

The warm, gooey, chocolatey goodness exploded on my tongue, chased with just the right kick of chili pepper. Orgasmic, as usual.

Emilio laughed as I shoved in a few more spoonfuls.

"Hey. Would you mind sharing?" he teased, nudging me in the ribs. "I did after all make them for both of us."

I scooped up a spoonful for him, cupping a hand under

his chin as I spoon-fed him. His mouth engulfed the entire end of the spoon, soft lips brushing against my fingers.

We took turns feeding each other, demolishing half the pan before we even took a break for milk. Then, we dove back in.

Finally, when I couldn't take another bite of the rich, chocolatey perfection, I set down the spoon and leaned back on the couch.

"That's it?" he asked incredulously. "There's still at least a third left."

"I can't eat another bite," I said.

"Lightweight." Emilio leaned back, putting his arm around me. I snuggled in close, inhaling his sweet, outdoorsy scent. Everything about him was so good, so warm, so... pure. It was a strange way to describe a lone wolf shifter, perhaps, but it fit. At a time where everything was going dark, Emilio was goodness and light.

"What are you thinking about, *querida*?" He asked softly, brushing his knuckles along my upper arm.

I turned to look up at his face, his deep brown eyes shining, his glossy black hair catching the soft lamplight, chocolate staining the edges of his lips. In that moment, he was the most beautiful creature I'd ever seen. He made me feel lucky to be alive, to be here, to be sharing this moment in time with someone so incredible.

And he was looking at me in the exact same way.

"Thank you," I whispered, my throat tightening.

He smoothed his thumb over the corner of my lips,

undoubtedly smeared with chocolate, just like his. "For the brownies?"

"Yes, for the brownies. But also for being in my life. For taking such good care of me. For keeping me calm and sane when everything around me is falling apart. For... for looking at me the way you do."

He cocked his head, a teasing smile playing on his lips. "How am I looking at you?"

"Like..." I swallowed the tightness in my throat, my heart thumping, everything in me hoping I was right. Hoping I hadn't misread his feelings. In a faint whisper full of that bright, gossamer hope, I said, "Like you want to kiss me."

He watched me a long moment, his eyes intense, his smile receding. For one mortifying, terrifying instant, I thought I'd made the wrong call.

Then he traced his thumb along the bottom of my lip, sliding his fingers along my jaw.

"I will always be in your life, *mi brujita*. That is a promise. As for wanting to kiss you..."

He held my gaze another agonizing moment, then dipped his head, capturing my mouth in a chocolate-infused kiss that was as hot as it was sweet, the spark of it traveling straight down to my toes.

I reached up and threaded my fingers into his hair, pulling him closer. Without breaking our kiss, he scooped me into his strong arms, lifting me up and carrying me back to his bedroom.

He laid me on the bed, kissing my lips, my neck, slowly

working his way down my body as he unwrapped the bathrobe, revealing my naked flesh. He took his time, exploring every inch of bare skin with gentle kisses and soft caresses, his tongue swirling over my nipple, then sucking, his fingers trailing down between my thighs.

I parted for him, welcoming the touch of his strong hands, his warmth. He slid two fingers inside me, his thumb tracing slow circles over my clit.

Everything about his touch was slow and deliberate, gradually electrifying my nerves, winding me tighter and tighter until I was certain I'd burst if I didn't feel him inside me.

He seemed to sense this, and gently made his way back to my mouth, capturing me in a deep, sensual kiss.

He pulled away just a moment, just long enough to strip off his own clothes. He stood before me then, naked in the moonlight, his beautiful, muscular form standing over me like the sculpture of a Greek god. I drank in the sight of him, my eyes tracing the broad lines of his shoulders, the defined muscles of his chest and abs, the trail of dark hair that led down to his cock, hard and massive.

I nodded, giving him a soft smile, and he climbed on top of me, graceful despite his hulking form. Slowly, he lowered his full weight over me, his warmth sliding over my skin like water, like the hot bubble bath I'd just taken, and we lay like that for several long, blissful moments, our hearts beating as one.

Wordlessly, we both sensed when it was time. Emilio shifted, and I parted my thighs, arching my hips.

There was no awkward fumbling or second-guessing, no nervous giggles, no questions, no fear. From the very first brownies he'd ever baked for me, everything between us had been building to this, an ending of one chapter and the beginning of something brand new.

As Emilio slid inside me, stretching me, filling me, I let out a gasp of pleasure, sliding my hands into his hair and pulling his mouth to mine.

"Are you okay, *querida*?" he asked.

"I'm… perfect."

He nipped at my lower lip and smiled. "Agreed."

His eyes turned serious again, sensual, and he rolled his hips, taking his time with every thrust, allowing me to get used to him. We found our rhythm easily, though, our bodies arching, our mouths seeking the warmth of a thousand kisses as we brought each other closer and closer to the edge of bliss.

After an eternity of delicious, deliberate kisses and touches and slow, languid thrusts, I felt my core tighten around him, my nerves tingling.

The orgasm took its time, teasing me, waiting just out of reach as my thighs grew slick with sweat, my breath ragged, my heartbeat pounding a fierce drumbeat behind my ribs.

Emilio pulled out slowly, cupping my face, then slid all the way back inside, his eyes rolling back into his head in a look of pure pleasure, a low, sexy moan rumbling through his chest.

And that was it.

The wave crashed over me, explosive, powerful, rocking me to my core. My thighs trembled with the force of it, the pleasure impossible to contain, and I let go, calling out his name in ecstasy, losing myself in the tumultuous spin as shockwave after shockwave rippled through my body.

Emilio came with the same electrifying force, his body shuddering against me as he gripped my hips, holding me close, breathing my name into the moonlit night as if he were casting his own spell.

I closed my eyes beneath him and felt the hot pulse of our connection, throbbing like a heartbeat that spread throughout my entire body. It bound me to him, and him to me, and us to Ronan and Asher and Darius. Darius might not remember it, Ronan wasn't allowed to act on it, Asher was still a prisoner, but that didn't change what we were.

A family. A *real* family—not the kind who jealously fought to control each other's power, or harmed each other out of spite and anger. But the kind that had each other's backs, no matter how ugly things got. The kind that took turns lifting each other up, stepping up when someone else couldn't, picking up the pieces when someone else's world was falling apart.

Spent and blissed out, Emilio collapsed on top of me, then rolled us so I was on top of him. I laid my head on his chest, listening to the strong, powerful beat of his heart as he traced figure eights on my back.

We stayed that way for a while, sinking into the peaceful moment, the beauty of it.

I lifted my head, resting my chin in my hands against his chest, staring into his eyes.

Emilio smiled, melting me. "What are you thinking, *mi brujita bonita*?"

"I'm thinking…" I arched an eyebrow, unable to hold back my own smile. "Those were some of the best brownies I've ever had."

"*Some* of the best?" Emilio laughed, grabbing me and rolling on top of me once again, tickling me.

"Top five at least," I teased, and the tickling intensified, making me squeal. "Okay, okay! The best! The absolute best! I swear it!"

"Good." He stopped tickling me, once again capturing my gaze with his soulful brown eyes. One look had the power to convey so much, and right now, I felt the force of his love for me. His friendship. His fierce desire to protect our pack.

And there, between my thighs, I felt the force of his love in an entirely different way.

"I'm making another batch tomorrow," he teased, kissing my jaw, his cock hardening further. "And the day after that." Kissing my neck. "And probably every day for the foreseeable future." My collarbone. "I hope you're okay with that."

He slid inside me once again, and I sighed happily, welcoming him in deeper, losing myself in his warmth.

"Emilio Alvarez," I breathed, closing my eyes, a smile stretching across my lips. "I am *more* than okay with that. *So* much more."

TWENTY-EIGHT

GRAY

Even in the arms of my powerful, protective wolf, I still couldn't resist the siren call of those brownies, and an hour after he'd fallen asleep, I slipped out of Emilio's embrace and padded down the hall in search of a midnight snack.

"Gray? Everything okay?"

I jumped at the voice, shocked to find Elena sitting at the dining room table in the dark, sipping tea. She stood up to turn on the overhead light, wincing at the sudden brightness.

"I'm... good," I said, tucking my hair behind my ears. I was wearing the bathrobe, my hair still damp from the shower Emilio and I had taken after our third round of... brownies. "Just looking for a midnight snack."

Elena frowned. "Oooh, I hope it wasn't brownies. I might've finished those."

"No!" I teased, letting out a playful gasp.

"In my defense, *someone* left them out on the coffee table. Abandoned. Clearly, they needed to find a good home."

"Clearly."

"Have a seat," she said, rising from her own. "I'll fix you something."

"You don't have to—"

"It'll be quick, don't worry. I was about to make some more tea, anyway. Do you like *yerba mate?*

"I'm... sure it's amazing," I said, no idea what I was getting into.

Elena buzzed around the kitchen, insisting I stay put and relax. No less than ten minutes later, she was back, with two steaming mugs of the *mate* tea and a plate of toasted, crustless sandwiches, pressed thin with three layers of bread.

"*Sandwiches de miga,*" she said. "This one is ham and cheese, the other are roasted red pepper and asparagus. Try one."

She handed me a plate. I reached for a ham and cheese, taking a bite. Gooey cheese melted into my mouth.

"You just made these?" I asked, marveling at the culinary skills of the Alvarez siblings. I could only imagine what their parents were like in the kitchen. "Wow. Thank you."

"*De nada,*" she said, helping herself to a red pepper sandwich.

We finished our sandwiches and sipped our *mate* through a round of small talk, then her eyes turned more inquisitive, and I knew what was coming next.

"Can I ask you something, Gray? It's kind of personal."

I nodded, smiling into my mug.

"You and the guys…"

My cheeks heated, my smile growing broader.

"You're connected to all of them?" she asked. "Like, romantically?"

"I know it seems… unconventional," I said.

"No, it seems like a lot to manage!"

"As long as they're okay with doing their own laundry, I don't foresee any problems." I laughed. "Honestly? Having a relationship like this… It's not something I ever thought about before they all came crashing into my life. For so long, there was only Ronan. I had such intense feelings for him. I couldn't imagine caring for anyone else on that level."

"Did things between you and Ronan cool off when you met the others?"

"No, just the opposite, actually. This might sound crazy, but being with Ronan, loving someone so deeply like that… I don't know exactly how to explain it. But it made my heart expand. The other guys came together to protect me after I started coming into my powers as a witch. A lot of crazy stuff went down, and we all bonded really quickly after that."

"I can understand that. Intense circumstances can definitely have that effect."

"The more time we all started spending together," I continued, "the more it just felt… right. Like we belonged together. It's not that we don't have our challenges, just like any relationship. And all of this is still so new—I mean, your brother and I are still… getting to know each other." I lowered my eyes into my mug, feeling myself blush again. When had Elena even gotten home? I really hoped she hadn't heard us. Then again, she was a wolf shifter, with wolf senses. Not to mention a cop. And it didn't take a detective to put the clues together.

I sipped my *mate*, then looked up at her again. "I trust them with my life. We have each other's backs, no matter what goes down. I never doubt that, even in the middle of the worst kind of craziness."

"Like this thing with Ronan and Sebastian?" she asked softly, her smile open and compassionate. "Emilio told me a little bit about the situation."

I nodded. I didn't expect we could keep many secrets in this house. Not with all of us living in such close proximity.

"I'm so sorry, Gray," she said.

At her kindness, a blade pressed against my heart, carving a fresh mark for all that Ronan and I had lost.

I nodded again, blowing out a slow, even breath. "Ronan and I will get through this. Don't ask me how, since I still don't fully understand Sebastian's head games. But a bond like we have—it doesn't end just because someone else says it has to. I have faith that we'll figure it out together. Darius, too. I have to believe he's still in there somewhere, even if he doesn't remember me yet. I'm not giving up on any of them, and I'm not giving up on hope."

Elena's eyes twinkled, and she winked at me over the rim of her mug. "Sounds like a pack to me."

"In a lot of ways, it is." Then, eager to shift the focus away from my own romantic entanglements, I flashed a teasing smirk and said, "Maybe you should try it. Get yourself a few boyfriends, do a little test run."

"That easy, right?" Elena smiled, but the laughter quickly dimmed from her eyes. "I can't, Gray. I'm the Alpha. We mate with one, and we mate for life."

"Well, that doesn't sound like such a bad deal if you find the right guy though. Right?"

She shrugged, noncommittal.

"What about Detective Hobb? I've seen the way you two look at each other."

She reached for another sandwich, breaking it in half. Melty cheese dripped from the center, still warm. "I care for Aiden," she said, taking a bite. "A lot. But he's not my mate. Not in the true sense of the word."

Her eyes glazed with a deep, dark sadness, the cause of which I could only begin to guess at. She set down the rest of her sandwich, and for a moment I thought that would be the end of the conversation.

But then she looked at me and said, "I already found my mate. A long time ago."

My eyes widened in surprise. I was almost afraid to ask the next question, but she seemed to be expecting it.

"What happened?"

"Well, we married young. He was human—totally forbidden." The mischievous sparkle in her eye told me *exactly* what Elena thought about that particular rule. But despite the momentary smile, it was clear she didn't enjoy talking about this.

"I… didn't mean to push," I said.

"It's not that. It's… I haven't talked about this in so long. I just…" She swiped a tear that had escaped down her cheek, taking a shuddering breath. "To make a long and tragic story as short as possible… Back in Argentina, our pack was betrayed. Our people were slaughtered. Emilio got me out—just barely—but our parents…" She shook her head, fresh tears gathering in her eyes. "And my… my husband and my daughter… She was only three at the time." A bitter laugh escaped her lips. "At the time. I say it as if she'll ever be any older."

"Daughter," I whispered. Her words punched a hole in my chest, reaching right in and grabbing my heart. "I don't… I can't even find the words for this."

"That's because there aren't any."

My heart was breaking for her, my mind racing with so many questions, colliding into one another and making my tongue feel fat. How had their pack been betrayed? How had she and Emilio escaped? And what had happened since that horrible tragedy to drive them so far apart? It sounded like they were the last two of their family—of their pack. And somehow, they'd become estranged. For nearly two decades, if I remembered it right.

I took a breath, trying to corral my thoughts into the right words, into a single sentence that could offer even the tiniest bit of comfort.

But when I opened my mouth to speak, Elena held up her hand.

"It's not necessary," she said. "I've read every book on grief and loss and recovering from trauma. I even went to a few support group meetings in Seattle a couple of years ago, hoping I could find a connection, another person who understood and could help me feel less alone in it."

"It didn't help?" I asked.

"Yes and no. It helped soothe the sting in the moment. But there's just no balm for a wound like this. You carry the burden, and you learn to live with the pain, making room for it like another person in the house. It follows you everywhere—to the grocery store, to work, into your bed at night. You make peace with it. You make friends with it. And you survive, despite the hole in your heart."

She held my gaze, her eyes suddenly fierce, and I nodded. I hadn't suffered the loss of a child—I couldn't even imagine what that would do to a person. But loss was universal, and in my own way, I understood what she was saying.

Finally breaking our gaze, Elena brushed the last of her tears away and forced out a laugh. "Goodness, what's in this *mate*? Truth serum?"

I returned her laugh, glad to lighten the mood, just a little bit.

Her laughter faded, and now she looked at me with kind, honest eyes. The eyes of someone who might become a friend.

Maybe she already had.

"As long as we're being honest, Gray..." She took a breath, searching for her words, then said, "My brother cares for you a great deal. It's... it's good to see him like that. Happy."

The words seemed to stick in her throat, each one pushed out with great effort.

God, there were so many layers to her relationship with Emilio. So many sharp edges and dark corners I could only guess at. But I truly didn't want to push, and I sensed she'd reached the absolute farthest end of her comfort zone.

Exhaustion was settling into my bones, anyway. Stretching into a yawn, I rose from the chair and cleared away the dishes, ready to give her some privacy and head back into the warm embrace of my wolf.

But when I exited the kitchen and headed toward the hallway, Emilio was already standing there, unbuttoned jeans hanging off his hips, a wrinkled T-shirt tossed over his shoulder. The sight of his massive bare chest sent a fresh pulse of desire to my core, and I ogled him openly, hoping I wasn't actually drooling.

But the severe look in his eyes told me this was not the time for ogling.

"Get dressed," he said to us both, just as Elena's phone started buzzing on the table. "That'll be Lansky. I just got off the phone with him. Gray and I have a visitor at the precinct."

TWENTY-NINE

EMILIO

Nine minutes and one harrowing drive later, we stood outside the RCPD interrogation room, staring through the one-way mirror at a witch I hadn't seen—in the flesh, anyway—since Sophie's murder.

Reva Monroe was so pale and thin, she was practically see-through. Dark circles lined her eyes, making them stand out starkly against her china-doll complexion. Her head had been shaved, covered now with the fuzz of new growth.

One of the female officers had helped her clean up, and now she wore a set of RCPD sweats. They were two sizes too big, but she looked grateful for the warmth, sitting at the table and sipping hot chocolate from a styrofoam cup.

I could only imagine what her living conditions had been like.

"She showed up here a little while ago, asking for you

and Gray," Lansky said to me. "She won't talk to anyone else."

"You get one of the EMTs to check her out?" I asked.

"Yes. She's refusing to go to the hospital," he said, "but they said she was stable. Dehydrated and hungry, a few scrapes, but no major injuries. She did tell us she hadn't been physically assaulted, but said that others had been... experimented on."

"Oh my God," Gray whispered, shaking her head. She clenched her teeth, her eyes sparking with rage. Her magic spiked—I scented it in the air between us. "Can I go talk to her?"

I put my hand on her shoulder, giving her a squeeze. "I'll go in with you."

Reva looked up from her hot chocolate as we entered, a smile stretching across her face when she saw us.

"I knew you'd come," she said.

Gray knelt before her, reaching for her hands. "Are you hurt? Did he hurt you?"

Reva shook her head. "Not like that."

"How did you even end up there?"

"Norah took me," she said. "Delilah too. She put Delilah under some kind of spell, but not me. She said there was only one way for me to help my friends."

"What way was that?" I asked gently, taking a seat across from her. I didn't want her to be intimidated. The kid had been through enough already—the last thing she needed was a bunch of hulking cops standing around, staring down at her, demanding answers.

"She sold me to Jonathan. I don't know how much she got, but probably not a lot."

Madre María, the sadness in those eyes.

I scrubbed a hand over my mouth, trying to keep my emotions in check. I glanced at the mirror, knowing Elena was there on the other side, thinking the same thoughts that I was.

Our theories about Norah were correct. She *had* betrayed her coven. Kidnapped Reva and Delilah, maybe others we didn't even know about. Likely she'd known about the vampire ambush at her house after Asher and Haley had been taken. Hell, she may have even sanctioned it.

"He has everyone in the cave prison," she said, glancing up at me. "Did you get my message before?"

"I did, kiddo. You did great. We searched the beach, right where you told us to, but the prison is fae spelled. Camouflaged." I glanced at Gray, then back to Reva. "But you're here now, physically. How did you manage to slip out of sight?"

"I knew there was another cave system behind that one, and it wasn't spelled. There was a shaft that led back out to the beach."

"How did you get out of the cell?" Gray asked.

"They said they were going to move us," she said. "Something about relocating into the city? When they came back to get us out of the cell, Asher and Haley started a fight with the fae guards, and I did my thing."

"Fae guards?" I asked. "Can you describe them?"

"Black uniforms, gold patches on their arms with a

weird swirly kind of design. It kind of looked like tree branches, maybe?"

I shot another glance at Gray. "Darkwinter," I mouthed.

"Did the guards say anything about where in the city they were going?" Gray asked.

"No, the fae guards didn't say *anything*. The guy in charge was human—a hunter. Asher said he's the guy who…" She swallowed hard, her eyes filling with tears as she looked at Gray. "Who killed your mother in New York."

"Dirty Beard," Gray whispered. She was positively ashen. "Jonathan's father."

Reva nodded.

"Reva," I said, "I'm going to need you to remember as much detail as possible about the prison and everyone in it. Anything the guards or the old man said, things Jonathan might've mentioned before, things about what happened with Norah, anything you can think of at all. Nothing is too silly or insignificant to mention. Do you think you can do that for me?"

She nodded emphatically. "I told those guys my plan would work. I knew I could find you."

"And I'm so glad you did." I couldn't help but smile. "You hungry, kiddo? How do you feel about cheeseburgers?"

She grinned, her smile lighting up the room. "I feel like I love them."

I waved for Elena to come in.

"Did I hear something about cheeseburgers?" she asked.

"Make mine a double," I told Elena.

"Mine too," Reva said.

My sister rolled her eyes, but she was nodding. I even caught a smile on that grim face of hers.

Turning back to Reva with a smile of my own, I pulled out my phone and hit the voice recorder, setting it on the table between us. "Okay, Reva Monroe, stealth spelunker and master escape artist. Tell us a story, and make it a good one."

* * *

"Story checks out," Elena said a couple of hours later. "We've got them."

"That fast?" I asked.

"All thanks to this one." She smiled at Reva, who beamed right back at her. "I might have to make you an honorary detective, kiddo."

Elena gave us the lowdown, pointing out the site on a map on her phone.

After hearing Reva's account, she said, she was able to narrow down the possibilities to the most likely locations in the city—abandoned commercial buildings that had plenty of space to imprison captors and set up labs for their ongoing experimentation, all without attracting too much attention. From there, she had her guys combing through security camera footage, and apparently, Hobb had hit the jackpot with a condemned three-story building down at the intersection of Granite Top Road and Spring Street, right on the seedy outskirts of the Cape's warehouse district. The place had been on the auction block for a year, dead to all but the rodents who'd made it home. Yet earlier that night, cameras picked up on six nondescript black vans rolling into the alley adjacent to the property, right where the service entrances would be. The footage was grainy, she said, but they were able to zoom in on a partial view of one of the divers.

"Jael identified the armband insignia as Darkwinter."

"Sounds like we've got our target," I said. "So what's our play here, Chief?"

"Surveillance. We need to gather more intel. Then?" She blew out a breath, meeting my eyes. "We'll make our move. Together."

THIRTY

GRAY

"Can you do it?" I asked.

Jael nodded, peering through the binoculars, scanning the scene below.

It was well after midnight, and Jael, Darius, and I were in position on the second floor of an empty office building adjacent to the prison site. We sat in darkness, hiding in shadow from our enemies across the alley. The operation would begin in earnest in twenty-five minutes.

Sunshine and Sparkle were here with me, as always, ready to pounce at the first sign of trouble. In our short time together, they'd become more like companions than guardians, and we'd finally begun to trust each other. They knew I wouldn't bolt—wouldn't leave them—and I knew they wouldn't hurt me. In fact, they'd do anything to keep me safe.

Now, they were as much an integral part of the plan as the rest of us.

"Luck is on our side. Their security spell isn't fully operational yet," Jael said. "They believe they've still got time. Right now, it's strong enough to keep the prisoners in and curious humans out of the area altogether. But there are still a lot of loose threads for me to exploit."

"Threads?" I asked.

"Think of fae magic like a weaving," he said. "Complex spells like this—spells that need to cover a lot of physical ground, for example—require millions of different threads, each of them precisely woven together. This spell is still in progress. I can feel its threads, so it's essentially a matter of finding the right one and giving it a good tug."

"Will it destroy the whole spell?" Darius asked.

"No. But it will temporarily weaken the magic—long enough to give us a window," Jael said. "Once I give the signal, you'll have less than two minutes to breach the physical security. The moment they see you, they'll know the spell was compromised and they'll go on the offensive. Killing you brutally, of course."

"Of course." I rolled my eyes playfully, desperate for a little levity to break up the heaviness. "No one ever accused you of seeing the silver lining, did they, Jael?"

"Fae don't see silver linings. We make them." Jael surprised me with a conspiratorial wink. Seemed he needed a little levity, too.

We fell into silence, taking turns scoping out the warehouse through the binoculars. I couldn't see much—an occasional fae guard patrolling the entrances, a hunter stationed at the corner of the building, playing with his phone. It was quiet outside.

Inside? I could only imagine what was happening. We were assuming the prisoners were being held on the third floor—Darius and the shifters had all sensed the concentration of fear there. But we had no other clues. Reva hadn't been able to shadow travel—not since she'd escaped the caves. I suspected she was just weakened from her ordeal, but she was understandably distraught about the loss of her powers, no matter how temporary it might've been.

Poor kid. Deirdre had concocted a mild sedative for her, and we'd left her home tonight, with one of Elena's officers posted outside. When we said our goodbyes earlier, she was already camped out on the living room couch with Elena's Netflix password and enough pizza, potato chips, and ice cream to tide her over. Emilio had expected her to protest, but I was pretty sure she was relieved to be left behind. Reva was tough, but she was also exhausted, scared, and hadn't even begun to process the trauma she'd endured at Norah's hands, let alone Jonathan's.

All of us had already lost so much. And there was still so much more darkness to come. I was certain of it. Freeing the witches tonight? Getting back to Asher? That was just the beginning of a long, bloody fight.

One I was supposed to lead.

"It's time," Jael said, his hand on my back. His yellow eyes glinted in the moonlight that streamed in through the windows. "We need to get down to ground level."

"Jael..." I looked into those catlike eyes, wondering

what he was thinking. He and I were connected by our love for Sophie, by the pain of her loss, but we had never spoken about her. Not really.

I hoped we'd get that chance someday.

"Doing this..." I continued, "There's no going back. If we fail and Darkwinter takes power, you'll be branded a traitor to your kind. They'll banish you from the fae realms, and probably worse."

"I am aware of the risks, and I fully accept any consequences, foreseen and unforeseen." He stood up straight, proud. But then his face softened, his eyes sparkling with new warmth. In a gentler tone, he said, "If Sophie were here, what do you think she'd have me do?"

The sound of her name on his lips brought tears to my eyes. But for once, they weren't tears of sadness. I felt his love for her. Felt the joy in her love for him. I was grateful she'd found that happiness, however briefly.

I smiled, blinking away the tears, and grabbed the lapels of his dark gray coat. "First of all, she'd probably add a little glitter to this jacket. It doesn't take much to go from drab to fab," I said, recalling one of her favorite lines.

Jael laughed, a sound that filled the room with warmth. When he met my gaze again, I saw my tears of joy reflected in his eyes. "Ahh, Gray. Sophie... She cared a great deal for you."

"She loved you, Jael."

He wrapped his hands over mine, giving me a reassuring squeeze. "How could I honor her memory if I turned my back on you? On our home?"

"You're taking a huge risk."

"Yes." He leaned in close, whispering in my ear. "But I'm fighting alongside the heir of Silversbane. I like my odds."

And then he was gone, disappearing down the stairs that would lead him out into the alley. In less than ten minutes, Darius and I would follow.

I turned to Darius, taking a deep breath. We hadn't spoken much since the staking, but he had mellowed out, just like Emilio had said. He seemed to have gotten past the bloodlust. He no longer needed the hawthorn sedative.

He was practically back to his old self.

Except for the part where he didn't remember any of us.

Shoving down the pain inside, I said, "We clear on the plan?"

He gave me a stiff nod, as uncomfortable around me as I was around him. "Crystal, Miss Desario."

I took out the comms device Elena had given me and pressed the button to check in.

"Jael's moving into position," I said. "Darius and I are ready to rock. Sunshine and Sparkle will bring up the rear."

"Message received," Emilio said. "All good here, too. Elena?"

"Ready and awaiting the signal," she shot back.

I took another deep breath, trying to calm the nervous energy buzzing through my body. This plan *had* to work. Our friends' lives depended on it. *Our* lives depended on it.

Once Jael had temporarily neutralized the spell weave, Ronan, Emilio, Detective Hobb, and Deirdre would hit the front of the warehouse, taking out the hunters and fae guards stationed there, working their way up to the second and third floors. Elena, Detective Lansky, and a few other shifters from her local pack would cover the back entrances.

Darius and I would enter last, with an assist from Jael to disable any additional fae security inside. Our mission was singular: locate and liberate the prisoners.

The witches.

Asher.

My sister, Haley.

Fiona Brentwood, the vampire who I still believed wanted to help us, despite her earlier loyalty to Jonathan.

And every last one of the beings imprisoned and experimented on. Tortured.

I looked out the windows, watching the fae guard pacing across the alley, and my heart rate kicked up. This was really happening. Jonathan's twisted, bloody legacy was about to come to an end.

I just hoped the rest of us survived the fight.

THIRTY-ONE

GRAY

The warm, gentle caress of a hand on my shoulder made my heart jump. Not because I didn't know who it was, but because I was surprised that he'd touched me at all.

"Darius," I whispered, my insides already heating, despite the protests of my brain. I couldn't deny our connection, even now, and being in his presence was unnerving enough without physical contact.

"Before we go into this," he said softly, "there's something I'd like to say to you. If you'll hear me."

I closed my eyes, unable to turn around. Unable to look into the eyes of the vampire I loved and not see that same love reflected back at me. I couldn't do it—not tonight.

I nodded, bracing myself for whatever twist in this tale was coming next.

"I didn't mean to be so cold to you, Gray," he said, the regret in his voice shocking in its pure nakedness. "So cruel. I am truly sorry."

At this, I finally turned around. I tilted my head back to meet his eyes, finding a tenderness I hadn't expected.

It wasn't love or recognition, but it was closer.

My heart dipped into my stomach, my breath hitching in my throat, stealing my words.

"Sometimes I look at you," he said, his voice silky and low in the darkness, "and I'm overcome with a... a strange feeling. Like we've known each other far longer than you've let on."

"Yes and no," I said, finding my voice, however frail it felt. "With us, it's kind of... complicated."

"I'd like to hear more about it, if you're comfortable sharing."

I closed my eyes and sighed. There was a time when "comfortable sharing" meant something entirely different between us. Briefly, I wondered how he'd feel if he could remember that night with Ronan, the love and passion and connection the three of us had shared with each other. It hadn't happened that long ago; I'd been so certain the three of us were forever. That our night together was only the beginning of something much bigger, much deeper.

Yet somehow, they'd both slipped through my fingers.

"You've known Ronan and the others much longer," I said. "You and I met several years ago, when I first came to the Bay. You... you helped take care of me when I was in no position to take care of myself."

Darius blew out a slow breath—an odd gesture for the vampire—and I felt the heat of it whispering over my lips. When he looked at me again, his gaze was heavy with sadness. "Several years of friendship, gone in a blink. How is that possible?"

"I wish I knew. Better yet, I wish I knew how to reverse it."

So much had happened since I'd talked to Deirdre on the beach, I hadn't had time to do any more research about blood magic. Part of me wanted to share my theory with Darius, but I wasn't ready. I needed more information. More... everything. And right now, we had other priorities.

"When I look at you now," he said, "I'm overwhelmed with..." He closed his eyes, took a deep breath. A scent. He reached out a tentative hand and cupped my chin, our skin barely making contact. Still, it was enough to set my heart on fire.

"I touch you," he continued, "and it's like I can *feel* everything we've lost. But I can't see the details of it. I taste your scent in the air around me, and it stirs something deep inside me, but brings back no memories." He opened his eyes, his honey-colored gaze intense and possessive and full of the same deep, desperate longing coursing through my veins. "I'm *certain* you've left footprints on my heart, Gray Desario, yet I can't recall the sound of a single step, and it's... it's breaking me."

His words mingled with the intensity in his eyes, the heat in his touch, the proximity of his body, the heartache in his voice, all of it wrapping me up in a spell I knew would soon shatter. But for the moment, I let myself take pleasure in it, indulging in the memories of *us*, the movie reel of our first kiss, the way we'd touched each other in the car outside Luna's, our shower at the safe house, the promises he'd made to take me to New York, the snow globe he'd brought back for me, our first time together in the Shadowrealm. Even the raw, lust-fueled night we'd shared in Elena's basement played in my mind, making my heart race, my core ache, everything inside me desperate for his touch, even now.

Each memory cut deep, but the pain was necessary, and I welcomed it. It reminded me that it was real. That everything Darius and I shared had really happened.

I'd lost him. I'd lost Ronan. I'd lost Liam. Each in very different ways, but each resulting in the same broken heart. Still, I wouldn't trade those moments and memories for anything, even if it meant a lifetime of suffering over this loss.

"Do you think it's possible that we might... become friends?" he asked suddenly, pulling me back to the present. "Maybe not overnight, of course. But in time, we might get to know each other again. Perhaps even enjoy each other's company."

"You mean starting over?" I asked, looking up at him. "From scratch?"

"I no longer have the memories that made me the man you knew and cared for. But in many ways, I'm still that man. It stands to reason that if you and I were destined to become friends once, it could certainly happen again."

"I think... I think I'd like that." I smiled. No matter how much I'd lost, no matter how hard life kept trying to hammer home the lessons of a broken heart, that glimmer of hope inside me refused to die. And now, at Darius's words, it surged brightly once again. It was only for an instant, but it was enough to buoy me for the battle ahead.

Because if Darius and I could become friends again, maybe we could fall in love again, too.

The comms device buzzed at my hip. It was time.

THIRTY-TWO

GRAY

From the moment Jael gave the signal, we were in motion. Darius and I ducked behind a Dumpster in the alley, watching as Emilio's team moved in on the front entrance, easily dispatching the lone fae and the hunter glued to his phone.

They were inside in under thirty seconds.

My heart was pounding in my ears, the dull thud threatening to drown out all else. I was relying on Darius's superior vampire hearing to let us know what was going on inside, because from the outside, everything was still and silent.

"They've been spotted," he said. "Ground floor. Fae guards are moving in."

That was our cue to release the hounds.

"Sparkle. Sunshine." I pulled out one of Ronan's T-shirts, letting them pick up his scent. "Go." I swatted

Sparkle on the butt, sending them bounding off toward the entrance in search of Ronan.

"Elena's group is attacking the hunters," Darius said, cocking his head to listen.

The echo of gunfire reverberated across the alley, and a flash of Deirdre's yellow-orange magic lit up the second floor of the warehouse.

They'd made it upstairs. Now it was on us.

"Here we go," Darius said, his arm strong and solid around my waist. "Hold on."

Holding me tight, he took off, the alley around me a blur as he sped to the entrance. I closed my eyes against a wave of nausea, but there was no time to be sick. In a blink, we were already inside, the discordant sounds of battle assaulting my ears. The clash of metal, the howl of the hounds, gunfire, the agonizing wail of a hunter who'd fallen to Sunshine's brutal attack... I caught sight of her just in time to see her rip out his intestines.

Elena was the only one holding a gun. The rest of her pack, including Emilio, had shifted into their wolf forms, the beautiful beasts attacking the fae guards armed with sleek, lightweight swords undoubtedly infused with magic.

The unmistakable song of a blade cutting through the air sent chills down my spine, and I spun around to see it slice through the shoulder of a magnificent black wolf.

"Emilio!" I shouted, but he was already retaliating, lunging for the guard who'd hit him. He sunk his fangs into the guy's arm before I'd even taken a single step toward him.

"Keep moving," Darius ordered. "Their blades aren't silver. He's fine." He grabbed my hand and hauled me toward the back of a huge, open space littered with old metal shelving and discarded office furniture. We wove through the melee, dodging Elena's shifters as they held off the hunters and fae, our focus on the metal staircases crawling up the back wall.

We slammed into the wall with a grunt, but my feet didn't even touch the first step. Darius hauled me against his chest, dragging me up the staircase in another nause-ating blink.

The second floor was a maze of cubicles and office equipment, all of it being decimated in the unfolding chaos. Fae guards darted around every cubical wall, leaping over office chairs and desks, desperately trying to get a piece of the witch at the center of the room. Deirdre wasn't letting anyone get close. The hum of her magic filled the air with a mix of smoke and an electric buzz that singed the back of my throat, and each time the fae charged, she shot out a burst of magic, forcing them back en masse. Sparkle fought by her side, mauling a particularly brazen hunter before he got within five feet of my grandmother.

Deirdre was a damn good fighter, but her magic wouldn't last forever. She was already losing steam, her shoulders trembling as she tried to focus her energy.

"We have to help her," I said, more to myself than to Darius. I knew we couldn't. There were too many obstacles between here and there, and we had to stay focused on reaching the third floor. On freeing the prisoners.

291

"Over there," Darius said, pointing to the next set of stairs. They were clear on the other side of the room.

I peered into the smokey haze, looking for a route. I'd just found a clear path when I felt two strong hands shove me from behind.

I stumbled to the floor and flipped around just in time to see Darius catch a hunter's blade in the chest—a blade meant for me. The hunter still had his fingers wrapped around the grip when Darius tore the man's arm clear out of its socket.

The arm and the body hit the floor. Darius pulled the blade free, wincing. The wound was already knitting back together.

I gasped in awe, but there was no time to wonder about the healing power of vampires.

"Move!" he shouted suddenly, and I rolled left, narrowly escaping the jab of a fae blade. The guard lifted his sword for another go, but Darius was already on him, tearing out half his throat with a vicious bite.

The sword clattered to the floor beside me. I wasted no time in picking it up and clambering to my feet.

I felt the ripple of its power immediately. It wasn't an electric buzz or even a hum, but a slow, silky current, clean and crisp as a mountain stream. An icy but not uncomfortable chill ran through my blood, and my own magic stirred in response, reaching to connect with this new power. I felt it the moment it happened—like a bolt sliding home inside me, locking itself into place.

The cold, new power raced through my body, twining with my magic, energizing me.

I knew nothing about how to handle a sword, but I swung it anyway, slicing through the air with an ease I didn't expect. The blade was light but solid, the edges glowing faintly.

"Looks like you've found a new toy." Darius grinned, wiping the blood from his mouth. "Take it to go."

Grabbing my free hand, he led us through the cubical maze, both of us ducking low to keep out of sight. There was a crash behind us, and I heard Ronan's gruff voice cursing up a storm. I turned, catching a brief glimpse as he jabbed a dagger into someone's neck. Hunter or fae, I couldn't tell, but the guy dropped like a sack of rocks. Ronan wiped his forehead with the back of his hand, blood pouring from a gash above his eye.

Please, please let him be okay at the end of all this. Let all *of them be okay.*

I sent the little prayer up to the universe, hoping someone, somewhere, heard it.

Turning back toward Darius, I caught sight of a pair of fae soldiers heading right for us.

"Darius!"

"I see them. You take righty, I'll take lefty."

He let go of my hand and lunged for the guy on the left, barely dodging the guy's sword before sinking his fangs into his neck. On nothing but instinct, I swung my newfound sword in front of me in a smooth arc. I had no proper form, no real idea what to aim for, but I connected anyway, slicing a diagonal gash down his torso. Magic surged through the blade, burning a clean line through the fabric of his uniform, right down to his skin. I watched in fascinated horror as his skin appeared to eat itself away, revealing muscle and bone and blood, unleashing the frantic howls of a soldier being devoured by his own magic. His and mine.

The combination was deadly.

And impressive as hell.

"This way," Darius shouted. "Now."

I ran to catch up, taking his hand once again. Darting past the last row of cubicles, we finally made it to the staircase and up to the third floor.

Only to find a locked gate at the top of the stairs, barring us from entry.

"Get back," he shouted, and I backed down a few steps. He crashed through the metal gate, sending it clattering to the floor.

We rushed in, my sword raised, but there wasn't a single guard or hunter in sight.

"Trap?" I whispered.

"No," a voice said from behind us. It was Jael, looking a little worse for wear, but unhurt as far as I could tell. His yellow eyes were alert.

He slipped between us and moved into the room, hitting a switch on the wall.

Harsh, white light illuminated an even harsher, whiter room.

"Self-contained security," Jael said. "The gate was just a holdover from the building's previous occupants."

The room was windowless and surgically spotless, with white walls that shone so bright, it was impossible to tell where the light was coming from. The space was full of gleaming steel tables and shelves—a sight that reminded me of a much more high-tech version of the morgue in Blackmoon Bay, where Darius and I had once fought off a trio of vampires.

"Where is everyone?" I asked, fear gripping my chest. "There aren't any other floors in this building. They *have* to be here."

"Gray," Darius said. "Look."

I followed his line of sight. It took me a beat to realize that the walls he was staring at weren't walls at all—they were glass cells. Seven in all.

"Oh my god," I breathed. There, huddled on the floor in each cell, were three or four witches. Dressed in dingy white hospital gowns, their heads shaved, their bodies brutalized, they clung to each other, looking up through their glass prisons with wide, frightened eyes.

"Break the glass," I said.

"It doesn't work that way," Jael said. "It's secured with magic. Much stronger than the outer walls. I need time."

"We don't have it!" I approached the glass, scanning the faces for my sister. They didn't move as Darius and I approached. I pounded a fist on the glass.

No reaction.

"They can't see or hear us," Darius said. "They know only that the lights were turned on."

"Another psychological torment," I said. If they couldn't see or hear outside their cells, then any time the lights came on, they'd have no idea what awaited them. Food and water? Or the hunter's carving knife? "Jael, what do we do?"

"We wait," he said simply. He sat on the floor in the center of the room and closed his eyes, his hands outstretched. "Quietly. I need to concentrate on unraveling the spell weave. This one is much tighter."

Darius and I exchanged a glance. The chaos below was fading—I hoped it was because Deirdre and Ronan had managed to win the fight, and not the other way around.

I paced in front of the cells, searching in vain for Haley, but it was impossible to know if she was here. All the women had shaved heads, and some of them weren't facing us.

"I don't see Asher," I whispered.

"Nor do I," Darius said.

"Can you sense him?"

"Not specifically, no."

The fear inside me surged again, tightening my throat.

"We'll find him, Gray." Darius's voice, even at a whisper, was confident and sure. I took a breath, trying to borrow some of that confidence. Darius was right. We'd come this far. We wouldn't leave here without him.

"Oh, shite," Darius breathed, all his calm confidence evaporating.

He pointed at the ceiling inside one of the cells. Some kind of sickly yellow-green smoke crept out from the vents. I didn't need to smell it to know it was poison gas.

One of the witches started coughing. Then another. And another. Then, all at once, the screams began. I spun around on my heel. Tendrils of poison curled into every single cell.

"Jael!" Darius shouted. "We've got a problem!"

"I'm working on it."

I pounded frantically on the glass, watching helplessly as four young witches choked on poison air. Their mouths were foaming, their eyes bulging, their skin turning purple.

"Jael! They're choking to death!"

"Almost there..."

"Jael!"

"Got it!"

A tremble rolled through the room, rattling the metal tables around us. The lights flickered, then popped. A dim set of emergency lights illuminated the floor.

When the room finally stopped shaking, I glanced into the closest cell. The witches were lying in a heap on the floor, unmoving. The poison had dissipated, the air clear once again.

Seconds later, the glass windows slid open in a single, unified hiss. I set down my sword, and Darius and I rushed into the nearest cell, slowly rousing the witches to consciousness. One of them coughed, then sat up on her own, sucking in deep breaths of clean air.

Slowly, agonizingly, the others came to.

"Gray? Is that you?"

At the sound of a familiar voice, I darted over to the adjacent cell, my heart hammering in my chest.

Haley Barnes stood before me, her hand over her mouth, her eyes wet with tears of relief.

Her head was shaved, her skin gaunt, her bones jutting out where before she'd had curves for days. But it was still her, those light green eyes sparkling.

I beamed at her, pulling her into a hug so tight I was probably cutting off her air supply again, but I didn't care. She was my sister. I wasn't ready to tell her about all I'd learned just yet—there would be time for that later. But now that I'd found her again, I didn't want to let her go.

"I'm happy to see you, too!" She laughed, finally wriggling free of my embrace. Her smile didn't last, though. How could it, after what she'd been through?

"Tell me you've seen Reva," she said.

"She's safe," I assured her. "She made it to the precinct and told us everything. That's how we were able to track you guys down. Is this everyone?" I asked gently, gesturing toward the witches stumbling out of the cells. They were all pale and thin and severely exhausted, but it looked like everyone could walk. That was a good sign.

"If you've got Reva, then there are twenty-three of us here." She scanned the room, doing a quick count. "That's all of us. The only one missing is Asher."

My heart leaped at the sound of his name.

"They put him in solitary. Down here," she said, leading me to a white door I hadn't noticed. She opened it up, revealing a dark corridor. "There's another cell back there."

"Go with Darius. I'll be right back." Not wasting another minute, I darted into the cell and down the corridor.

I found the cell at the very end of the hall. It was smaller and dingier than the others, with bars rather than glass, and bare concrete walls and flooring that looked like they hadn't been cleaned since Nixon was in office.

And there, slumped in the center of the floor, sat a man in camouflage pants and a black T-shirt that had been torn to shreds. At the sound of my approach, he lifted his head, revealing a face covered in bruises, his nose clearly broken, a fresh gash carved from his ear to the corner of his mouth.

But then he smiled, and I let out a cry of happiness, drinking in the *very* welcome sight of one long-lost, sexy-as-sin, bad-boy smirk and a pair of piercingly beautiful eyes the exact color of the deepest part of the sea.

"Hello, Cupcake," Asher croaked. "You miss me?"

THIRTY-THREE

ASHER

Gray really was magic. One look at her, and all the fucked-up shit around me disappeared in a blink.

No longer electrified with fae mojo, the bars of my cell pushed open easily, and I stepped out from behind them and took a breath. I knew we weren't out of the woods yet, but I still felt free. It'd been a long time since I'd seen anything from this side of a cell.

And an even longer time since I'd seen anything as beautiful as her.

"You're hurt," she said softly, the spot between her eyebrows wrinkling. Tentatively, she reached up and touched my face. "They really did a number on you."

I pressed her palm to my cheek, soaking up the feel of her touch. "Nothing I can't handle."

"Tough guy."

"*Me*?" I laughed. "You're the one who made it through the Shadowrealm."

"Hell, too."

"Hell... what?" I closed my eyes, shaking my head. "To quote our friendly neighborhood vampire, I seem to have lost the plot."

At the mention of the vampire, sadness filled her eyes.

"What is it?" I asked, my heart thumping. "Is he—"

"He's okay. Just... there's a lot of plot to cover."

I sensed the weight of her words, the depth of everything that must've happened while I'd been locked up in these bullshit prisons.

"And Jonathan?" I asked. "Tell me you blasted that motherfucker into oblivion."

She shook her head. "I blasted him, all right. Multiple times. And he fell right into my magical realm. Liam is still hunting him. But that's—"

"More plot," I said.

Gray nodded. "We should probably stock up on bourbon and tequila on the way home. We have a *lot* of catching up to do."

Silence came between us, and I took her hands, stroking her soft skin with my thumbs. Just having her near me again, feeling the heat of her skin, my body was already responding, my wounds knitting back together, the force of her healing energy pulsing through my veins.

"When I didn't see you in that other room," she said, her voice breaking. "I thought..."

"You thought I'd checked out?" I smiled, pressing my forehead against hers, taking another deep breath of her sweet scent. "Not a chance. You kept me alive in there, Cupcake. You know that, right?"

"I'm glad my magic gave you strength. It—"

"No, not the magic. A thought. One simple thought." I pulled back and took her face in my hands, trying my damnedest not to tremble. I could seriously drown in those blue eyes. "I couldn't die in that fucking hole knowing I'd never kiss you again."

At this, her eyes sparkled, a smile playing on her lips.

"Is that right?" she teased, that smirk of hers driving me wild. She stood on her tiptoes and put her arms around my neck, pressing up against me. My body responded to her instantly, in all the obvious ways. I didn't even bother hiding how turned on I was. "Who says I *want* you to kiss me again?"

"Oh, let's not play games." I nudged her nose with mine. "I'm pretty damn sure you want me to kiss you again."

"Kiss a guy in camo?" She wrinkled her nose. "I don't know about that."

"Maybe you want to find out."

"Yeah. Maybe I do," she whispered, all the teasing gone. The look in her eyes turned ferocious, a passion that would never be tamed, and I crashed against her lips, stealing a bruising, breathtaking kiss. She moaned my name into my mouth, and I slid my fingers into her silky blonde hair, pulling her closer, closer, closer…

Fuck, I couldn't get enough.

I wanted to devour her, kiss by devastating kiss.

But that, too, was a plot we'd have to catch up on later.

Without another word, we broke apart, linking hands and heading out into the main room to join the others.

"If it isn't my favorite witch and my favorite pain-in-the-ass incubus." Haley beamed as Gray and I entered the room, her hope-o-meter off the charts.

"At your service, Hay," I said, giving her a wink.

"So, the witches are accounted for, but where are the rest?" Gray asked, looking around the room. "Fiona Brentwood? The other shifters and—"

"Not here," I said. "As far as we know, they only transferred witches to this facility. I'm only here because Dirty Beard can't get enough of beating me with his big stick."

I couldn't be sure, but I swore I heard Gray growling.

"Do you think they're still back in the caves?" she asked.

"No," Haley said. "It sounded like they were clearing out from that area altogether. My guess is they didn't want Jonathan coming back and screwing up the new world order."

"Alright, everyone," a commanding voice called from the other side of the room. "We still need to get ourselves out of the building, and that's going to take a group effort."

Darius.

"Good to see you again, bloodsucker." I crossed the room, pulling him into a hug that seemed to surprise him.

"Oh. Right, well, it's... lovely to see you, as well." He patted me on the back, then turned away, focusing his attention on the witches.

I looked at Gray, confused. Why had he been so stiff and

awkward with me? We weren't exactly besties, but I thought we'd made some inroads.

"Later," she mouthed, picking up a badass looking sword from one of the metal tables. It glowed faintly at her touch.

Shit, a lot of *plot* to catch up on? Looked like I'd missed the whole fucking movie.

Shifting gears, I said, "I take it the rest of the boys are downstairs, beating those fae fuckholes into a glittery pulp?"

"Ronan and Emilio are," Gray confirmed. "With the help of the local pack. Emilio's sister is the chief of police. That's... another long story."

"What about Liam? I never thought I'd say this, but I actually miss his spooky ass."

Gray shook her head, her eyes glazing with pain. Before I could even ask about that, Darius was calling for us again, urging us to follow him down the stairs.

"With any luck," he said, "our people have cleared the way for our exit. But if there's any trouble, stay together, and stay down. We'll handle the fighting for now. Clear?"

The witches mumbled their assent, too exhausted to argue.

With Darius and Jael taking point and Gray and I bringing up the rear, we led the witches down the stairs.

Most of them could barely walk, let alone use their magic. Even Haley, the strongest of the group, was fading on me.

"You good, Hay?" I asked, putting a hand on her shoulder.

She turned to me and smiled, flashing a double thumbs-up. "Hungry as hell, but I'm hanging in."

"How's that hope-o-meter?"

"At least half," she said. "Let's see what happens when we got out of this shithole."

I had no idea what had been on the second floor before, but now it was a wasteland, littered with burning paper and overturned desks, dozens of gray cubicle walls smashed to bits.

We had to watch our footing, stepping over fae corpses. I hoped none of our guys were in this mess.

"Second floor cleared," Darius said, leading us to the stairs at the other side of the room, then slowly descending.

I could tell from the explosive chaos emanating from below that the first floor would be another fucking story.

And from the looks of things, this one wasn't going to have a happy ending.

THIRTY-FOUR

RONAN

In all our preparations, all our planning, and in every fucking scenario we'd run through, it wasn't supposed to go down like this.

I saw the scene unfolding in my mind before the wolf even made his move. It would end in blood—Emilio's—and there wasn't a damn thing I could do about it. No one else had seen it coming, and I was simply too far away to stop it.

I charged ahead anyway, shoving aside bloodthirsty hunters and dodging fae attacks, shielding my eyes against the bright bursts of Deirdre's magic. Gray's hounds were at my heels, taking down would-be assailants. I was fifty feet away from the wolf, and closing in fast. *Forty. Thirty.*

Time slowed. Still in human form, Elena whipped around, taking out a hunter with the butt of her gun.

Twenty feet.

From behind, another hunter attacked her, grabbing a fistful of her hair and wrenching her to the ground.

Fifteen feet.

"Emilio, no!" I shouted over the melee, reaching out for him as I ran.

But it was too late, as I knew it would be. Fighting on instinct, the wolf lunged for the hunter that had nabbed Elena, knocking him to the floor. He rose up on his hind legs, his sharp claws glinting, ready to shred the bastard who'd attacked his sister.

But Emilio was oblivious to the fae soldier hiding behind the wall.

Ten feet.

Orendiel stepped into view, a silver dagger positioned perfectly, flashing like fire in the yellow-orange light of Dierdre's spells.

Five feet.

Orendiel was quick. Efficient. The blade cut through Emilio's soft underbelly like a hot knife through butter.

The wolf yelped, then dropped, hitting the floor with a thud that rattled my bones.

Elena screamed.

And shattered my fucking heart.

"Ronan! Incoming!" Deirdre shouted, and I jumped on top of Elena, shielding her from the blast of magic that exploded behind us. Something burst into flames, but it wasn't Orendiel. He was already running away from the destruction, fleeing our brutal assault like the coward he was.

I crawled over to Emilio, gently turning him onto his back. I gasped, unable to swallow the raw horror of it.

Elena said nothing, her face a mask of pure shock.

Her brother was covered in blood, more of it pumping out with every beat of his heart. Muscle and torn flesh glistened, the jagged edges of broken ribs protruding. The silver was pure poison, amplifying the effects of a regular dagger by a thousand. I couldn't even decipher where the blood was coming from—where the worst of the damage was. Confused by the silver poisoning, Emilio's body was stuck in limbo, parts of him shifting back into human form, while other parts remained wolf.

"*No!*" A gut-wrenching scream rang out across the room, and I looked up to catch Gray and Asher pushing through a group of witches, running toward us from across the room.

I caught her eyes and knew in an instant that she'd seen everything. That she'd watched the man she loved get gutted by the Darkwinter captain while I couldn't do a damn thing to stop him.

"Emilio," she breathed, falling to her knees before him. She took his human hand, tears spilling into her mouth as she reached up to touch his wolf snout.

He was stuck, half wolf, half man, his face twisted in excruciating pain. The sounds coming from his mouth were indescribable, each one tearing a chunk out of my heart.

Behind us, the fire crackled, superheating the air around us.

"Put pressure on the chest wound," I ordered, snapping

my fingers in front of Elena's face to yank her out of her shock. "Now, Elena. Now!"

The sharp command woke her up, and she did as I asked, pressing her palms to the wound near his heart. Blood leaked out through her fingers.

"He needs to shift back into wolf," she said. "His body is using too much energy trying to shift back and forth between the two. We can't heal him like this."

"We damn well need to try," I said. "Unless you can force him to shift."

She shook her head.

I whipped the T-shirt over my head and tore the fabric into strips, tying them tight around his limbs, anywhere I thought might help slow the bleeding.

But nothing I could do was helping. Emilio's breath was shallow, fading. Blood pooled on the concrete floor beneath him, a glossy black slick that reflected the flickering firelight surrounding us.

"You fucking listen to me," I shouted at him. "You're not going anywhere. Don't even *think* about it. You hear me, asshole?"

A gentle touch on my arm made me flinch. I didn't need to feel the burn to know it was Gray.

"Ronan," she said, her voice broken and soft. I didn't even want to look at her. Didn't want to see the hopeless-ness in her eyes. The resignation.

Behind us, the flames surged, licking up the walls, consuming everything they touched. We had five minutes, maybe ten before they crawled across the ceiling, and then we'd all be fucked.

"Ronan," she whispered again, that soft voice trembling. I'd never seen her so scared. Not in the Shadowrealm. Not with Sebastian. Never. "Do something."

I finally met her eyes, the fierce need to protect her rising up inside me.

"Go with Ash and Darius," I said, blinking the sweat from my eyes. This place was quickly becoming an oven. "You need to get the others to safety. I'll take care of him."

Gray's eyes were wide in a pale face as she looked him over. Then, she turned to me again and nodded, locking her gaze on mine. Instead of the hopelessness I'd feared, I saw the exact opposite. Hope, so much of it, it made me dizzy. She was pinning it all on me, and I felt the weight of it on my heart. The importance of it.

"I won't let him die," I said. "I swear to you, Gray. I *will* get us out of here. *All* of us." My promises weren't worth much in her eyes these days, but it was all I had to give, and I gave it honestly. Emilio would survive this. He was the best of us, and he needed to be there on the other side when we got out.

Gray got to her knees and leaned forward, still holding Emilio's hand. She pressed her mouth to mine, her kiss fiery and all-consuming, hotter than the flames behind us. She tasted like smoke and ash and everything—*everything*—I'd ever loved. Everything I'd ever lived for.

When she pulled back, her mouth was red and swollen, her lips blistered.

"Don't you let go, Ronan Vacarro."

Asher hauled her up to her feet, and they followed Darius and Jael and the hellhounds, leading the witches out the front entrance, leaving a trail of bloody footprints in their wake.

Emilio's blood.

Elena gasped, and I turned back to feel a strange wind on my face that had nothing to do with the fire.

A majestic black raven flapped its giant wings before us, alighting on Emilio's chest as softly as a curl of smoke.

Emilio stopped breathing.

And there, from the space between his lips, the thin silver mist of his soul floated out.

"Colebrook!" I shouted at the raven, terrifying in its darkness. "Liam! Don't you dare take him from me. Don't you *dare*."

I screamed at him until my throat was raw, until I was coughing up ash, until I could no longer make a sound.

And still, the soul floated out, perfect and beautiful, made of pure silver-white light.

I lunged for the raven, but he opened his massive black beak, releasing a howling wind that blasted me and Elena onto our backs.

The flames behind us receded, the air immediately cooling.

When I got back on my feet and the dust finally cleared, Elena was still on the floor, unconscious. The few remaining hunters had scattered. The flames were out, leaving black, roiling smoke in their place.

In the space where Emilio had fallen, where the great black raven had sat upon his chest and ignored my desperate pleas, there was nothing more than a single black feather, floating in a glossy pool of blood.

How will Gray and her rebels endure this devastating loss? When it comes to fighting for the ones they love, will they ever catch a break? Find out in *Death Untold*, book five in the Witch's Rebels series. **Get Death Untold now!**

If you loved reading this story as much as I loved writing it, please help a girl out and **leave a review on Amazon!** Even a quick sentence or two about your favorite part can help other readers discover the book, and that makes me super happy!

XOXO
Sarah

ORIGINS OF THE WITCH'S REBELS

I was primarily inspired to write this series by three things: my fascination with Tarot, my love of all things witchy, and my desire to see more kickass women telling stories for and about other kickass women.

I've always enjoyed books, movies, and TV shows about witches, monsters, and magic, but I never found exactly the right mix. I wanted a darker, grittier Charmed, an older Buffy, and most of all—as much as I love the brothers Winchester (who doesn't?)—I *really* wanted a Supernatural with badass bitches at the helm, hunting monsters, battling their inner demons, and of course, sexytimes. Lots and lots of sexytimes.

(Side note: there's not enough romance on Supernatural. Why is that? Give me five minutes in that writers' studio…)

Anyway, back to The Witch's Rebels. We were talking about badass bitches getting the sexytimes they deserve.

Right.

So I started plotting my own story and fleshing out the character who would eventually become our girl Gray, thinking I had it all figured out. But as I dove deeper into the writing, and I really got to know Gray, Darius, Ronan, Asher, Emilio, and Liam, I discovered a problem. A big one.

With so many strong, sexy guys in the mix, I couldn't decide which one would be the hero to win Gray's heart. I loved them all as much as she did!

I agonized over this.

It felt like the worst kind of love triangle. Er, love rhombus? Love—wait. What's the word for five of them? Pentagon! Yes, a love pentagon.

Pure torture!

But then I had my lightbulb moment. In the face of so much tragedy and danger, Gray fights hard to open herself up to love, to trust people, to earn those hard-won friendships. Her capacity for giving and receiving love expands infinitely throughout the story, so why the hell *shouldn't* she be able to share that with more than one man?

There was no reason to force her to choose.

So, she doesn't. And her story will continue!

You, dear reader, don't have to choose either—that's part of the fun of reverse harem stories like this. But if you happen to have a soft spot for a particular guy, I'd love to hear about it!

Drop me a line anytime at sarah@sarahpiperbooks.com and tell me who's winning your heart so far! I'll tell you mine if you tell me yours! *wink wink*

Paranormal romance fans, I've got even more sexy books ready to heat up your bookshelf!

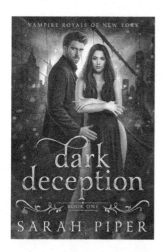

VAMPIRE ROYALS OF NEW YORK is a scorching paranormal romance series featuring a commanding, dirty-talking vampire king and the seductive thief who might just bring him to ruin... or become his eternal salvation. Sizzling romance, dark secrets, and hot vampires with British accents abound!

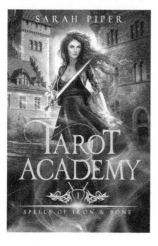

TAROT ACADEMY is a paranormal, university-aged reverse harem academy romance starring four seriously hot mages and one badass witch. Dark prophecies, unique mythology, steamy romance, strong female friendships, and plenty of supernatural thrills make this series a must-read!

ABOUT SARAH PIPER

Sarah Piper is a Kindle All-Star winning urban fantasy and paranormal romance author. Through her signature brew of dark magic, heart-pounding suspense, and steamy romance, Sarah promises a sexy, supernatural escape into a world where the magic is real, the monsters are sinfully hot, and the witches always get their magically-ever-afters.

Her works include the newly released Vampire Royals of New York series, the Tarot Academy series, and The Witch's Rebels, a fan-favorite reverse harem urban fantasy series readers have dubbed "super sexy," "imaginative and original," "off-the-walls good," and "delightfully wicked in the best ways," a quote Sarah hopes will appear on her tombstone.

Originally from New York, Sarah now makes her home in northern Colorado with her husband (though that changes frequently) (the location, not the husband), where she spends her days sleeping like a vampire and her nights writing books, casting spells, gazing at the moon, playing with her ever-expanding collection of Tarot cards, binge-watching Supernatural (Team Dean!), and obsessing over the best way to brew a cup of tea.

You can find her online at SarahPiperBooks.com and in her Facebook readers group, Sarah Piper's Sassy Witches! If you're sassy, or if you need a little *more* sass in your life, or if you need more Dean Winchester gifs in your life (who doesn't?), come hang out!